A Female Doctor in the Civil War

Another American Journey

by

Richard Alan

Village Drummer Fiction

www.villagedrummerfiction.com

ISBN: < 978-0-9974546-3-5 > (print edition)
ISBN: < 978-0-9974546-4-2 > (eBook edition)

Also by Richard Alan
American Journeys From Ireland to the Pacific Northwest Book 1
American Journeys From Ireland to the Pacific Northwest Book 2

Meant to Be Together series:
Finding a Soul Mate (formerly called Meant to Be)
The Couples
Finding Each Other
Growing Together

Contents

Chapter One: Field Hospital...1

Chapter Two: Life as a Surgeon..19

Chapter Three: More Wounded..35

Chapter Four: Directives...47

Chapter Five: On the Battlefield...69

Chapter Six: The March 85

Chapter Seven: Dr. Connolly..105

Chapter Eight: Wounded 113

Chapter Nine: One Mystery Solved – Another Continues....119

Chapter Ten: Tired..143

Chapter Eleven: First Leave 151

Chapter Twelve: Evaluations..167

Chapter Thirteen: Expanding Educations.............................173

Chapter Fourteen: Maggie Disappears...................................197

Chapter Fifteen: A Major Battle 201

Chapter Seventeen: The Enemy Gets Close 215

Chapter Eighteen: Bromine..231

Chapter Nineteen: The Chemist...235

Chapter Twenty: Second Leave...255

Chapter Twenty-One: Dialogue Between Friends..................263

Chapter Twenty-Two: Dr. Scharf..275

Chapter Twenty-Three: The End in Sight...............................283

Author's Notes and Resources..293

Dedication

This book is dedicated to Surgeon General William Hammond, who, during the early years of the Civil War, wrestled American physicians away from medicine as an art and into scientifically based practice. This led our medical community to the forefront of medicine.

Secondly, this book is dedicated to the light of my life, my grandson, Zane Noah Roberts. His melodic laughter and calm demeanor fills our hearts with joy.

Last and most significantly, this novel would never have been completed without the devotion, encouragement, love and sacrifice of my wife, Carolynn. She has enriched my life in all my personal and intellectual pursuits since the day we met.

A Female Doctor in the Civil War

Chapter One: Field Hospital

June, 1862

"You're a woman...doctors know...and you should have learned in medical college, young lady...too much stimulation isn't healthy for a woman."

"Thank you for noticing my gender but," Abbey's attempt at an upbeat voice became tinged with anger, "at the risk of...over stimulation...I'm willing to put my life in harm's way just like the men." She struggled to remain calm. "I've worked hard to earn a degree at medical college, pass the medical board examinations and earn contract employment as a surgical assistant with the military."

The older man she addressed wore a uniform with major's rank which fit loosely on his slender frame.

"Dr. Fellows," she handed him a folded copy of her orders. "As I said, I was told I'd be training with you."

He clenched his jaw numerous times while he read then shook his head. "No…No…I'm sorry but assistant surgeons work in field hospitals which are close enough to combat that we occasionally take fire."

The six-foot-tall, buxom woman pursed her lips while her attempt at an upbeat demeanor evaporated. "The men risk their lives for the sake of the Union. Why shouldn't I?"

His neatly trimmed but sparse salt and pepper beard framed an expression of incredulity. "I was informed I'd receive a recent medical school graduate who's had surgical…I mean…but no way…a woman?" He took a step back from the tall woman as if distance would change the situation. The chief surgeon's shock slowly turned to anger. He put his hands on his hips then leaned toward her. "You…you're the Dr. Kaplan I've been expecting?"

"Doctor Abbey Kaplan…"

"But…you can't be." Slowly shaking his head, he thought for a moment, swallowed hard then continued. "I'm expecting someone I can train as an assistant surgeon."

"Sorry to disappoint you but I'm the new assistant surgeon."

His chin began to quiver. "There has to be a mistake."

"No mistake. As my orders state, I'm your new assistant surgeon."

His eyes raced through her orders a second time. "No…the person I'm waiting for passed the medical exams with…"

"Peerless scores, one of my examiners told me."

"His essay was brilliant."

"I wrote about the symptoms, diagnosis, pathology and treatment of erysipelas and gangrene."

He raised his eyebrows. "How did you know about…?"

"Encountered them during my years in the Northwest so spent time researching those diseases during medical college. To prepare for my service assisting the military, I've also been reviewing the circulars, directives and documents coming from the Surgeon General in Washington and the National Medicine Museum."

Dr. Fellows snorted. "When one of those damn pieces of paper can perform surgery, they might be useful." He stammered. "This must be some kind of mistake…a woman…disgusting…I can't be burdened with a woman." With his chin trembling like a leaf, he practically shouted, "My next surgical assistant will be replacing a first-class surgeon. He had nerves of steel, excellent dexterity and therefore was promoted from assistant surgeon to chief surgeon of a Connecticut regiment." The doctor glared at her. "Seventy-five-percent of the surgeries are amputations. I need someone with steady nerves who won't blanch at their first limb removal or run away at the first sound of battle."

Abbey said through clenched teeth, "I assure you, I realize I have much to learn but the gruesome nature of surgical intervention doesn't bother me. Plus, while I haven't experienced combat, I have assisted in surgery during College.

I've even treated a gunshot wound. In addition, I'm a contract surgeon so not concerned with promotion."

With an expression of disgust he waved a hand of dismissal at her. "With our nation at war…I get a woman." He snorted. "You're not fit to be…"

Abbey's countenance, indeed her mood and posture, no longer made any attempt to contain her rage. With fury in her eyes, she interrupted. "Not only do my exam scores recommend me, I have a burning desire to learn more about medicine…particularly surgery plus study mental state. By joining the war effort and doing my part to keep the Union together, I'll be exposed to more diseases and surgical procedures than numerous decades of civilian practice." She added in a slow and succinct voice, "That's why I'm here."

He returned her glare. "I need someone I can depend on. You should be at home, raising a family. Casualties might be arriving any moment."

Abbey's anger swelled like a river swollen by spring's melting snow. Her hands slowly moved to her hips. She shouted, "With casualties about to arrive, perhaps you should get your gaze off my chest and we could begin my training."

He coughed and cleared his throat, then stared at her shoes. "Training? No. No, I won't let you." He turned to one of the medical helpers. "Pvt. Silver, escort…Miss Kaplan…and her gear to the tent she's been assigned. She'll wait there for new orders." He turned to Abbey and smirked. "I'll have you reassigned within the hour."

***

"Do I call you Lieutenant or Dr. Kaplan?" Pvt. Dan Silver said as he walked down a row of tents set up for officers. He carried her duffel bag on his shoulder.

In one hand, the six-foot-tall doctor carried a leather covered, briefcase-sized container which held her surgical instruments; a carpetbag in the other. "I understand, as an assistant surgeon, I'm considered rank equivalent of lieutenant but I'd prefer being addressed as Dr. Kaplan."

The private pulled a tent flap aside. "Your quarters, Dr. Kaplan."

Abbey stepped out of the bright, mid-morning sun, into a ten-by-twelve-foot tent which was tall enough for her to stand along the center line. The interior smelled of mold and a slightly earthy scent, reminiscent of recently turned soil. A cot occupied each side wall and a desk with a single oil lamp occupied the center of the space. Pvt. Silver dropped her duffel on one of the cots.

"I'll tie both flaps open to air out the place," he said.

"Thank you, Private." The doctor removed the pin which held her hat in place then placed it and the hat on top of her duffel. She ran her gloved fingers on the edge of the desk and examined them, then mumbled, "Filthy."

"I'll get some supplies and clean that for you, Ma'am."

"Some rags, soap and a bucket of water, please, and I'll do it myself...even though I may not be here but a short time."

Four-hours later and Abbey sat at the desk in her tent reviewing documents on new medical practices. She glanced at her duffel. "Wonder if it's worth unpacking?"

In the distance, she heard thunder. "Wonderful," she said under her breath. "Hot and humid as the seashore in August and now it's going to rain…more humidity." She wiped rivulets of sweat off her brow. "That's just what I need." Abbey walked to the tent opening and glanced skyward. "That's odd. Clear and sunny." She heard thunder again. A number of officers ran out of their tents, leapt on horses and galloped in the direction of the deep rumble. She heard a new sound, higher in pitch and more of a pop.

"Damn," she thought. *"That must be cannon and rifle fire. A battle is starting. I should be putting my skills to use and saving lives."* Abbey cursed, then walked to her desk and opened a medical text. *"I'll review wound repair. With a battle started they'd be foolish not to use my skill."*

During the next hour, the gun and rifle fire continued. If anything, it seemed to intensify. Abbey's ears perked up. Someone was calling her name. She moved to just outside the tent.

A tall, clean-shaven, barrel-chested man with muscular build and wearing sergeant's stripes hurried down the row of officer's tents. "Looking for Dr. Kaplan," he shouted.

"Over here." Abbey yelled.

He double-timed up to her and saluted.

Abbey returned his salute. "I'm Doctor Kaplan."

"I'm Scharf, Ma'am. We need your immediate presence at the medical tent."

"Which way?"

"Your medical instruments?"

"Oh yes." She quickly retrieved her government-issued case.

"Your apron?"

"Don't have one."

"That frock will be covered in blood and guts shortly."

"To hell with the dress. We have men who need medical intervention."

The Sergeant grinned. "Follow me, Dr. Kaplan."

As they approached the three medical tents, indicated by the red flag which waved in the stiff breeze, men on stretchers were gently lifted out of two-wheeled, single-mule-drawn carts. Each cart carried from two to four wounded on stretchers. Tens of injured were arrayed in rows, waiting treatment. Some of them moaned. Others yelled for their mothers. Still others lay motionless, simply staring skyward. Abbey noted many had opened their shirts.

The sergeant's eyes followed her gaze. "They're checking to see if they've been gut-shot," Sgt. Scharf said. "It's an always fatal wound."

"Always?"

He nodded. "That's what I'm told. Tragic we can't fix that type of injury. But…" he grinned, "maybe you'll figure out how, Doctor."

They entered the center tent. Dr. Fellows stood at an operating table, his blood-covered hands gripped a bone saw which rasped its way through a man's femur. His apron, once white, but now covered in splotches of bright-red, fresh blood stains and dark, nearly brown, old stains. The acrid scent of chloroform reached her nose.

"Next patient," Dr. Fellows yelled. With the corner of his apron, he wiped flecks of blood off his sweat covered face.

"Here," Sgt. Scharf said, throwing Abbey an apron which she quickly looped over her head then tied.

"Across the table from me," Dr. Fellows growled upon seeing her.

The next patient was placed on the table. A cloth containing chloroform was put on a holder then placed above the patient's mouth and nose. When bandages were removed from his right foot; the soldier's foot bones were shredded.

"We'll amputate at the ankle," Dr. Fellows said then nodded at the bandages across the soldier's eyes. "Miss Kaplan, remove the wrapping."

Using scissors, Abbey cut through them at the side of the patient's head then gently lifted the wrappings off the front of the man's face.

The man who administered anesthesia cursed and turned his head so as not to view the empty eye socket and missing nose.

Abbey noticed the others watching to gauge her reaction to the gory sight. "He has scalp and facial lacerations which should be sutured."

"Then get busy," Dr. Fellows growled. "And be quick." He picked up a scalpel and cut through the tissue around the man's ankle.

Abbey picked up a needle and thread then pulled the two sides of the six-inch wound together. She started carefully tying the sutures in a continuous row.

Dr. Fellows glanced at her work. "Faster Miss Kaplan," he said in a mocking voice. "I've nearly removed this foot and you're still making pretty stiches." He picked up the bone saw and glanced at Abbey then cursed. "Time counts, damn it. Not pretty. The faster we finish, the faster we can move to the next patient."

"Yes, Dr. Fellows," she said while tying off the end of the stiches.

"Ligation Doctor. This blood vessel." He pointed.

Abbey moved to the other end of the table and tied off the bleeder.

"Too damn slow," Dr. Fellows grumbled. He performed the balance of the amputation himself.

Abbey finished closing the man's facial lacerations then with the help of a nurse, bandaged the area.

"Next patient," the older doctor yelled.

A man, whose eyes pleaded for Abbey's help, was without his lower jaw.

"Do what you can for him," Dr. Fellows said. "Lt. Smith, prepare the other surgical table and put the next patient on it. I'll work there while Miss Slow does what she can for this man."

"During my brief stay, I'd appreciate being referred to as Dr. Kaplan," red-faced Abbey stated.

Dr. Fellows muttered an indistinct vocalization which sounded to the medical team like, "Harrumph."

Seven-hours later and Dr. Fellows grabbed his lower back and stretched. He announced to the surgical team, "Thirty-minute break. Get something to eat then report back here." He turned and walked away.

A tall, lanky lieutenant with a long nose and large Adam's apple approached and held out his hand to Abbey. "I'm Lt. Smith, head of the medical assistants. There's ten of us depending on assignments. Mess is this way, Doctor."

Sgt. Scharf joined them. She asked, "Do the helpers have medical training?"

The lieutenant tried but couldn't suppress a laugh. "No, Ma'am. We're band members and a few men not fit for combat. Our medical knowledge is limited to what you doctors teach us. I believe you've met Sgt. Scharf."

"I have," she said. With barely disguised sarcasm, Abbey asked him, "What instrument do you play?"

"I'm lead percussionist, Doctor," said the powerfully built man who was slightly taller than Abbey.

"What qualifications do you possess which recommend you to the surgical team?"

He smiled. "I can precisely follow orders."

She laughed.

"Food is this way," Lt. Smith said with a wave of his hand.

"We're glad you're here, Dr. Kaplan," Sgt. Scharf said. "An assistant surgeon is a key member of the team."

"Won't be here but a short time. Dr. Fellows is having new orders cut for me."

The lieutenant and sergeant exchanged worried glances.

"We've been without an assistant surgeon for a number of weeks," the sergeant said. "They don't grow on trees. I can't imagine why they'd get rid of a capable surgeon."

"Capable? With the exception of today's surgical interventions, I'm only school experienced, not exactly capable yet."

"You hung in there damn well, Ma'am," the lieutenant said.

"Thank you." Abbey stared at her food for a while then asked, "Doesn't bother either of you, I'm female?"

Sgt. Scharf said, "Today's wounds were as ugly as they get and you did fine."

"Our chief surgeon didn't think so."

The two men again exchanged further worried glances.

The lieutenant said, "We'd best eat, Ma'am."

After an additional six-hours of surgery and constant ridicule from the chief surgeon, Abbey collapsed onto her cot. *"With his constant demeaning remarks, I doubt I'll be here much longer,"* she thought. *"I'll bet I assisted in three-dozen amputations today and even performed two myself…all performed to the melody of our chief surgeon's derogatory remarks."* She shook her head. *"This experience is what I prayed for but I can't imagine he'll keep me."*

***

Not long after sunup, Abbey reported to the medical tent. Dr. Fellows and the medical helper staff gathered there.

The chief surgeon addressed her. "While I'll have you out of here shortly, help with camp disease for now. Treat that line of men queued up in front of the small desk and chair. I've assigned three assistants."

Abbey examined a large abrasion on a soldier's lower leg.

"Sgt. Scharf. Please clean this. He'll need a couple stitches."

The tall man washed dirt from the area then dried it. "I've spent many hours in my grandfather's tailor shop so I have experience sewing cloth; if that would be useful."

"Which is not the same as suturing," Abbey said while closing the man's laceration.

"Yes, Doctor."

Abbey examined a man's dislocated shoulder. "If we need you to acquire that skill, we'll setup an arrangement with the cooks."

"Cooks?" the sergeant asked.

She put a fist into the soldier's armpit then pulled out and down.

"Ouch," the man yelled then smiled as he flexed his hand and arm. "Thanks, doc."

"Don't put excessive strain on your shoulder for the next two-weeks and you'll be fine."

Abbey turned to Sgt. Scharf. "Cooks will give you cuts of meat which I can use to simulate the work you may be asked to perform. I learned suturing from that plus joining cooked pasta. They'll be useful until you're proficient."

In an angry voice, Dr. Fellows shouted, "I'll decide what training he gets. Enough chit-chat. Concentrate on your patients."

Abbey cared for a stream of non-battle injuries ranging from boils, which she lanced and bandaged, to splinting and setting a fractured tibia which resulted from a mule's kick, plus minor scrapes, rashes and cuts.

"These are soldiers," Dr. Fellows growled. "Not delicate flowers. You have to work faster. They don't need a delicate touch and you have many more in line."

"Yes, Doctor," Abbey said while wondering why the major wasn't treating some of the men himself...although he appeared to have difficulty standing straight.

The chief surgeon leaned over to examine the wound Abbey was about to treat. He belched.

The scent of cheap bourbon assaulted Abbey's nose. *"This early and he's been drinking?"* she thought.

A deep rasping cough emanating from one of the men in the middle of the line caught her attention.

"Come up here," she called to him.

The watery-eyed sergeant approached, then coughed into a bloody rag while holding an arm against his chest.

"How long have you been coughing?" Abbey asked.

"Over three-weeks, Ma'am."

"Coughing up blood?"

"About four-days."

"Night sweats?"

"Yes, Ma'am."

"Chest pain?"

"Terrible when I cough."

She turned to Dr. Fellows.

"Tuberculosis."

In a voice loaded with sarcasm, the chief surgeon said, "Of course it is." His voice changed to one of sympathy and, putting his hand on the man's shoulder, he nodded to Lt. Smith. "Follow this man, Sergeant. You're going to the recovery hospital and he'll arrange transportation."

The soldier hacked loudly and spit blood into the rag. "How soon can I return to my men?"

"When your cough is gone and your lungs have healed. Recovery will take some weeks."

The man's eye's pleaded with the chief surgeon and his assistant. "Just give me something so I can get back with my men."

"If you don't let us cure you, you'll die of bleeding lungs."

"Major," he pleaded, "I'm a squad leader and some of my men are new to combat. I have to train them before we hit the shit again."

"Someone else will have to do the training. You need rest in order to heal so you will proceed to the recovery hospital. That is a direct order Sergeant."

The man said, "Yes Sir," straightened and respectfully saluted the major who returned his salute. As he walked away, his shoulders slumped and he hung his head.

The chief surgeon turned to Abbey. His sarcastic tone and sneering facial expression returned. "Why are you watching me? Keep working."

Abbey did her best to suppress the anger she felt. She splinted, with Sgt. Scharf's assistance, a man's wrist.

"Keep in mind," Dr. Fellows lectured, "the men feel a tremendous responsibility to return to the men they serve with. Sometimes against medical advice."

"Next," Abbey shouted.

"Tried to break up a knife fight, Doc," A short burley man said. He held a rag up to his lower right-side jaw. "Won't stop bleeding."

Abbey put nine stiches along his jaw line.

The chief surgeon peered at her over the tops of his glasses. "Miss Kaplan, you mentioned an interest in mental state. Why?"

"A classmate from college committed suicide without any outward signs she was troubled. We believe she was upset by her inability to keep up with the workload and her grades were barely adequate."

Dr. Fellows grinned and turned to the men around him. "You see? A woman kills herself because she has poor grades. A perfect example of and surely the result of, over stimulation."

Abbey added, "Her main goal in life was community medicine. I believe that's laudable."

He snorted. "She tried to compete in a profession which requires a man. No surprise it led to suicide."

"I believe the reason was more complex."

"Teach you that in school, did they? This is the real world, Miss Kaplan. Strong men with strong minds don't commit suicide. It's that simple." He chortled. "Keep going, Miss Kaplan. You're on your own. I'll be talking to some of the senior officers at the west end of the camp if you require my assistance."

Anger swelled in Abbey. "I would appreciate being referred to as Doctor Kaplan."

He didn't reply immediately but said, "Of course…" Dr. Fellows hesitated as if her title and name were stuck in his throat then rapidly turned and walked away.

"Problem?" Abbey inquired of the next soldier in line.

"I ripped open my arm." The man held a cloth over his bicep. He lifted the cloth.

"Sit on this bench and don't move. I'll have to close this with sutures."

"Go ahead. Ah…what kinda' name is Kaplan."

"A Jewish name. I'm sorry but this will be painful."

He grinned. "Not as painful as being treated by a woman." The other soldiers in line snickered so he added, "Is we so worthless, all they can find is some Jew-lady to treat us?"

Abbey felt a tear form in her eye which she quickly wiped away with her shoulder. She regarded the man's sarcastic grin. Her sadness quickly turned to anger. "Private, I strongly urge you not to move—and that includes talking—or I might have no choice but to let you bleed to death."

The soldier gritted his teeth and stared to the side away from the wound but didn't move while she sutured the laceration. Sgt. Scharf applied a bandage.

A lieutenant approached Dr. Kaplan.

"How may I help?" Abbey asked.

"Boil on my ass. Burns like hell if I try to sit."

She moved to the chair. "Please turn around and drop your britches."

"You're a lady. I can't just expose myself in front of you. How about the other doctor?"

"I'm not a lady. I'm a doctor and unless I treat this today, your infection will worsen."

"I'll come back tomorrow."

In an angry tone, she said, "Who do you think will be here tomorrow? Turn around and drop your britches."

The officer's face reddened while he stared daggers at Abbey. "What is this shit? Treated by a damn woman? And I damn sure…I ain't takin' orders…from some…goddamned, cow-tits, Jew-doctor!"

Out of the corner of her eye, she noted some of her helpers grinning. Abbey unfolded to her full six-foot height. She slammed a fist into the lieutenant's jaw. He spun around and pitched onto his belly then moaned. She loosened his suspenders, jerked his britches down, lanced the boil then yelled to her helpers, "Bandage that and get him out of my sight."

"Yes Doctor," the suddenly serious-faced helpers said in unison while quickly moving to comply.

She yelled, "Next."

The next man turned to leave.

Abbey was dumb-struck but Sgt. Scharf wasn't. In his deep voice, the big man thundered, "When your limp worsens, and it will, we'll meet again when your leg requires amputation." The soldier stopped walking. "Get the fuck over here, Corporal!"

The soldier turned to the sergeant and shouted, "Yes Sergeant." He quickly returned, spun around and pulled up one leg of his britches, mumbling, "Ain't this some shit."

A few quick motions, a bandage and Abbey yelled, "Next."

Sgt. Scharf commented to Abbey. "Your sutures are neat and equidistant."

She shrugged. "I've been practicing since childhood…but apparently I'm too slow."

"Everyone is at first. Your speed will improve with repetition."

In the distance, Abbey heard Dr. Fellows screaming, "But she's a woman. Damn it. I will not be humiliated. Get me someone else."

She muttered, "I may not be here long enough to improve."

The Sergeant raised his eyebrows but didn't comment.

Abbey glanced at the grinning men around her.

Sgt. Scharf noticed them as well and yelled, "Next…and wipe the damn grins off those faces or I'll have the lot of you shoveling horse shit until this fucking war ends."

Following the last man's treatment, red-faced Dr. Fellows returned. In a bitter, angry voice he spat out, "Congratulations, at least for now, you're my assistant surgeon." Putting his hands on his hips, he eyed her with contempt. "I don't know who the hell you knew to get this assignment but don't get comfortable. If I have any say-so, you'll be out of here within a matter of days."

Abby spoke in a conciliatory tone. "I'll appreciate any training to advance my career as a doctor and surgeon."

In an accusatory voice and through gritted teeth, he said, "No way in hell, women should be doctors let alone surgeons in the medical corps."

A distant but furious volley of cannon fire was heard followed by the sound of the shells exploding. All glanced in the direction of the sound.

Still seething, Dr. Fellows said in a sarcastic voice, "Welcome to your second day in the war. We can expect casualties within the hour. Let's see how you manage another day of blood and gore."

Chapter Two: Life as a Surgeon

"Only five-hours of surgery today," Sgt. Scharf said as he approached the mess area. "Must have been a skirmish."

Abbey returned an expression of confusion. She sat at a mess table, eating lunch from a container all the soldiers carried. It appeared as a cross between a mug and a bucket so the soldiers called it a mucket. In reality, it was an oversized metal cup.

He continued, "A small battle is considered a skirmish. At times they test the lines to determine where each side's troops are located to try to get an estimate of strength."

She noticed a number of soldiers twenty-yards-distant glancing at her and snickering.

Richard Alan

"May I join you?" Sgt. Scharf asked.

She nodded and he sat across the table from her. "Not joining your friends over there?"

He glanced at them. "Not my friends. We just happen to work together. Mostly I find them boorish and crude."

Abbey's eyebrows went up.

He continued, "Outside of our work we have nothing in common."

"Nothing?"

"They have different backgrounds than I do. Besides, I have to give them orders. I've found it's best not to be friends."

They ate in silence for a number of minutes.

"How are your knees?" Sgt. Scharf asked.

"Uncomfortable. How did you know?"

"Happens to most people after their first surgeries. Didn't think I'd make it when the first series of surgeries I attended ran fourteen-hours. My back was killing me as well. As tall as we are, the damn, pardon me Ma'am, tables are low. It's rough to work all bent over."

"My cutting instruments aren't nearly sharp enough."

"I'll take care of that as soon as we finish eating," Sgt. Scharf volunteered. He grinned. "They'll be sharp enough to shave the hair off a gnat's…ah…eyebrow."

"Thank you, Sgt."

Abbey thought, "*A man with a pleasant smile and concern for polite conversation. Not many of those in the lower ranks.*"

Sgt. Scharf ate quietly for a bit then cleared his throat. "I don't want you to feel offended but a number of our team have asked to be transferred to other duty."

"Because I'm female?"

He nodded. "I suspect they feel emasculated because they're taking orders from a woman."

"None of them took orders from their mothers?"

The sergeant laughed.

Abbey sighed and shook her head. Without looking at him, she asked, "Are you one of them?"

"No Ma'am." They moved and sat leaning against a tree. He glanced down and waved his hand in the grass they were seated on. The tall man closed his eyes and smiled as if reliving a pleasant memory. "I have three, kind and gentle, older sisters plus parents who didn't put up with crap from any of us." He laughed. "Been taking orders from multiple women since the day I was born."

Abbey laughed. "Perhaps as my skill increases, they'll learn to respect me."

He sighed. "Maybe, maybe not. Skill has little to do with how they feel. For whatever reason, most seem threatened by an educated woman. The fact you're rank equivalent of a lieutenant may help as they'll respect the rank if nothing else."

"Did Pvt. Wilson ask for a transfer? He constantly watches my hands."

"He and I have worked with a number of surgeons since the first battle of the war. I'm sure you realize you have much to learn and you're slow, but we think you're going to be a good one…despite what Dr. Fellows thinks."

"*At least two of them believe in me*," she thought. Abbey thanked him and they ate quietly for a bit.

"Dr. Fellows told me," the sergeant said, "he had limited surgical experience before the war."

"I wonder how he was chosen to be the regiment's chief surgeon."

He shook his head. "Don't know for sure but political appointment I'd guess. Lots of those initially but they have exams now. Many of the old-timers and those who don't want to learn new techniques will get pushed out of the medical corps."

"As they should," Abbey said. She closed her eyes as a warm breeze wafted over them, the leaves in the trees around them rattled. The wind carried an acrid scent which assaulted her nose. She twice sniffed the air then turned to the sergeant.

"The smell is gunpowder after it's been fired. You'll get used to it," he explained. "I believe your recent education should help as you should have been trained in the latest techniques."

"Yes, but as you mentioned, I have much to learn. Prior to my arrival, I'd only treated one gunshot wound. Compared to the surgeries I attended recently, it would be considered a minor injury. However, the thought that my lack of experience could further damage or kill one of these brave soldiers scares me to death. The Medical Board in Washington has provided numerous articles on treatment of battle wounds and camp disease. I've been trying to memorize them so I can apply their guidance."

His voice now sounded enthusiastic. "If you come across an article which will help me with the wounded, I'd be glad to read it."

"Medicine is progressing and the War Department is demanding doctors move our profession into scientifically-based medicine. The lessons the British learned in the Crimean War will save numerous casualties if we apply them."

"How do I learn about those lessons?"

"I'll write up a summary and you can review it. Plus I have medical text books you can read."

They rinsed their muckets, filled them with coffee then seated themselves at the base of a tall oak tree.

Abbey examined an acorn then asked, "How did you happen to become a surgical helper?"

"Dumb luck. When I joined the Army, I volunteered for the band. I thought it would be fun." He gazed at the ground and slowly shook his head. "I had absolutely no idea what war entailed. Like many of us who enlisted, we thought it would be a short war; a few months at most."

"Seems to have been common thinking."

"It's none of my business but as a woman, don't you miss having a family?"

"Since childhood, I've concentrated on becoming a doctor. Didn't take a moment to think about anything else."

The sergeant became pensive then glanced around to ensure they were away from anyone else's hearing and said in a quiet voice, "Dr. Kaplan, it's not my place to give you an order…but…it is imperative you develop your skills as fast as possible…and never…ever…slug anyone again."

"He deserved it."

"I agree. But you need your hands in good condition." The sergeant stared at the ground briefly then continued, "If anyone mouths off again, I'll be in charge of slugging."

She giggled then asked, "You said, imperative, I develop quickly; imperative is a strong word. Why would you say that?"

He sat up straight and glanced around a second time before continuing. "Sooner or later, and I suspect sooner, you'll have to work in place of Dr. Fellows."

Abbey's eyebrows went up and her jaw dropped. "A frightening thought as I have much to learn. I've only seen a fraction of the types of injuries I must learn to surgically repair."

"Our former assistant surgeon asked me to convey something to his replacement," he glanced around again, "but I'd get my butt burned if anyone found out I told you this."

Abbey briefly studied the broad-shouldered man whose discomfort was written in his furrowed brow. "Sgt., tell me what?"

He spoke in a near whisper. "I've worked with Dr. Fellows since just after First Bull Run. He's saved many hundreds of soldiers. I respect the hell out of him but his drinking…"

"I smelled it. Cheap liquor."

"Yes, Ma'am."

"I've seen no ill effects."

"Watch close and you'll see his hands shake. My uncle was a real boozer and his tremors got so bad he couldn't pick up a spoon."

"Hopefully, Dr. Fellows won't reach that point."

"Also, when our former assistant surgeon became proficient, Dr. Fellows seemed not to worry about his drinking as his assistant could perform in his place."

A shudder went down Abbey's spine. "I'm a long way from proficient."

He pleaded, "Dr. Kaplan, I'd appreciate if you could keep this between us?"

"Of course...but why hasn't anyone reported his drinking?"

"This is the military. You learn early on not to make waves. If he was a political appointee, that means someone powerful got him the post and would likely destroy anyone who complained about him." He hesitated then continued, "You understand?"

"A person with influence got me this post, so I understand completely."

The sergeant appeared relieved. In the distance, a tremendous fusillade of cannon fire plus the sound of small arms erupted.

"Likely the sound of the main battle starting," Sgt. Scharf said, scrambling to his feet. "I should get back to the medical tent, assemble the men and verify things are prepared for surgery. You'll be needed shortly, Doctor." He helped Abbey to her feet.

He smiled at her. "I'll pray Pvt. Wilson is right about you."

"Concerning?"

"He believes you've got golden hands. We watched close during the surgical interventions. You use an economy of motion and precision any surgeon would envy."

She shook her head as she suddenly wore a worried expression . "I need months of learning and experience before I'm anywhere near the...golden hands...level."

"For the sake of the wounded, I'll pray you get there quickly."

She stared at the sergeant briefly. He stood straight, saluted and left after she returned his salute.

Within the hour, a trickle of wounded turned into a torrent.

Abbey primarily handled light injuries, bandaged and set broken bones plus occasionally closed for Dr. Fellows.

As the next to last wounded combatant was placed on the operating table. In a sarcastic voice, Dr. Fellows said to Abbey, "Go ahead, Doctor. This one's yours."

The patient, unconscious from the chloroform anesthesia, was missing his right hand, torn off slightly above his wrist. Abbey ligated numerous blood vessels then smoothed the ends of the sawed off bones so they wouldn't be sharp and therefore pierce the tissue she'd use to cover them. She pulled the flap of skin from his forearm over the ends of the bones then neatly sutured the wound closed.

Dr. Fellows growled. "If you always work this slow to make sure your work is pretty, half the men will die waiting for treatment."

Abbey kept her eyes on her work and said, "Yes, Doctor." When she glanced up she noticed many of the team members grinning...until they encountered Sgt. Scharf's glare.

Doctor Fellows said to the hospital attendant and head of the helpers, Lt. Smith, "Next patient." The doctor turned to Abbey. "Have you read the directive about hygiene?"

"I have."

"Keep it in mind but remember time is of the essence at the field hospital. Prompt treatment and rapidly moving the wounded to a nearby recovery hospital is what will save them." Dr. Fellows wiped his scalpel on his blood and pus-stained apron then used it to slice into the muscle of a man's thigh.

***

The following morning and having just completed fifteen-hours of surgery, Drs. Kaplan and Fellows checked on the soldiers waiting for transport to the recovery hospital. He lectured her on elements of triage.

One soldier, lying on a cot, tugged on Abbey's skirt.

"Can I help you?"

"I was told your name is Kaplan."

"I'm Doctor Kaplan."

"Kaplan is usually a Jewish name."

"I'm Jewish."

"I know I got a bad wound but could you do something for me?"

He closed his eyes and his entire body shuddered momentarily; as if a wave of pain coursed through him.

Abbey dropped to her knees, opened his blanket and lifted the bandages covering his abdomen. He'd been shot there; an untreatable and fatal wound.

"Gut-shot?" the soldier asked.

"Yes."

"Thought so." He closed his eyes and pursed his lips. "Damn."

Abbey waited until he opened his eyes again then said, "Something I can do?"

"If I die, there won't be a minyan to say *Kaddish* for me. You know. Ten men are needed to say the prayer."

Abbey nodded toward the rows of fresh grave markers in a nearby cemetery. "If you don't make it, I guarantee there will be enough holy souls to constitute a minyan."

He pleaded. "But who's gonna recite it?"

"I know I don't count for a minyan…but I will."

His face evidenced great relief. "God bless you, Doc."

"Hang in there Mushy," a soldier on a nearby cot called out.

"Thanks Tilden. You too," the solider replied in a weak voice.

"Mushy?" Abbey asked.

The man smiled. "My name is Moshe but since we started training, the guys call me Mushy. I don't mind. I'm the only Jew in this outfit and they all treat me good." He thought for a bit then added, "Good, like a brother." He winced then closed his eyes and held his breath for a number of seconds. He peered into her eyes, took a deep breath then continued, "I know this is a lot to ask but would you mind holding my hand?"

She gripped his hand and glanced around at the other wounded. A number gazed at her. Abbey smiled at each of them; most returned her smile. The doctor felt the hand she was holding briefly tighten then go limp. She checked for a pulse and found none. Tilden raised himself on one elbow. Abbey slowly shook her head. Tilden closed his eyes and laid flat.

As a tear rolled down her cheek, Abbey pulled the blanket over Moshe's face and began reciting the Jewish mourner's prayer. "*V'yit g'dal…*"

Dr. Fellows waited until she'd finished the prayer then growled, "Get something to eat then take care of the men lined up for camp disease treatment. I'll be in my tent."

***

A line of soldiers stood before the medical tent for camp medicine treatment. Abbey, with two helpers, busied herself with their care; suturing or closing minor lacerations, lancing and bandaging boils and blisters, plus applying a Sulphur compound for rashes.

Dr. Fellows approached and addressed the medical team. "I've just finished a meeting with senior staff. We may have a battle in the next few days." He turned to his new assistant. "Abbey, when you're finished here, verify our surgical supplies are ready and cutting instruments sharpened." She didn't respond but continued to work on a soldier. "Abbey," he repeated. Apparently incensed at her lack of response, he shouted. "ABBEY!"

She gritted her teeth, stood up, spun in his direction and with fury in her eyes, shouted, "YES, ALPHONSE?"

His eyes widened and his cheeks reddened. The doctor whipped his head left and right to see if any of his friends had heard Abbey voice his first name. "Don't you every call me by my first name…" He prepared to shout again but apparently realized his mistake. He cleared his throat then in

29

a more reserved but still agitated voice, said, "Dr. Kaplan, please verify our surgical gear is ready."

"Yes, Dr. Fellows," she replied while continuing to glare at him.

She proceeded to the surgical tent then examined a table where her instruments were laid out. "All cleaned and sharpened?" she asked Lieutenant Smith.

"Yes, Doctor, but we're running low on rubbing alcohol."

"In a pinch, you can use wine. White, hopefully."

Dr. Fellows entered the medical tent. A corporal approached, saluted, and handed each of the doctors a document. Abbey reviewed hers and then announced, "Orders are we move out at first light in three days. The regiment will be on the march for a number of weeks." She handed the document to Dr. Fellows.

Abbey turned to their hospital orderly. "Lieutenant…"

He interrupted, "We'll begin breaking down the field hospital and readying it for transport, Doctor Kaplan."

She said, "Another thing Lieutenant Smith. I'd appreciate a clean apron to begin each day."

The lieutenant seemed surprised but said, "I'll arrange it."

Gazing past the lieutenant, Abbey saw Dr. Fellows raise his eyebrows, then snort at her request. She ignored his mocking gaze.

She turned to Sgt. Scharf who said, "I'll have your instruments sharpened and packed within the hour, Doctor."

After reviewing his own document, Dr. Fellows said to Abbey, "You and I are being sent to the recovery hospital until the move is complete. This will be an opportunity for you to learn additional skills." He sneered. "There's less pressure over there so you're snail's pace surgical technique likely won't kill anyone." He glanced at his pocket watch. "Pack your belongings for a four day stay at the recovery hospital. The team will move the balance of your gear. We leave in two-hours."

***

When Abbey arrived at her tent, she found a short, somewhat pudgy, middle-aged woman, standing in front of it calling her name.

"I'm Doctor Kaplan."

The woman did a double take then said, "Sorry…I didn't realize who you were. I'm Martha Warshawsky. Lieutenant Smith sent me. He said you have laundry work for me. He gave me extra aprons which I will keep clean for you plus I pick up laundry every Monday, Wednesday and Friday then return it the next day." The woman held out her hand with a glowing smile. "It's an honor to meet a lady doctor."

Abbey said under her breath. "It would be nice if everyone thought that." In full voice she continued, "Maybe I should wear a sign so there's no confusion."

"I don't understand. A sign?"

"So people know I'm a doctor. Just joking. Do you live locally?"

The woman laughed. "My daughter and I live in my wagon and follow the regiment."

"A pleasure to meet you. Please come in. I have a pile of clothing you can wash for me plus an item that needs mending."

Abbey noted the woman's uneven gait as she entered the tent.

"Why are you limping?"

"It's nothing. A small irritation on the bottom of my foot."

"Sit on the chair."

"Doctor…"

Abbey raised her voice and pointed. "Sit!"

The woman grimaced while her boot was removed. A laceration beneath her heel was weeping pus.

"I have to drain and bandage this. Don't move."

"You don't have to bother with me."

Abbey smiled. "Mrs. Warshawsky, you'll be my first civilian patient."

The woman squirmed on the chair but remained seated.

Abbey cleaned out the wound, closed it with two sutures and wrapped it. "Any chance you can stay off this for a week?"

She laughed. "Oh no, Doctor. I have to work."

"Keep it clean and try not to put pressure on your heel. I want you to find me each time my laundry is delivered. I'll have a nurse put on a clean bandage and make certain you're healing."

"How much I owe you?"

"Nothing. Just take care of your foot."

Mrs. Warshawsky stuffed Abbey's laundry in a large cloth bag. "I never met a lady doctor before." Martha stopped moving, stared at Abbey briefly, then said, "Um…would you mind if I bring my daughter to meet you. I want Talia to see a lady doctor. I don't want her to end up like me. You know, washing clothes."

"I'd love to meet her."

The woman smiled broadly. "You clothes going to be real clean and in good repair…and you gonna see when I bring them back, people will know you're the doctor." She stuffed the balance of Abbey's laundry into a large cloth bag and limped away.

Sgt. Scharf stood outside the tent and asked permission to enter. Abbey invited him in and returned his salute. "You said you had documents for me?"

"Here," she said, handing him a number of pages. "Details on suturing technique and lessons from the Crimean War. Get down to the mess area. Get a section of pork belly. Use a scalpel to create lacerations like you've seen then practice closing them. When the meat is full of stiches, bring it here and I'll make some cuts and observe you closing them."

"Dr. Fellows is okay with this?"

"He is if you don't tell him."

Chapter Three: More Wounded

"I'm a farmer. Name's Tom Martin. From just west of Brookline, Mass." said a trembling, pale soldier who was lying on a stretcher in front of the field hospital following their latest move. Blood soaked bandages wrapped both his lower legs.

"I heard we'd be treating soldiers from another Massachusetts regiment. You men ran into a large force," Abbey said. She'd been walking among the wounded performing triage. The doctor opened his bandages and examined his wounds.

"Whatever you do, please remember I'm a farmer and I need my legs."

"I'm Dr. Kaplan. We'll take the best care of you we can." She turned to Sgt. Scharf who trailed her. "The soldier from Brookline is first."

The sergeant turned his back to the soldier and whispered, "Double Amputation?"

Abbey nodded then entered the medical tent and assisted Dr. Fellows.

The following morning, Abbey walked among the post-surgery patients who were on beds at the recovery hospital. She observed one soldier, with his arm folded across his eyes. The doctor recognized the farmer from Massachusetts. He whimpered quietly.

Abby smiled and said, "Farmer from Brookline, if I remember."

He uncovered his eyes. "Farmer no longer."

"We did our best to save you. The next step is up to you."

"I won't be taking any damn steps."

Abbey took a deep breath. "Can you see the men working beyond the stand of cottonwood trees?"

He lifted his head sufficiently to glance out a window. "Yes."

"Those men are digging hundreds of graves. You survived."

"A legless farmer isn't my idea of surviving."

Her voice becoming agitated, she insisted, "The Lord has given you an opportunity those men don't have."

Continuing in a bitter tone, he said, "The Lord took my legs. I'm angry as hell at Him."

"He must have other plans for you."

"Like what?"

"It's your responsibility to discover your future."

He shook his head in apparent disbelief. "Something must be wrong with your thinking. You really believe, He has plans for a legless farmer?"

Abbey leaned down and put a hand on his shoulder. "You still have your mind and two good hands."

He brusquely shoved her hand away. "For what?"

She stood straight and said in a motherly tone, "You have a number of week's recovery ahead of you. Ask one of the nurses for books. They may provide ideas for a new occupation."

He turned away then folded an arm across his eyes.

Her voice pleaded, "Investigate careers which utilize brain instead of brawn."

He spun his head back to Abbey and glared at her. The legless farmer opened his mouth as if to reply but remained silent.

As she moved to the next patient, he found his voice and shouted. "You're fucking crazy, Doc."

***

Two weeks later, Dr. Kaplan approached the field hospital. The three large medical tents were surrounded by a grove of tall maples. The red flag hung limply in the hot, humid air.

"*How appropriate*," she thought while shaking her head. "*The indicator of the medical-aid tent is the color of blood.*"

The acrid smell of gun powder wafted through the air while the sound of distant battle portended a stream of casualties.

"Dr. Fellows told me, it would be quiet for another week or so," Abbey said.

"I guess someone forgot to tell the Confederates," Lt. Smith said.

She giggled.

When the wounded were carried from the two-wheeled-ambulances, some moaned, a few yelled, and some were silent. By now, Abbey knew the men who had strength to yell could wait but the quiet one's needed immediate care. A few of the men pleaded with anyone nearby to have their limbs repaired rather than removed. She didn't see Dr. Fellows so she began triage.

"In this order," the doctor said then pointed, "One, two, three, four, five, six…"

A light rain fell causing a rhythm on the medical tent's top and sides. Abbey entered and walked to the surgical table.

"Dr. Fellows?" she asked.

"Indisposed," Sgt. Scharf said.

"What? For how long?"

He mimed a man drinking, then said, "Dr. Fellows was blind drunk last night. His request for your replacement was denied again. The doctor also carried on like a jilted lover concerning the humiliation of having a female assistant surgeon."

"*The bastard*," Abbey thought.

The Sergeant barked orders at the team to prep for surgery and bring in the first patient. The men quickly complied.

"We'll begin…without Dr. Fellows," Abbey said in as confident a tone as she could fake.

Abbey approached a table with supplies on it and unfolded one of her recently cleaned aprons. She smiled briefly. The words, Dr. A. Kaplan, were embroidered in two-inch-high black letters across the top. She said quietly, "Thank you, Mrs. Warshawsky."

Abbey glanced through the entrance of the tent. While cannon fire rumbled in the distance, a long line of ambulances were queued to unload their damaged human cargo.

Trembling, she mumbled to herself, "It's all on me until the bastard sobers up."

Sgt. Scharf, standing at her side, whispered, "One at a time doctor. We treat them one at a time."

Abbey took a deep breath to steady herself, turned to the Sergeant and nodded.

She checked her medical instruments were complete and laid out the way she preferred. Abbey viewed the faces of her team.

"Anyone feel they are unable to help repair the wounded by following a female Doctor's orders?"

Sgt. Scharf gave an angry expression to a few of the team members then said, "It won't be a problem, Doctor."

"Pvt. Wilson," Abbey said, "prepared to take notes as senior medical staff requested?"

"I reviewed the directive you gave me so I'm prepared, Doctor."

"Sgt. Scharf," Abbey said to the lead percussionist. "Your practice with pork belly was sufficient, in Dr. Fellow's absence, I'd appreciate you assisting me."

"Yes, Doctor." He moved from her side to across the table.

"Ready Pvt. Lawrence?" she asked the man administering the chloroform anesthesia.

In a barely audible voice he said, "Yes."

She glared at him until he added, "Doctor."

"We're presented with an otherwise healthy soldier who is missing his left foot, severed just below the termination of his tibia."

Wilson wrote feverishly as she described her work. When the next soldier was placed on the operating table she examined his wounds and said, "We'll be doing circular amputations today because these men will have to be transported a long distance to the recovery hospital. I'm amputating mid-thigh."

A tourniquet was secured by Sgt. Scharf where Dr. Kaplan indicated. Abbey began the incision at the top of the thigh and ran the scalpel down each side and below to the bone. As she cut, Sgt. Scharf pulled the lower muscle away from her work area. She left a flap of skin from the section to be removed which would serve to close the wound. Abbey picked up the bone saw and severed the femur. She picked up a file-type instrument and rounded the sharp edges of the bone so they wouldn't penetrate the skin flap. Abbey ligated many blood vessels, instructed Sgt. Scharf to tie off a few then sutured the covering skin in place.

Dr. Kaplan did her best to appear and sound confident but her tension was revealed when her voice quivered as, for the fiftieth time, she yelled, "Next patient."

The next amputation, a man's right arm, had just begun when Pvt. Lawrence said, "He stopped breathing, Doctor."

"Damn," Abbey cursed.

The deceased man was removed and the next put on the table.

"There is a bullet entry just inside his left shoulder joint." She briefly probed for a bullet, didn't find one so began closing the wound.

"He's not breathing," Cpl. Lawrence said.

"What? It wasn't much of a wound." She rolled the soldier onto his side...and saw the large exit wound. "Shit. He bled out because I didn't check for an exit wound."

"All surgeons make mistakes," Lt. Smith said.

"This mistake killed someone."

"Next patient!" Lt. Smith shouted.

Abbey stood unmoving with furrowed brow while contemplating the mistake which, in her mind, she caused.

"Dr. Kaplan," Sgt. Scharf said, "the next patient needs your attention.

Abbey glanced at the sergeant then nodded. She closed a six-inch curved laceration on a soldier's scalp.

Three patients later, Abbey was closing an amputation when Pvt. Lawrence said, "He's gone." She checked for a pulse, swore under her breath, then shouted, "Next."

After seven-hours, a man was placed on the surgical table with bandages on his left shoulder and missing his left arm. Sgt. Scharf removed the bandages. A couple inches of his humerus remained but had torn loose from the shoulder socket. The tissue surrounding the area reminded Abbey of raw ground beef covered in a thin layer of tomato sauce. "I'll remove the dead tissue and humerus bone." She did then watched Sgt. Scharf as he followed her directions while closing the wound.

Dr. Fellows appeared at her side. He was unsteady but took over as lead surgeon. She moved across the table from him to assist. The stench of bourbon and cigar smoke caused her to regularly bring the back of her hand up to her nostrils. She decided it was better to breath shallow breaths to avoid the disgusting odor. His bourbon scented belches still assaulted her nose.

"*His work is rapid but sloppy,*" Abbey thought. And he didn't describe his work so Pvt. Wilson could record it. The private glanced at Abbey. She shrugged.

Two-hours later, Dr. Fellows nodded to Dr. Kaplan to perform another amputation. He observed for a while then said, "Fast counts, Doctor. Not goddamned pretty."

"The patient is no longer breathing," Cpl. Lawrence said.

"Your slow work killed him," Dr. Fellows said, giving Abbey a disdainful gaze. In a contempt filled voice, he added, "That's why a man is needed to do this work. Continue to lead…Doctor."

Another patient was placed on the table. Abbey closed a laceration across his pectoral muscles then set his broken lower leg bones.

The hot, humid conditions caused sweat to form on her brow. Beads of sweat ran down her back and chest. She noted her clothing sticking to her skin. Salty droplets stung her eyes. She kept wiping with her shoulders until Sgt. Scharf wiped her forehead and cheeks. Abbey nodded a thank you.

"Next," she yelled.

Dr. Fellows took over as lead again.

"You and you, raise the tent sides," Lt. Smith shouted. The men scrambled to comply.

Mercifully, a cool breeze wafted across the medical staff. As if it wasn't sufficiently humid, a light rain began.

Five more surgeries and Dr. Fellows noticed his staff staring at his trembling hands. Just prior to making an incision, he dropped his scalpel. "Dr. Kaplan," he growled, "finish here. I…I…hurt my wrist last night. I'll be in my tent if you need me. And try not to kill anyone else."

Through gritted teeth she replied. "Yes, Doctor Fellows."

He spun on his heal and hurriedly left the medical tent. Sgt. Scharf moved across the table from Abbey and assisted as she completed numerous surgeries.

Seven-hours since she'd begun and three-hours since the shooting died down, Abbey addressed her team. "Seems to have slowed down. Get something to eat and rest for a bit. We'll return in sixty-minutes or sooner if casualties needing surgical intervention arrive."

They were exiting the medical tent when a shell whistled into the area and exploded fifty-yards beyond the tent.

Abbey flattened herself to the ground, copying the example of the others. A few minutes silence ensued.

"Is it over?" Abbey asked.

"I suspect so," Sgt. Scharf said. He helped her to her feet.

"Why would they fire at a medical tent?"

He shrugged. "Not sure. The Confederates are good about respecting medical facilities; even trains with wounded. They most likely didn't know what they were aiming at. I think it's called probing."

Abbey held up her trembling hands. "The explosion shook me up almost as much as being lead surgeon." She brushed off her clothing. "Wonder how many soldiers I killed today?"

"Don't be hard on yourself, Doctor. We always have patients die on the operating table. Some are just too torn up to make it."

"My mistake in not checking for a an exit wound cost someone his life today. I always like to think there was more I could have done and there certainly was for that poor man."

The Sergeant moved directly in front of her and stared in her eyes. "Don't kid yourself. There wasn't anyone else in the tent who could have done what you accomplished."

She turned away briefly then said, "I appreciate your support...and assistance, Sergeant."

"Thank you, but it's become part of my job since you've been training me." He became pensive for a while then said, "Rumor is, this battle will be continuing."

***

Dear Mom,

It's late August as I write this. The second Battle of Bull Run ended ten-hours-ago.

Despite the lack of battle, the acrid scent of burned gunpowder still hangs in the muggy, hot air. Twelve-hours prior, I was sitting on a bench and leaning my exhausted body against a tree. I could barely lift my arms. After thirty-six-hours of surgery, I was desperate for sleep but knew, even as exhausted as I was, it wouldn't come easily as my mind still functioned at the breakneck pace needed to devise surgical interventions for the seemingly endless stream of casualties. My right hand was, and is, sore when I flex it. The palm is red and still pulses from the exertion of gripping a bone saw while its teeth chatter their way through the bone of, yet another, soldier's appendage. I can't count the number of limbs I've removed from these brave young men. Prior to their loss of consciousness due to the chloroform anesthesia, they beseeched us to repair but not remove their torn appendages. At some point my dominant hand was cramping. I tried placing sutures with my other hand. It didn't work.

Like two boxers having savaged each other, the two armies retired to their corners to assess their own and their opponent's damage before eventually re-engaging.

I've learned, initially, most believed the Civil War would last but a few months. Governor Sam Houston of Texas, just before secessionists forced him from office, predicted a long and bloody struggle.

Sadly, he was correct.

We discovered two soldiers walking around aimlessly. They didn't respond to questions but babbled unintelligibly. I suspect their emotional balance was altered after participating in numerous battles. We need to know more about what causes this. Any ideas?

My ankles, knees and hips ache when I stand. I regularly arch forward to stretch my sore back muscles then rotate my shoulders. This helps relieve tension besides loosening my musculature.

Before I forget, I've been told it may be difficult for the post office to find me if you send letters so don't concern yourself with a reply.

As I write this, just after dinner and outside my tent, I see a two-wheeled, covered cart rumbling toward our three medical tents. Two similar units trail it. A nurse has just examined the first wagon's contents and is yelling for me… ironically, this is the same nurse I'd overheard speculating as to what type of woman could perform the removal of limb after limb with "an utter lack of emotion."

I'm needed.

Love to all, Abbey

Chapter Four: Directives

"Dr. Kaplan, this is my daughter, Talia. She's fourteen," Mrs. Warshawsky said with a proud grin.

The doctor said, "Pleased to meet you."

Talia held out her right hand but kept her left in front of her mouth.

"Let me examine that."

Talia was embarrassed but let Abbey examine her hare lip.

"New techniques are discovered all the time. If I learn of a way to repair the opening, I'll let you know."

"Please Lord, that should happen," Mrs. Warshawsky said while stuffing Abbey's laundry into a canvas bag.

"Soon, I hope," Talia whispered.

***

"Dr. Kaplan," a young corporal called out. He was helping remove a man from an ambulance. "This one is pleading to talk to a surgeon."

Although sunny, the brisk air of a cool fall day whipped around them.

Abbey, performing triage, approached the man's stretcher as it was placed near the entrance to the medical tent. The man wore a large bandage on his left hand. His face was dirt-smudged and tear-streaked.

"Are you a surgeon?" he asked. She nodded. "My name is Lawrence Solomon. Remove the contents of my left pocket. You must help me."

Abbey nodded at the corporal who removed a rag from the pocket, opened it and showed three fingers to Abbey.

"You have to replace them," the wounded soldier said. "I've spent my entire life studying piano. I need my fingers. You must re-attach them."

"I'm sorry. We'll do the best we can so the rest of your hand can heal but we're not able to re-attach fingers."

"My ability to share Bach and Mozart gives my life meaning. I have no head for business or technical pursuits. Music is the gift God gave me and playing piano is my gift to Him."

Abbey kneeled at his side and put an hand on his shoulder. "I'm sorry. You need to discover other ways to use your musical gift."

The soldier's eyes filled with tears.

Abbey noted his *mezuzah*. "You're Jewish."

He nodded. Abbey showed him her *mezuzah*.

The pianist pleaded, "You're sure there's nothing you can do?"

"We'll give you the best care possible but are unable to do what you ask."

His heart rending sobs filled the air.

On her way to the surgical tent, she encountered a soldier wearing captain's bars sipping a cup of coffee. "I need a favor, Captain."

The warmly smiling officer stood. "Yes, Doctor Kaplan," he said, after reading her name from her apron. "I'm Captain Ascari. How may I be of assistance?"

"One of the casualties I'll be working on shortly was a pianist. I used the word 'was' because he lost three fingers today."

"How tragic."

"If possible, can you send word to have a Jewish chaplain report to me? I believe it may help the soldier if he speaks to clergy."

"I'll ask around, Doctor."

***

"Dr. Kaplan, Thank you for asking for me." He stood in line next to her while mess soldiers served coffee late the same day. The term bookish would have described the man who addressed her; short, on the chubby side, with thick lenses in his glasses which sat half way down his nose, his face surrounded by a dark, curly full beard.

"You're welcome, Rabbi. How was your conversation with Pvt. Solomon?"

"Difficult. He mostly cried but we did recite a few prayers." He gazed at Abbey for a while but then said. "You are a woman working in a sea of men in what is, considered by most, a man's profession."

Abbey stiffened. "But more importantly, I'm a surgeon repairing a sea of wounded soldiers."

"Yes, of course. For certain you are."

Abbey motioned him to sit across from her at a mess table.

He took a sip of dark brew. "If I may ask, what goals have you set for yourself?"

"Become a skilled surgeon…and learn to exist in a man's profession."

"How do you relate to your superiors?"

"With difficulty. My immediate superior resents my gender, speaks to me disrespectfully and continually reminds me, I'll be replaced soon."

The rabbi cleared his throat and said, "How do you manage such a difficult situation?"

"I bury myself seven-days-a-week in medical work including research, reading and writing reports. Haven't considered much else; although I try to light *Shabbat* candles on Friday night and *Havdalah* Saturday evening as long as I'm not performing surgery."

The Rabbi smiled. "What do those simple acts do for you?"

"Reminds me of my family and allows me to feel a sense of home for a few minutes."

"That's all?"

"The light reminds me, as a Jew, I have a responsibility to use the gifts the Lord gave me even if my environment tries to prevent their use." Abbey thought for a while then added, "My spiritual self takes a beating on a regular basis."

"How so?"

"I've been thrown into a wartime environment, where I must work at the limits of my, admittedly, beginner surgical ability while acquiring new techniques...all the while enduring daily reminders, most believe I should be home raising a family."

"You are a contract surgeon?"

"Yes."

"You can leave."

"As a doctor...and a Jew...I have a responsibility to the wounded whether they approve of my gender or not. And my goal is to become an accomplished surgeon and learn as much practical knowledge about disease as I can."

Rabbi Schulman folded his hands and leaned toward her, saying in a quiet voice, "You're putting immense pressure on yourself."

"My job and my future as an accomplished doctor require it."

"Your mental balance may suffer."

"How?"

"Irrevocable sadness. Also depression, difficulty sleeping, becoming easily provoked."

"You've witnessed this?"

"I served with the British during the Crimean War. Those with altered emotional state may also injure themselves or commit suicide."

"Injure themselves? Such as?"

"Shooting themselves in the foot or hand, even shooting off a trigger finger…all to get out of combat."

"I've treated wounds that, I suspect, were self-inflicted."

"I believe you are to report them to your superiors."

"Yes, but I had no way to be sure." Abbey became pensive, taking long sips of coffee then asked, "Did the British discover methods to treat injuries of the mind?"

"None I'm aware of. A soldier's altered mentality isn't even considered a disease, let alone a treatable one."

"According to my chief surgeon, strong men don't commit suicide."

The Rabbi appeared surprised then asked, "Your thoughts?"

"Along the lines of…how much horror can one mind endure…whether strong or not."

The rabbi smiled, "You've been thinking about this." He nodded and stroked his beard. "This is an area of medicine painfully lacking in solutions."

"I try to accumulate information on the environment of soldiers who have lost their mental balance."

"Excellent…you're working on helping them." The Rabbi nodded with a smile then sighed. "It's painful you lack respect."

"Most assuredly."

"My brother will be traveling to the Middle East in a number of weeks to visit the city of Hebron in Palestine. Have you heard of Menucha Rochel Slonim?"

"No."

"She provides warmth, love and Torah wisdom to the women of Hebron. Perhaps you'd like to write her a note asking for a blessing? My brother would be honored to present it to her."

"Thoughtful of you Rabbi, but…"

"What would it hurt? A small note in an envelope. No one sees it but you and her. Besides, I have a feeling she'd enjoy knowing you and what you're accomplishing."

"You've met her?"

"Yes. My wife and I have a sixteen-year-old son whose hips are twisted." He sighed. "Max was born disabled. He suffers substantial discomfort when walking. During a trip to Hebron some years ago, my wife asked Menucha for a blessing to heal him."

"And?"

"They had a long talk which I wasn't privy to. When we returned home, my wife stopped acting like she and our son were suffering a punishment. My beloved spouse found new strength to take care of our crippled son and our other children. Suddenly, instead of coddling him, she expected the same good behavior and scholarship as our other three children."

"So Menucha didn't heal him."

"As it happens, she realized my wife needed the healing."

"Your son?"

The rabbi smiled with pride. "As his siblings before him, off to college."

"I don't think I need healing."

"A little note…perhaps asking for strength or patience when dealing with your detractors…what would it hurt?" He shrugged then leaned toward her and said, "I fear your environment, as you put it, is more painful than you realize…which may lead to a deterioration of your mind"

***

A number of days and countless surgeries later, Abbey, pen in hand, wrote medical summaries at a small table in her tent. In addition, she put collected tissue samples in alcohol filled containers. They would be shipped to the Washington Medical Museum. Each was labeled with a description and the condition of the soldier. It was early evening. The last of the sun's rays provided scant illumination. A single oil lantern on the table cast long shadows on the tent walls.

"Dr. Kaplan," the chief surgeon called from the opened entrance.

"Come in, Doctor Fellows."

He stood across from her desk, wobbling slightly, obviously intoxicated. "I reviewed your notes from your surgical interventions of the last few weeks."

Abbey explained, "In your absence, I complied with the circular-two directive from the Surgeon General's office concerning reports on each patient."

She put the back of her hand up to her nose as he reeked of cigar smoke and bourbon.

"Yes, Yes. The circulars. I appreciate the effort you put into them but they don't need so much detail."

"Circular-two requires it…we're responsible to write and forward to the Medical Museum, detailed reports on all our patients."

"I know but we have so much to do, we don't always have time…"

"Circular-two isn't a request. It's a direct order…" She picked up a different document, "as spelled out in circular-five."

"Damn you. No one wants you here. You belong at home, raising a family…not pretending to be a man. The soldiers are all grumbling because they don't want a woman doctor treating them."

Abby stood. At six-feet and nearly a head taller, she looked down at Dr. Fellows. With fury in her expression and an angry voice, she declared, "Seeing as the surgical patients are unconscious due to anesthesia, we won't hear complaints from them." She gave Doctor Fellows a long glare, raised her hands to her hips and spoke in a sarcastic tone. "Besides, I'm sure the chief surgeon, who holds the rank of major, won't let resentment I'm female become a problem for his assistant surgeon, however briefly her stay may be."

Dr. fellows appeared momentarily flustered by her angry outburst then recovered enough of his own anger to mumble, "Well…don't bet on that."

Dr. Fellows hesitated as if he was contemplating what he would say next. Now visibly trembling, he shouted through liquor scented breath, "Damn it. I'm a major. You don't argue with me. I'm sure you enjoy knowing your name will appear in the museum's records…"

She interrupted. "As it specifies in circular-two, we're doing it to put American medicine on a scientific basis."

Now rage was written in his face and demeanor. "God damn it." He ripped his hat off and threw it on the ground.

He shook a pointed finger in her face. "I've been a doctor since long before you were born. You're doing this to make me look bad."

Abbey brought her hands to shoulder height, palms up. "By following the surgeon general's orders?"

"I don't have time for asinine paperwork! Sending preserved samples to Washington is a bunch of crap." He shook a fist at her then shoved a bunch of her papers off the desk. They fluttered to the ground. "I will not be made a fool."

Abbey struggled to maintain her composure. She spoke through gritted teeth. "If I'm the lead surgeon, as I was while you were…indisposed…then I'm responsible for compliance and I will do as ordered."

He ignored her response then shook his head. "Another thing. You will not, I repeat, not, open bodies of dead soldiers for any reason."

"Autopsies are recommended by Washington to enhance our learning of internal organs and their placement. We also preserve diseased tissue from autopsies for later examination."

"You get permission from me before you do any desecrations of soldier's bodies."

Abbey turned away and folded her arms across her chest.

His eyes widened and he suddenly seemed consumed with righteous anger. The chief surgeon's entire body shook. "God in heaven. You…fucking…bitch, you've already been doing them."

Her head spun in his direction. She growled, "Yes. I have. I asked the recovery hospital to notify me of soldiers who died of erysipelas and gangrene plus gut-wounds so I could examine them."

The vane's in his neck throbbed. "How dare you desecrate soldiers bodies!"

"We can learn from them to help save others. I believe most soldiers would approve."

"How do you know? Did you ask them? You have permission from their families?"

Abbey was filled with fury but spoke slowly and succinctly, "The soldiers deaths are tragic but we can learn from an autopsy so we can improve techniques and save other wounded. What better final service for a deceased soldier than to help his fellow soldiers survive their wounds?"

He raged. "I've never needed autopsies to perform my work."

"I had little exposure to the inside of a human body during college."

"Because autopsy is illegal in most states. The rest of us manage to take care of our patients without it. As will you…Dr. Kaplan."

"Doctors who have the money, go to Paris where learning from cadavers is accepted practice. The more I know about the inside of the body, the more effective my surgical technique." She glared at him and waved a pointed finger in his face. "You could learn from them as well."

The neck veins of the red faced doctor visibly pulsed. He screamed, "You work for me, you fucking bitch! Who the hell do you think you are?"

Abbey shouted, "A recent graduate with much to learn and directives to comply with."

"While you're learning, you'll do what I say and you'll not work in a way which makes me a…laughing stock."

A colonel appeared just outside Abbey's tent. He shouted, "Major Fellows! Please join me out here."

Dr. Fellows, trembling and panting heavily, glared at Abbey for a second, retrieved his hat, jerked it onto his head then angrily spun on his heel and left the tent.

She heard agitated whispers, the word bitch and the Lord's name used in vain numerous times, then Dr. Fellows constantly repeating the words, "Yes Sir."

Abbey sighed, stared at the stack of papers on her desk and thought, *"What am I doing here? I'm leered at, not respected by members of my team…not to mention the chief surgeon…and without a single friend to talk to."*

She walked to and closed the entrance to her tent. *"Isn't it enough, I take the same risk as anyone else at a field hospital? I'm not respected because I have different genitals?"* Abbey stared at the tent walls, slowly shaking her head then thought, *"Wonder what Mom would say when gender becomes an issue?"* She thought briefly, smiled and then laughed out loud as she heard Myra's voice telling her, "Ask your detractors, how someone will provide the troops with better medical care because of a difference in their genitalia."

The doctor slumped onto her cot, leaned back and closed her eyes. She thought, *"My goal in coming here was to learn more medicine. Particularly surgery."* She looked over the stack of reports and directives piled on her desk. *"I'm achieving that…but the damned lack of respect is painful…well…I hear you Mom…to hell with the detractors. I'm not going to let it stop me. I came here to learn and that's what I'll do until they drag my butt out of here."*

Abbey took a few more deep breaths, trying to relax then stretched her arm and back muscles. The doctor returned to her desk, adjusted the wick of her oil lamp and continued writing.

Around midnight, she took out a sheet of paper to write a letter to her mother. Abbey thought for a while then put the paper away. *"Mom doesn't need to know how difficult things are and I certainly have little pleasant news to write about. When I have success to write about, I'll put pen to pap*er."

Later that night, Abbey stood outside her tent looking at the stars when three soldiers came up to her. They saluted and a corporal said, "I believe you're Doctor Kaplan?"

"How can I help?"

"A member of our squad is talking funny. Sgt. Scharf said we should talk to you."

A second man said, "We don't think he's getting any sleep."

"Is he injured?"

"No, Ma'am."

"I doubt I have a cure for sleep disorders."

"If you got time Doc, we'd appreciate you looking at him."

Abbey nodded and said, "Lead the way but let me get a notebook from my tent first."

Another of the soldiers volunteered while they walked, "He and his brother got separated during a battle a few weeks ago. We walked over this rise and found the brother. He'd been blown in half and his face was all messed up."

They stopped in front of a man sitting on a small barrel. He was using a knife with a four inch blade to whittle a small stick.

"I'm Doctor Kaplan."

He stood, grinned and saluted. "Pvt. Dennis, Ma'am. What can I do for you?"

She returned his salute. "Please sit down." One of the soldiers quickly provided a stool so she could sit next to him. "Your friends are concerned about you."

"Thank you but I'm fine Ma'am." He began whittling again.

"I understand you lost someone."

"It's a war. Loss of family members is going to happen."

"Your hand is bleeding."

He opened the hand which held the stick revealing a number of lacerations. "Must have been holding it too tight," he said with a laugh.

"Come to the medical tent. We'll bandage your hand."

"I'll be alright Ma'am." He began whittling again.

She stood. "Private, this is an order. Put down the knife and stick. One of your friends and I will accompany you to the medical tent."

The man dropped the items and jumped to attention. "Yes, Ma'am."

Abbey turned to his friends.

One of them mouthed, "Thanks, Doc."

At the medical tent, Abbey cleaned his hand and Cpl. Silver began wrapping it. "How long have you been in combat, Private Dennis?"

With pride in his voice, he stated, "Since First Bull Run, Ma'am."

"Are you having trouble sleeping?"

"Occasionally. But I'm alright."

"Sad about your brother."

"He's fine."

Abbey watched his eyes. He seemed to be communicating with someone behind her and Cpl. Silver but no one was there.

She asked, "What do see?"

"James. My brother."

Abbey hesitated then asked, "Is he talking to you?"

"Sure. Talks to me all the time."

"Private, I'm going to keep you here so you can get a good night's rest."

"No, Ma'am. We might be going into combat and my squad needs me."

"You need to sleep."

He started fidgeting; not knowing where to put his hands. "I won't. I mean I can't."

"Why?"

"I get this…" The man began to tremble.

"This what?"

"James. Tell her why I can't close my eyes."

"Corporal. Listen to me. James is not here. He died."

The man laughed. "No…ain't true. Ma said we must watch out for each other…I promised her. He's my little brother and I wouldn't…" he glanced past her. "Tell her, James."

"Private, tell me why you can't sleep."

"I'll see…" His trembling increased and the color drained from his face.

"What?"

"Shit. Terrible shit."

"Like what?"

The man's eye's went wide as an expression of terror spread across his face. He screamed and leaned back, crossing his arms in front of his face as if trying to ward off a terrifying apparition. Abbey grabbed his wrists and yelled his name. The private abruptly quit trembling, his eyes seemed to glaze over. The soldier's arms slowly went limp, then dropped to his sides; his expression went blank. He stared straight ahead.

"Pvt. You'll see what?"

She shook his shoulders. "Private Dennis? Talk to me."

Abbey thought for a minute then slapped his face. There was no reaction. She tried harder; hard enough to leave red marks on his cheek, but still no reaction from the soldier.

The doctor turned to his squad mate. "You can head back to your unit. He appears exhausted. We'll send him to the recovery hospital and see if rest will help."

"Speaking of which, you look exhausted yourself, Doc."

***

When Abbey arrived in her tent a few weeks later, a letter from Hebron was on her desk.

"Dearest Doctor Abbey Kaplan, Just enjoyed reading your letter. Your diligence, hard work, and devotion to your patients has strengthened my spirit. People have been telling me to slow down, as now I'm sixty-six. However, having been inspired by the example of your work ethic, I will find the strength to do more for my community.

I've told my friends of your dedication to medicine and specifically surgery. You've strengthened our resolve to perform *mitzvot*. Every *Shabbat*, we will say a *Mi Sheberach* for your patients and light an extra candle until the war between the states ends. I hope you find time to light *Shabbat* candles as well. The world always needs more light. Please know, the women of Hebron are praying for you.

Remember, Dr. Abbey, even when you seem alone, the Lord is with you. As you are performing such good works, I know He will send you the appropriate assistance.

When you have time, I'd love to hear from you again.

Love from Hebron, your friend, Menucha."

Abbey stared at the letter then leaned back and closed her eyes. She smiled and thought, *"How ironic. Women half way around the world are supporting me."*

***

Four-weeks later Dr. Kaplan was again performing the role of lead surgeon.

"Only gut-shot patients out there," Lt. Scharf said, after seven-hours of surgery.

Abbey finished cleaning her instruments then said, "Bring one in."

A soldier was placed on the table with a wound to his lower-right abdomen.

Abbey inspected the injury. "I'll remove the ball, clean the wound of debris and attempt to repair the torn intestine."

She worked feverishly for over an hour.

"Find another gut-shot patient."

Lt. Smith asked, "Aren't gut-wounds always fatal?"

"NOW!" she shouted.

Abbey attempted repair of three more abdominal wounds.

***

At the recovery hospital five-days later, Abbey examined the gut-shot patients.

One was near death, one was suffering terrible pain, and both their wounds wept pus.

She cleaned the wounds as best she could then asked, "Where's the third and fourth men?"

"Down there," a nurse said. "One's doing better but the other is in lots of pain and the same as these men."

Abbey walked to the man's side and lifted the sheet covering his injury.

The man moaned.

Her jaw dropped. His repaired gut-wound was healing. The area wasn't warm to the touch nor showed signs of infection. Dr. Kaplan applied gentle pressure on the area above his appendix.

"Don't," the soldier screamed.

She turned to the nurses. "I need chloroform, alcohol, and my surgical instruments."

Two nurses ran from the ward but returned quickly.

The nurses prepped the man for surgery. Abbey, after cleaning her instruments, removed his appendix.

"I want his bandages replaced daily," she told the nurse.

"Consider it done, Doctor."

"And clean your hands before you change the bandage." She glanced at the other men with gut-wounds. "If their condition changes I wish to be notified immediately."

She noted a major talking to a few of the wounded. Abbey asked a nurse if he was a doctor.

"No. He does something at headquarters but visits the wounded troops regularly. Name of Sokolov, I believe."

**

Just before Abbey began camp medicine, Dr. Fellows approached. Sgt. Scharf whispered to Abbey. "Take a gander at the wisp of a fellow with our chief surgeon. A good puff of wind would carry him away."

"I learned of your adventures with abdominal wounds. Don't do it again," the old doctor grumbled at Abbey.

A skinny young man with a shy expression stood at his side. He glanced briefly at Abbey then stared at the tops of his shoes.

The lady doctor explained, "But two of them recovered despite having pierced intestines…which I repaired."

He sneered. "Even a broken clock is correct twice a day you fool. You'll not experiment on soldiers again."

Abbey was incredulous. "Experiment? I used procedures as specified in a directive and saved two lives."

"Gut-shots are fatal. Everyone knows except, apparently, some bureaucrats in Washington. You'll treat those wounds as such; not waste time on them. Do I make myself clear?"

She replied sweetly with no intention of complying, "Yes, Doctor."

"This is Dr. Albert Nelson. He'll be training with us."

"Pleased to meet you, Dr. Kaplan." He held out a thin hand, glanced at her face then returned his gaze to his shoe tops.

"Dr. Nelson, in honor of your arrival, please join me in my tent for a drink."

"I don't."

"What?"

"Drink alcohol."

Dr. Fellows glared at the new arrival.

"Then go with her and she'll begin your training. I'll be at the recovery hospital." As he left the area, Abbey heard him mumble, "Is this command's idea of a man?"

Five-hours of camp medicine followed with Dr. Nelson observing and occasionally assisting.

"Time for lunch," Abbey said after she directed a nurse to bandage a wound she'd just closed.

"Tell me about yourself," She said to the newcomer as they filled their muckets.

"From Vermont. Lived in a small town near Lake Champlain."

"Beautiful country I hear."

"Incredibly peaceful once you're away from the city."

"Which city?"

"Burlington."

They ate quietly for a bit then he volunteered, "My father is a doctor so everyone expected me to go into medicine."

"If you were to choose a career…"

"Short story writer." He gazed skyward with an expression which made Abbey think he was enjoying a pleasant memory. "I'd extol the virtues of sailing and fly-fishing."

"The only sailing I've done was on the ship which took us to the Northwest. I hated it."

"Not large boat sailing. I'm talking small boat. Only the sound of the water gently kissing the hull and the creaking of the rigging to listen to. My boat is nineteen-feet-long. I worked in a boatyard after school for three years until I had enough money to buy it."

"Seems a long way from medicine."

"My father decided my career." He sighed. "Also insisted I join the military as our family's contribution to the cause."

Abbey stared at his thin body.

"I know. Skinny and, although I'm twenty-one, I don't shave yet."

"I'm sorry…"

"Don't be. I was sickly as a child."

Abbey sighed then asked, "Are you my replacement?"

"I was asked not to discuss my future with you."

She nodded over her shoulder. "Ambulances approaching. Let's prep for surgery."

In the surgical tent and closing a large laceration on a man's thigh, Abbey's ears perked up as high-pitched-whistling sound screamed at them.

Someone screamed, "Incoming!"

"Hit the dirt," Sgt. Scharf yelled.

Abbey glanced at him, her surgical instruments still in hand. He bounded over the surgical table, roughly shoved her to the ground then covered as much of her body with his as possible.

She tried to push him away as they heard more high pitched sounds followed by explosions. Each explosion's pressure-wave hitting them milliseconds before the sound reached them. Two nearby explosions, each making the earth to tremble, assaulted their ears and caused constant ringing.

The Sgt.'s barely audible words, "Stay Still," were punctuated by an explosion which cut holes in the tent making its sides and roof appear like Swiss cheese. A soldier screamed as his intestines spilled from his body. He grabbed at them screaming in a tremulous voice for his mother…while trying to return them to his abdomen. Abbey prayed, "Please Lord, don't let me end up torn to pieces."

Chapter Five: On the Battlefield

Abbey's ears were ringing so loud, she heard little else as Sgt. Scharf helped her stand. She saw rather than heard him say the words, "We have to get out of here."

"The patients," she yelled.

"Later," he screamed. "We're being overrun."

She didn't move. They cringed as more explosions occurred nearby.

He screamed in her ear, "You can't help them if you're dead."

A large explosion knocked them off their feet a second time. She quickly stood, this time helping Sgt. Scharf stand. The sergeant grabbed Dr. Nelson's arm and pulled until he began moving with them. The threesome ran opposite the enemy's direction and into the surrounding woods.

A few more shells exploded in front then behind them.

"We need to keep going," Sgt. Scharf screamed.

"*I haven't run this hard since I was a child,*" Abbey thought as her feet slapped a terrified rhythm into the dry soil.

They'd run seventy-yards when Abbey's ears recovered sufficiently to hear the angry-bee sound of the enemy's lead balls as they whizzed past. Her leg muscles were tiring and she was winded.

Dr. Nelson, running ahead of Abbey and panting deeply, slowed and turned to glance behind. A roughly half-inch red hole appeared at the front of his skull, just above his nose. The rear of his head and a red mist of blood and brain-matter exploded out the back. Abbey cursed then dug deep inside to find the strength to ignore her muscle pain and increase her torrid pace.

They reached the middle of a field bisected by a fence line. Four squads of Union soldiers wearing Michigan insignia were arrayed along the mostly open rail fence which utilized two horizontal beams roughly three-feet apart and X-shaped supports every ten-feet. Sgt. Scharf leaped over the barrier and Abbey ducked through the middle. They each took adjacent positions in the battle line. One squad was to their left and three to their right as they faced the enemy. Two of the soldiers were cut down. Sgt. Scharf kneeled next to one while Abbey checked the second. They looked at each other and shook their heads. The Sergeant picked up the dead soldier's lever-action Spencer rifle, fired seven rounds then began reloading.

Abbey flattened herself to the ground at his side while bullets whizzed overhead. A cannon shell exploded twenty-five-yards behind them. With shaking hands, lungs on fire and heart pounding with the intensity of a galloping horse, the doctor picked up the other soldier's lever-action rifle. Lying flat on her back, the doctor took a handful of cartridges, pulled the spring from the rifle's butt and inserted more rounds. She swore as her sweaty fingers allowed one of the cartridges to drop into the dirt. When the rifle Sgt. Scharf was using emptied, they traded and she began reloading again. The enemy small-arms-fire intensified. They heard the whistling sound of another shell. Abbey rolled onto her belly, covering her head with her hands.

Sgt. Scharf's sweat covered face evidenced anger. "Keep Low," he yelled.

The doctor thought, "*I can't get any damn lower 'cuz my buttons are in the way.*"

Bullets whizzed past them like angry bees. A large whump sounded behind them. Abbey dropped her rifle, rolled over into a fetal position and covered her head.

They were showered by dirt and the remnants of a hedgerow. Abbey grabbed for the rifle, which was now covered in soil. She momentarily considering wiping the dirt off it and her hands but with the enemy's rifle fire getting closer, her mind screamed, it was time to shoot…not clean.

Sgt. Scharf and now Abbey as well, began firing at the line of advancing enemy soldiers. They were within fifty-yards of the twosome's position when a tremendous fusillade of enemy rifle fire rang out. Numerous Michigan soldiers screamed and collapsed. The doctor dropped three enemy soldiers and the man carrying the unit flag. Another man picked it up and they continued advancing.

"*This could be the end*," she thought, briefly glancing around at what might become her final resting place. "*What an ugly place to die.*"

Out of the corner of her eye, Abbey spotted movement thirty-yards to their left. Seeing a kneeling soldier wearing a gray uniform aiming a musket at them, she swung her rifle in his direction. The enemy soldier fired and a bullet struck a nearby infantryman who moaned and pitched forward. Abbey wrenched the lever of her Spencer to chamber another round then aimed center mass and fired; her bullet knocking the bark off a tree just above and behind the enemy combatant's left shoulder. He stood to reload. She racked the lever action again, aimed slightly left and down from center mass then fired again. This time she struck him mid-chest and he toppled backwards. Sgt. Scharf glanced in the direction she'd fired. "More gray coats over there," he shouted then partially stood and surveyed the terrain behind them.

"We're being flanked." He screamed to the soldiers on his left, "Corporal, take your squad, drop back, and cut off the flanking movement." Sgt. Scharf turned to his right and yelled, "Lieutenant, I suggest you move one squad to my left to cover that part of the line, then we'll gradually fall back. There's a dry streambed behind us which we can use for cover."

"You heard the Sergeant. Move your asses!" the lieutenant screamed at the top of his lungs while trying to sound confident…but his shaky voice betrayed his fear.

"Abbey, we need to get out of here."

Abbey didn't move but stared at the last soldier she'd shot. Sgt. Scharf grabbed her shoulder and shook her. "We have to move." He took the rectangular leather pouch that was the dead soldier's cartridge box and placed it's strap over his shoulder. Abbey did the same. Rifles in hand, they belly-crawled, keeping their heads as low as possible while small-arms-rounds, now sounding like an angry hornet's nest, buzzed just over them. Rounds hit the dirt space which separated them. A high pitched sound approached them.

"Incoming," Sgt. Scharf yelled putting his body over Abbey and one arm over his head. The ground shook and again, they were showered with dirt and debris.

"Damn," Abbey cursed, realizing the right side of her face landed in warm manure. She wiped her face on her shoulder while they continued crawling. The doctor was forced to pull herself along primarily using her hands, forearms and elbows as her long skirt limited effective assistance from her legs.

"Keep moving!" the sergeant shouted.

A shell exploded in a nearby stand of cottonwoods. The shell's fuse caused it to explode before it hit the ground. Splintered wood, branches and bark struck them; killing three of the infantry soldiers, wounding numerous more plus cutting and bruising Abbey and Lt. Scharf.

They continued crawling, dragging themselves over sharp gravel and branches which cut and tore at their bodies. The duo and the remaining soldiers withdrew another twenty-yards then took cover in the dry streambed. Crouching, Sgt. Scharf moved up and back among the soldiers to direct their fire. He and Abbey continued shooting. When she ran out of ammo, she belly-crawled to dead soldiers or those too injured to fire their weapons, utilizing the rounds in their cartridge boxes. The line of enemy soldiers was now only twenty-yards away. A handful had advanced close enough to their line, some of the combatants were engaged in hand-to-hand fighting.

They were running out of ammo and the doctor thought they'd have to retreat again when multiple squads of Union soldiers and horse cavalry came up behind them and engaged the enemy force; pushing them back until, sixty-minutes and many deaths later, the bulge in the northern line would no longer exist.

Abbey rolled onto her back. Only now did the doctor take stock of how frightened she was. She experienced difficulty catching her breath; her entire body was covered in sweat and trembled. Her hands to wiped more of the cow manure off her face and neck then wiped them on her skirt. Small cuts on her arms bled. The distant shooting and cannon fire gradually died down. The doctor rolled onto her right elbow and sat up. Sgt. Scharf held out a hand to assist her in standing.

She closed her eyes and still sitting, held up a hand, palm out. "Please let me rest," she said, in between deep breaths.

"Take your time."

Abbey examined her trembling hands then examined nicks and scrapes from the tree detritus plus the damage to her forearms and elbows from pulling herself along the ground.

"You okay?" the sergeant said.

"Other than frightened out of my mind, I think so. Minor cuts. That's all. I stink like horseshit. Tough to crawl across the ground in a dress."

"You need britches…and, just like the other officers, should likely keep a pistol on your hip just in case."

"I agree about the pistol…but wearing britches…someone might mistake me for a man."

Without looking at her, Sgt. Scharf said. "Not from the front or side."

Abbey glared at him momentarily then burst out in tension-relieving laughter.

He smiled.

She closed her eyes and took a few deep breaths. "That was some shit."

"It was." He reached out with both hands and helped her stand.

"We should see what we can do for the wounded." Abbey removed her underskirt; tearing it into strips. She and the sergeant began applying bandages.

"These three will need surgery."

"Let's get back and I'll send men to recover them."

Abbey examined her hands. "First time these hands have shot someone."

"Either that or the sniper would have killed us. How many do you think you shot?"

"Not sure. Too busy shooting. Maybe four, five; maybe more." Abbey sighed. "I came here to learn medicine and surgery; learn to save people."

"And that's what you do."

She slowly shook her head. "Not all the time, apparently," she mumbled. Her mind replayed the memory of the Confederate soldier as he crumpled to the ground. She shuddered.

The Michigan company's lieutenant approached them. He and Sgt. Scharf exchanged salutes. "Thanks for the direction, Sergeant. That was my first time in combat. Not at all certain what to do. It hurts to admit but I didn't notice we were being flanked."

"Your Wolverines acquitted themselves well."

"Thank you. During training we were told we could rely on experienced Sergeants like yourself." He saluted.

The sergeant smartly returned the salute. The lieutenant walked away.

Abbey compared her rifle to the sergeant's. "The barrel on my rifle is shorter."

"It's called a carbine."

"Less accurate?"

"Not at these distances. A carbine is easier to maneuver in close-quarters battle."

"This wasn't your first time in combat?" Abbey asked her helper.

"Possibly sixth or seventh. I've lost count." He sighed. "In case we run into more…stuff, I'll get permission to hang on to the rifles and cartridge boxes. Besides bullets, I'm going to carry an extra box filled with bandages and lint."

Returning to the field hospital, they found felled and wounded soldiers of both armies scattered about. The field hospital's tents were in shreds from the cannon and rifle fire. The pole which held the red flag was lying on the ground having been splintered near its base.

Abbey searched for her surgical instruments. She found the remnants of their case. Most of her surgical tools were bent and twisted. Abbey secured a bowl of water and washed off as best she could.

Sgt. Scharf walked up with armloads of bandages and lint then handed them to team members who busied themselves with the wounded. He glanced around and said, "I need to get more." He turned away and Abbey yelled at him to stop.

"You have blood all over the back of your shirt and right buttock."

"I think I was nicked when the first shell hit then by the damn airburst in the trees."

"Take off your shirt. Pvt. Silver, over here. Clean his back, please." She found a serviceable pair of forceps and poured alcohol over them. Abbey began removing wood and steel shrapnel from the area over his shoulder blades. He winced and gritted his teeth each time she probed. The private held a tin cup which clanked as Abbey dropped pieces of metal shrapnel in it. The doctor closed two of the wounds with sutures. "Lower your britches."

He did and two jagged pieces from his left butt cheek clanked into the tin cup. "Stay still until the private finishes bandaging your wounds then we need to find Lt. Smith and get setup for surgery."

"Yes Doctor," Sgt. Scharf said, while he pulled up his britches.

"And thank you," Abbey said.

"For what?"

"My face was against your shoulder when the explosion in the tent occurred. The pieces of shrapnel which struck your shoulder blade would have been in my face."

"Your accurate shooting…taking out the sniper…you probably saved one or both of us."

The doctor relived a pleasant memory. "I learned about guns from my brothers and an old trapper." She shrugged. "It was little more than a game then."

The hospital attendant ran up. "The tents are worthless. We have to setup in the open, Doctor."

"Most of my instruments were destroyed."

"I noticed. Have an extra set squirreled away. I've sent a private to recover them."

"Lieutenant, have you seen Dr. Fellows?"

"He's collapsed in his tent."

"Wounded?"

"Passed out. Drunk."

She stepped over two bodies. One blue-coated and the other in a gray uniform. One's head split open and the other's body nearly ripped in half. She took a deep breath and while letting it out slowly, thought, "*Young boys who look to be the age of my brothers. They should have been out fishing or flirting with girls or learning a trade.*" She sighed and slowly shook her head. "*Now their torn bodies are only fit for stuffing a pine box.*"

Abbey stared at them without moving. Her mind replayed a vision of the soldier she'd shot as he crumpled to the ground. She said in a subdued voice, "Someone's son. A mother will be grieving due to my carefully aimed shot. If one of my brothers died, it would tear my mother's heart out." Abbey continued in a quiet voice with bowed head as if she were praying, "I'm sorry I was the instrument of your death, whoever you were."

She approached the surgical table and gazed at her assembled team. "Where's Wilson?"

"First shell killed him."

"I'll cover for him," Lt. Smith said.

After nods from the trumpet-playing-chloroform-administrator and her now helper, Sgt. Scharf, Dr. Kaplan concentrated her remaining mental and physical energy on numerous surgical interventions until well after nightfall.

Working by lantern light, she said, "Please try to keep the damn insects away from the surgical field. And try to keep the lamps still."

"Difficult to swat bugs with one hand and keep the lamp still with the other," one of her helpers complained.

While suturing a head laceration, she said, "Do your best, please."

Around one in the morning, they completed the last surgery. She tried to eat but only managed a few bites. Exhaustion overwhelmed her. Abbey dragged her tired body back to her tent. She noted three pairs of waist overalls on her desk. She thought, "*Where the hell was our chief surgeon today?*"

***

The sounds of battle decreased. Abbey, lying five-yards from Sgt. Scharf, spotted an enemy soldier aiming at him. She carefully aimed and fired. The soldier toppled fell onto his belly. They approached the fallen man.

Sgt. Scharf turned him over.

She gasped and her heart pounded.

"Abbey," her brother William said, "you shot me."

"I wouldn't," she said.

The doctor awoke with a start; jerked up to a sitting position. Covered in sweat, her breathing rapid and heart pounding. "What an awful dream," she announced to the empty tent.

Abbey poured water into a basin. She moistened a rag and rubbed it with her last sliver of the perfumed soap she'd brought from home. As she washed off the previous day's dirt, she thought, "*Wish I could wipe away the memory of killing that soldier as easily as I remove the dirt from this soiled body.*" The doctor stared into the gray water. "*I used Kentucky windage like my brothers taught me, squeezed the trigger instead of jerking it like Andre taught me…and extinguished the life of some mother's son. At least those dying from surgical errors weren't intentional.*" She shrugged her shoulders. "*Either way, dead is dead. But why the dream about my brother?*"

***

Dr. Fellows appeared late the following morning just as Abbey was getting a mug of coffee at the mess tent. He gave her a disapproving glare when he noticed her waist overalls then rapidly puffed a few times on a cigar which was clamped between his teeth. "I haven't seen Dr. Nelson."

"Sorry to say, he died during the attack. Poor man. He was a gentle soul."

The older doctor's eyes widened. "He was to be your replacement. I moved heaven and earth to get him out here."

He cursed again, took a deep breath and let it out slowly. "I'm told the surgeries you performed yesterday went well."

Abbey nodded.

"No experiments, I trust."

"Do you really want to know?"

"Absolutely not." The Major puffed hard on his cigar then slowly shook his head. "Just received a note from the recovery hospital, two of the soldiers with gut-wounds you treated died but two, including the one whose appendix you removed, are doing well. They are well enough, they should recover completely."

"Thank you for telling me. I wanted to ask…we examined a number of seemingly able-bodied men who were unconscious, had no visible wounds yet died."

"When a shell lands near a soldier, the force of the explosion, even without shrapnel striking the individual, can cause internal organ damage. We find the liver, spleen and other internal organs sustain severe damage which causes profuse bleeding into the abdominal cavity."

"Is it possible to repair?"

"Not at this time. Attempts to perform surgery inside the abdominal cavity result in death of the patient." He glared at Abbey. "Unless the surgeon gets lucky, of course."

"Are there symptoms we can look for to determine if this is the case?"

"If the individual is conscious, check to see if he has a sore abdomen. If unconscious check for a swollen or abnormally firm belly. Either would indicate internal damage and bleeding."

"Thank you for the discussion, Dr. Fellows."

"By the way, Dr. Kaplan, gangrene is showing up at the recovery hospital."

"Odd how it isn't present but then, once found, many fall ill with the disease."

"It's the body's reaction to being wounded. Nothing can be done about it."

"But we didn't have it at the recovery hospital until recently then it seemed to spread to many."

"In each soldier's body, different wounds react differently."

Abbey considered his thought then said, "It seems more likely something is spreading the disease."

Dr. Fellows replied with sarcasm. "Learn that in school did you? Or did you just make it up?"

"I'm speculating on what I've observed and my reading."

"And how would it spread?"

"Nurses and doctors move from patient to patient…"

His face turned red, the veins in his neck throbbing. Dr. Fellows interrupted, shouting, "Are you mad? Doctors and nurses spreading disease? In case you hadn't read it somewhere, I wish to inform you, we are healers…not spreaders of disease." He stared at her as if she just arrived from another planet then added, "I can't imagine how you think…but take it from a doctor who's been in medicine most of his life…you couldn't be more wrong."

"Yes, Doctor." Abbey briefly considered telling him about recent research on gangrene but decided it was unlikely he'd believe the reports.

He slowly shook his head then said, "Another thing. The leader of the infantry company Sgt. Scharf directed during the recent enemy incursion put him in for a medal."

"He deserves it."

"The sergeant will be asked to join the infantry."

"We need him."

"I agree and let them know. He's not going anywhere but may be promoted to lieutenant."

"Thanks for keeping me informed. Please excuse me, I need to relieve myself." She hurried away because, even at an early hour, his breath and clothing reeked of bourbon and cigar smoke.

"By the way," he shouted after her, "we'll be on the march for a couple weeks starting day after tomorrow."

Chapter Six: The March

A light rain began the second day of the march.

Dr. Kaplan peered over the scarf which kept some of the dust out of her nostrils and mouth, at the leaden gray cloud cover. She thought, *"Hopefully, a little moisture will keep this damn dust down."* She eyed the column ahead. Soldiers, wagons and horses constantly raised a choking cloud of dust. Without a breeze to move it, it hung in the air in sufficient density to sting eyes and burn throats. Like many of the soldiers, Abbey wore a bandana over her nose and mouth.

A wide brimmed hat kept sunshine out of her eyes initially but now kept the rain out of her face. Thunder rumbled in the distance. She viewed black clouds coming their way. Heavy rain drops struck and occasionally penetrated the canopy of trees which arched over the road. They thumped her hat like acorns. "Damn," she cursed, as she pulled the handkerchief off her face. The dust was turning to mud...sticky mud which pulled at her boots necessitating extra effort to raise each foot out of the mire. Her breathing rate increased. She felt the rain soaking through her clothing then mumbled, "At least it's still warm or I'd be shivering my butt off."

Abbey joined soldiers as they grunted and groaned while shoving carts and wagons out of mud holes and ruts. Mules brayed as they strained against their traces while the muleskinners yelled, shouted at and cussed their cantankerous four-legged charges to pull harder. The doctor cursed as her right boot filled with muddy water.

"Not what I'd thought a doctor would be doing before I arrived here," she thought as she wedged her shoulder against the spoke of, yet another, mired wagon then shoved.

By late in the afternoon and having fallen a few times, her clothing, "Hell, my entire body," she mumbled, was covered in mud. Strained thigh, buttock and abdominal muscles ached. The column's progress slowed as animals, men, and wagons became mired in the ooze.

Word came down the column to make camp.

"Finally," she said.

Soldiers hastily erected tents for those of officer's rank. She entered an unoccupied tent. It was smaller than the tent she'd become accustomed to. It contained three cots with a folded wool blanket on each.

"Dr. Kaplan," she heard a voice shout. Abbey stuck her head out of the tent, into a driving rain. "Over here," she shouted.

Lieutenant Smith and newly-minted Lieutenant Scharf, plodded through ankle-deep mud to the tent.

"Ma'am," Lt. Scharf said, "We thought…"

"Don't stand out there. Come in," she shouted.

They entered but stayed just inside the entrance. Lt. Scharf carried a lantern.

"We've been told officers are to sleep three to a tent," Lt. Smith said.

"We thought it might be easier if people from your staff stayed with you," Lt. Scharf said.

"Of course, of course," Abbey said. They didn't move. "I'll take this one." She pointed to an end cot.

"Thank you, Ma'am," Lt. Smith said, then removed his knapsack and sat on one of the cots.

Lt. Scharf hung the lantern then did the same.

Abbey reached into her knapsack and pulled out a towel. One end was damp but the rest was dry. She pulled her boots and socks off then examined her feet. "No blisters, thank God." Abbey wiped the accumulated grit from between her toes then wiped dirt off her feet and lower legs as modestly as she could manage. She noted the two men kept their gaze averted.

"Any blisters or foot problems?" she asked.

"Had a blister earlier in the day," Lt. Smith said. "It popped so I wrapped it."

"Want me to examine it?" she asked.

"I'll keep it wrapped and clean. It's smaller than a dime." he said.

"I have one set of dry clothing in my knapsack which I'd like to put on," Abbey said.

They both turned away while she changed. She then kept her eyes averted while they changed.

"I've got something to eat," Lt. Scharf said. He pulled out a half loaf of bread and a block of cheese. He opened his pocket knife and sliced the cheese into sandwiches.

More thunder rumbled. The intensity of the rain noisily pelting their tent increased.

"Getting worse," Lt. Smith said, raising his voice to be heard over the driving rain.

"What a simple joy to be in dry clothing," she said. The others nodded.

Abbey took a bite from her sandwich, chewed for a while then declared, "A bit dry." She sipped water from her canteen. She shivered. "I'd love a steaming hot cup of coffee."

Lt. Scharf stood. "I can see what I can find, Doctor."

"Sit," she said while motioning. "You just dried off."

"Likely impossible to light a fire in this weather," Lt. Smith grumbled.

An hour later someone called from outside their tent. Lt. Scharf opened the tent flap then yelled to the others, "Get your mucket. The mess soldiers have coffee."

Abbey returned to her cot and sipped the hot liquid. "Wonder how they got a fire started?"

"Stove in a tent, one of them told me," Lt. Smith said.

The three exhausted officers finished their coffee, wrapped themselves in blankets and slept like logs until...

***

At three in the morning, a number of successive lightning strikes illuminated their camp and assaulted their ears.

The sharp bark of soldiers shouting could be heard. A soldier came down the row of officer's tents yelling for a doctor.

"Over here," Abbey yelled while pulling on socks and boots.

The threesome left the tent and into a light rain then followed a lantern-carrying soldier.

Abbey saw a number of wounded soldiers. Some with burns moaned while others yelled. All with wounds from either the lightening itself or the tree which exploded when lightning struck it.

"Damn this rain." She cursed as she wiped water off her face and hunched her shoulders in a vain attempt to prevent cool rain-water from running down her neck and back while examining the soldiers.

"Lt. Smith, we need medical supplies and a tent for surgery."

He pointed to two groups of men. "You three and you four, come with me." They quickly disappeared into the inky night.

Abbey noted a smell she hadn't encountered previously. She wrinkled her nose.

"Burned flesh," Lt. Scharf said. "As a young teen, I helped pull people from a burning building and remember the stench."

"Find blankets and try to keep the wounded dry and warm."

"Ambulances are coming," someone said.

Pvt. Silver approached. "Lt. Smith sent me. Medical tent will be up in fifteen minutes. We can begin transporting to the area now."

"Pvt. Silver. See if you can find Dr. Fellows."

"We did."

"And?"

"Ah…he's not in a useful state, Ma'am."

Abbey swore under her breath. "Lt. Scharf, I count twelve wounded needing immediate surgical attention."

Men with stretchers arrived. She pointed. "These men first."

"I'll setup your surgical supplies," Lt. Scharf said, and hurried away.

Abbey, with a nurse at her side holding a lantern, examined a few more wounded. "Pvt. Silver, guide me to the medical tent."

The same afternoon, Abbey checked the patients waiting to be transported to the recovery hospital.

"You the one who patched me up?" a soldier with bandages on his thigh and lower leg asked.

"I'm Doctor Kaplan," she replied. "I closed those wounds."

"Thanks. I'm Tom Raymond from Brooklyn."

"You're lucky. No crush injury or we might have been forced to amputate your leg.

"Will I be able to walk?"

"You should heal completely in about ten- or twelve-weeks barring infection."

"Bless you, Doc." He smiled. "It's good I'll heal completely. I'm the best shot in my company. Feeling kinda' guilty getting hurt and not being with my buddies."

Abbey kneeled at his side. "You need time to heal, soldier."

"Didn't know but a few of them before I joined up."

"I'm sure they'll manage without you."

"We're like a team, Doc. When one guy with special skills goes down there ain't always a replacement."

"You may re-injure your leg if you return without taking time to fully recover."

"Whatever you say." Raymond took a deep breath. "Surely, I want to heal completely." He smiled then asked, "You ever been shot at?"

"A few weeks ago. First time."

"Still shaking?"

Abbey giggled. "As it happens, yes. And I jump when I hear the sound of cannon fire; even if it's some distance away."

"You'll get over it." He stared into her eyes for a bit, then asked in a subdued voice, "You have nightmares?"

"Yes. Why?" She nodded.

"Seems them what keeps having nightmares kinda," he shrugged, "I don't know no medical terms but they get continual sad and quiet. A guy in our company was so bad he quit talking. Didn't even seem to recognize us. He was in all the same battles as we were but began having this awful nightmare he couldn't get his musket to fire." The private closed his eyes, seemed lost in thought then slowly shook his head. He gazed up at Abbey. "Anyway, he'd wake up in the middle of the night with the sweats, yelling and carrying on. After a while, I think he was afraid to sleep because of his nightmarish dream. They sent him home."

"We doctors have much to learn concerning the mind."

"Would you consider telling me about your nightmare?"

Abbey leaned toward him as if whispering a confidence. He laughed and said, "Hey, I can keep a secret."

She laughed as well then in full voice said, "I shot a man."

"That's the dream?"

"Partially. In my dream, I walk up to the body and discover I shot one of my brothers."

"Scary one. Don't worry. It should go away."

He reacted to Abbey's concerned expression. "Hey, Doc. Don't let me get you down. I'm sure you got better stuff to do than gabbing with me."

Without smiling, she said. "You take care of your leg and I'll keep an eye out for soldiers with nightmares and continual sadness."

"You do that. Thanks again for patching me up."

Abbey moved to another patient and thought, "*So many with disturbed emotions which make it difficult or impossible for them to accomplish even simple tasks. When do we start to heal them?*"

***

A month later and just as daylight was filling their latest encampment, Abbey heard a single gunshot then shouting for a doctor. She ran to a group of soldiers who'd surrounded a stricken man. "Make room. I'm Dr. Kaplan."

The crowd parted, the doctor kneeled and examined the man. A bullet had gone through his head from right to left. A still smoking pistol lay at his side. Abbey tilted his head. The entrance wound was surrounded by powder burns.

Lieutenant Scharf approached.

"He shot himself, sir," one of the men said.

Her helper turned to those assembled. "Any idea what or why?"

"Cold as hell six nights ago, sir," one of the soldiers said. "He and a buddy slept in each other's arms to stay warm. During the night, someone slit his buddy's throat. He woke up hanging on to a dead man. Scared the hell out of him. He joked about it at the time but I think the incident bothered him more than he let on. His squad mates said he quit talking and couldn't sleep."

Abbey was deeply saddened and slowly shook her head.

"Don't feel too bad, Dr. Kaplan," a corporal said. "From what I hear, there's no medicine to fix the ones who go crazy."

"Crazy?" Lt. Scharf asked.

"What else do you call it?" another man asked.

A third added, "Some who've been in lots of battles get this kind of facial expression where they just stare into the distance all the time." He turned to Abbey. "What would you call such a condition, Doc?"

"Possibly some type of tiredness," she speculated and stood up.

"Hell, we're all tired," the corporal said. The other men laughed.

Dr. Fellows approached the group. "What's going on here?"

"This man shot himself," Abbey said.

"Why are you all standing around? Why is the body still here?"

She stated, "I'm investigating his death."

The chief surgeon's jaw dropped. "What? Why the hell would you investigate a man who's dead"

"I'll make notes on the circumstances of his demise. With enough information, perhaps we can head off these incidents," Abbey said.

"He shot himself. What else if there to know? Weak men don't have the constitution for war."

"Begging the major's pardon sir," one of the enlisted men volunteered, "but the sergeant's been with us since first Bull Run. A good man and great leader. Likely one of our toughest. If it happened to him, it could happen to any of us."

Dr. Fellows snorted and said, "Then why did he give up and shoot himself?"

Abbey said, "We don't know why which is what I'm trying to learn."

Dr. Fellows face turned red. "There is nothing to learn and these men have work to accomplish which is where they need to be." He snorted in Abbey's direction. "Not helping our lady doctor, who won't be here much longer, investigate any damn thing. Lt. Scharf, have a team collect this body and you men get to your posts."

Lt. Scharf replied, "Yes, sir."

The men dispersed but the enlisted man who'd stepped forward, mouthed to Abbey, "Thanks, Doctor."

***

Abbey and Lt. Scharf sat across from each other eating dinner.

She asked. "Where did you grow up?"

"Boston. I hope to complete an engineering degree when I return."

"Congratulations on becoming a lieutenant. You were a hero out there."

"A hero? Not me. Just doing my best to keep us alive." He laughed, "When I signed up I thought, for a few months, it would be fun to be in the band." He nodded at a group of soldiers. "I get tired of hearing their disgusting remarks about the few women we have out here."

"Me?"

Lt. Scharf nodded. "And anything else in a skirt."

"So then instead of band, you turned your drummer hands into medical ones."

He held up his hands and examined them. "With your help. I never expected to become an assistant surgeon's assistant."

Abbey smiled. "You handle it well."

"Outwardly yes."

"Bloody sights don't seem to upset you."

"Because I save my nausea until we're done. As you say, I manage the disgusting sights adequately. If I spend much time taking stock of how many men are crippled for life, I get teary."

"Miss your family?"

"Certainly. Makes me feel lonely as hell at times."

"Sad and lonely…and yet you are one of the team's most diligent workers."

"As a band member I didn't feel useful. But being part of the medical team, I feel like I'm contributing. The men we treat are in desperate need of care. I honestly believe the best way I can help these brave men is by working with you." A warm smile formed on his lips. "You, Doctor Kaplan, like the other doctors, are a hero."

Abbey folded her arms across her chest. "A hero doesn't kill patients. I'm just a doctor doing what she was trained to do and trying to acquiring additional skills." She stared at her lap briefly. "I do wish our chief surgeon appreciated my effort."

"He does but won't admit it because you're a woman. I've seen how he watches you."

"Watches?"

"With pure admiration." He chuckled. "Or maybe it's envy. Dr. Fellows may have more experience than you but the Lord has given you marvelous dexterity and you learn so quickly."

"Thanks." She rolled her shoulders to try and ease some tension. "So after the war, why an engineer?"

"Like my father but hope to design buildings and bridges." He gazed at their surroundings. "One day, I will forget this ugliness and lead a normal life."

"You won't remember what's happened here?"

"I hope not." He shrugged again. "Find me after the war and I'll tell you."

Abbey giggled.

"One thing I'd like to ask, Doctor. Lt. Smith and I were talking. We think the team should be learning each other's jobs. One of us gets hurt and anyone else could cover."

"I agree." Abbey sipped her coffee then asked. "I wonder why Lt. Smith didn't ask me?"

"Most of the guys are intimidated by you."

Shocked and wide-eyed, she sat up straight. "By me?"

"When they make a mistake, you get upset, give them your demeaning facial expression then use your first-class vocabulary to make them feel like idiots."

"If they do something stupid…"

"I agree they've got it coming; but sometimes they just make a mistake."

"You said, they…are intimidated. Not you?"

"No, Ma'am." He gazed in her eyes. "Besides being an accomplished doctor and surgeon, I see the gentle, caring woman inside the tough exterior."

Abbey stared at her lap. "Thank you, Lieutenant."

He continued, "I understand your brusque behavior is needed to earn a place of respect in a male-dominated world."

Abbey stared at him briefly. "Amazing. You…do understand." She stopped conversing to watch a robin trying to pull a worm out of the grass. "Then let me ask you…don't you think your use of profanity with the men is demeaning?"

"When I give an order, it must be followed or people die."

"If they question the order?"

"No questions allowed. Just compliance. Profanity allows me to speak the enlisted men's language."

She leaned back and closed her eyes.

He took a deep breath and said, "Sad about the suicide this morning,"

"Tragic. Some men's minds seem to collapse."

The lieutenant stared at her for some time.

"What?" she asked.

"Insightful, Doctor Kaplan. Although, I'd say it's a matter of how much they can endure. Kind of like boxing. Each horror experienced is like a blow to the mind. Some guys can't endure as much as others."

Abbey stared at her lap and mumbled, "Blow to the mind…endure as much…" She sipped her coffee then turned to Lt. Scharf. "We know so little about a person's emotional balance."

"Would you agree the mind can endure only so much?"

"I'm just speculating but from what I've seen here…I'd agree with you but different men have different endurance." She became pensive for a bit. "Possibly because the blows to their mind are bigger or smaller or occur more often? Again, just speculation."

"How do we get beyond speculation?"

Abbey thought for a bit. "We may need doctors to specialize in areas to concentrate their energy in solving medical conditions like problematic mental conditions…using scientific methodology, of course."

"So no more doctors as generalists?"

"Generalists will be needed but specialists, I believe, will also be needed."

"So, getting back to emotional balance, what treatment is available?"

"No clue. No clue whatsoever." She sighed. "Not even for my own painful demons."

"Demons? Would you like to talk about them?"

Abbey was deciding how much to tell him when the sound of cannon fire rumbled across their encampment.

The lieutenant jumped up. "I'd better make sure things are prepped for surgery."

"Lt. Scharf, I appreciate your taking time to talk to me."

"My pleasure, Doctor."

She watched him walk a few steps then called to him. "I have medical books you could read during the slow time between casualties."

He stopped walking, turned slightly back toward Abbey and said over his shoulder, "I'm no doctor."

"The more you learn, the more help you'll be…not just to me but the wounded as well."

He scratched his head while considering her request, then smiled. "I'll pick them up, Doctor Kaplan."

The lieutenant walked ten paces, glanced over his shoulder and smiled at her.

"I can have a word with him," a soldier wearing captain's bars said.

"Concerning?"

"Enlisted men are not to fraternize with women of officer's rank."

"He's been promoted to lieutenant but hasn't received his insignia yet."

"I apologize then." He removed his hat. "My name is Francis Ascari."

"I remember. I'm Dr. Abbey Kaplan." She offered her hand then motioned him to be seated.

"A pleasure to meet the doctor who's skilled hands repair so many of our men."

"It's an honor to serve." She eyed him for a bit. "You found the rabbi for me."

"I did. Should be a beautiful sunset this evening. Perhaps you'd accompany me on a walk after evening meal?"

"Thank you, Captain Ascari, but I have numerous medical write-ups to complete."

"Perhaps another time?"

Abbey smiled at him. "I'll look forward to that."

***

Dear Mom,

I hope this letter finds all of you at home in the state of Washington, healthy and happy as possible.

I received your letter. So great to hear from you. As you suggested, I'm doing my best to stay healthy and ignore my detractors.

I'm learning medicine and surgery at a furious rate; just as our community doctor predicted. Although I'm an assistant surgeon, the regiment's chief surgeon has a constant romance with liquor which forced me into the role of lead surgeon. Due to my lack of experience, I was frightened nearly to death. One of our team members watches out for me and helped me get past my fright and adjust to my leadership position.

I receive regular correspondence from the Medical Museum in Washington which detail new medical and surgical techniques. I struggle to memorize and implement them.

The chief surgeon, a crusty old codger, hates having a woman as a surgical assistant. I perform my work as best I can, despite his withering criticism and unwillingness to accept me as a doctor or surgeon. Holding the equivalent of lieutenant's rank gets me some grudging respect from those around me.

You'd be astounded at my dress. I wear britches and soldier's boots all the time plus carry a pistol on my hip. Yes, Mom, we are close to the fighting, so the pistol is necessary.

I ended up fighting along-side infantry soldiers some days ago. It gave me insight into what they must endure during each battle. The fighting was an emotional and physical horror. Those brave men, on both sides, look death in the face and still do their duty to the best of their ability.

I'd prefer no one else knows I was in combat or what I'm going through with the chief surgeon. I'll tell the others when I come home. I need to tell someone; so you're the lucky (?) one. Would love to have a female friend to talk to but that's unlikely out here. My surgical staff treats me adequately and as I previously wrote, one of the team members has been a rock of support for me. He's a good man from the Boston area.

Remember my brothers and Andre the trapper teaching me shooting? I put all their training to use during the battle and likely saved a few lives as a result.

Please keep my letters to yourself and please save them. If nothing else, after the war, they will provide me with a reminder of what I'm going through. For now, I'd prefer others don't know. When I'm home, I'll tell them. If I don't make it home, they can read the letters.

I miss my family. I'd give anything to make a pot of tea and sit on the porch with you to discuss what goes on here. I can't wait to get home.

Love,

Abbey

"Dr. Kaplan," a voice called from outside her tent. "It's Cpt. Ascari. Do you have time for a walk?"

***

On their seventh such excursion in as many weeks, he asked, "How are things in the medical section?"

"I've come to the conclusion, we have an odd existence."

"In what way?"

"We live in a peaceful location." Abbey gazed at the surrounding hills and indicated them with a wave of her hand. Tall trees swayed in the evening's moderate breeze. "Pretty enough here I'd enjoy bringing my family to see these beautiful hills once the war ends." She took a deep breath and continued, "Then without warning, we are exposed to and must work on the most ghastly sights, sounds and smells of combat. We must concentrate on men who are never going to have a normal life. They will go home with permanent disabilities…"

He interrupted. "Best not to think about it."

Abbey walked in silence for a while. "I try to bury as much as possible but at night, when there's nothing else to think about, I get anxious and depressed."

He smiled. "I didn't bring you out here to become upset."

Abbey put a hand on his arm. "You're right. I apologize." They walked in silence, admiring the orange western sky, whose few clouds displayed fanciful shapes. "One thing Captain. I'm Jewish. We won't ever be more than acquaintances."

"You're a fine conversationalist. I'll be proud to be one of your acquaintances."

They exchanged smiles and continued walking.

Abbey was admiring the shapely red clouds in the western sky when a shot rang out. They both hit the ground.

Chapter Seven: Dr. Connolly

Abbey scanned in the direction the shot came from. From behind her, a second shot rang out. Abbey saw a gray-coated soldier pinwheel out of a tree forty-yards to her front. She turned to Captain Ascari. "Captain…"

Three Union soldiers ran up. One said, "You okay Ma'am?"

"Yes, thank you." She turned over the unmoving Captain. "Damn. Shot through the throat."

"Fuckin' Rebel snipers," one of the men said then quickly added, "Pardon my language, Ma'am. We'll escort you back to camp. A doctor from the recovery hospital wishes to speak with you."

***

"I'm Dr. Connolly. I'm in charge of the recovery hospital. A number of patients are experiencing problems which indicate they've been given chloroform for too long or the anesthesia is being administered in a way which doesn't let in enough air." He stared at Abbey. "I think I should be talking to the surgeon who's actually operating on the men."

"I'm the one performing surgical interventions at the moment."

"But you're a…"

Exasperated, she interrupted, "Yes. I'm female and I have breasts which you don't need to stare at."

He looked to the side. "Sorry, Ma'am. Actually, I need to talk to Dr. Fellows."

"I'm Doctor Kaplan. Now that you're finished examining my body, we need to discuss the problem."

Red-faced and staring at his feet, the doctor continued "Perhaps I should be talking to Dr. Fellows."

Exasperated, Abbey said, "Perhaps you should." She looked about. "Pvt. Silver. Take this man to the chief surgeon."

Fifteen-minutes later the Captain returned. Obviously embarrassed, he addressed Abbey, "Dr. Fellows was…well…incoherent."

"As I said previously, you and I need to discuss the chloroform problem."

"When do you quit giving anesthesia?"

"Once the most painful part of an operation is complete. For instance, during an amputation, we stop after I complete work with the bone saw."

"Do you have confidence in the man administering the drug?"

"He has over two-years' experience. Joined the unit just before Bull Run. When did the problem begin occurring?"

"Roughly three months ago. Possibly longer but we may not have noticed."

"Nothing's changed I'm aware of. If it's quiet tomorrow, I'll travel to the recovery hospital. You and I can examine some of the patients then discuss this further."

***

A sergeant stood in front of the men's ward at the recovery hospital. "Sorry miss. You can't enter. It's an all-male ward."

"I'm Doctor Kaplan."

He laughed. "And I'm the king of England."

"Dr. Connolly asked me to come here."

"Say what you want, lady. Dr. Connolly says no women in the men's ward so despite your britches…you ain't getting in"

"Shit. This is so goddamned frustrating."

"So I guess you ain't no lady either."

Fuming, Abbey returned to her quarters at the field hospital and sent Dr. Connelly a note explaining her difficulty in gaining access to the patients.

"*More crap because I'm female,*" she thought. "*Does it never end? I have so much work to perform and shouldn't be wasting my time on this. Will I spend the whole damn war demonstrating that I'm just as capable as a man?"*

***

"There are male and female wards at the recovery hospital." Abbey said. She and Doctor Connolly stood in the middle of her tent.

"Yes," he replied.

"And you've setup restrictions such that male doctors are allowed to visit their female patients in the female ward but a female doctor isn't allowed to visit her male patients in their ward?"

"You're a woman. It wouldn't be appropriate."

Abbey clenched her fists. "I operated on many, if not most, of them. Do you have any idea how damn stupid you must be to establish those rules?"

His eyes grew large. "How dare you talk to me like that! You have no business being here in the first place. The very idea of a female doctor is abhorrent." He stood tall. "I'm an officer and a gentleman who doesn't appreciate nor will tolerate your language or tone of voice." Dr. Connolly removed a leather glove from his belt. He slapped her across the cheek as if he were remonstrating a child. If he had ever seen Abbey's father David's expression when he became angry, the Captain would have known what was coming next.

Red-faced and with fury in her eyes, Abbey slammed her right fist into the doctor's face quick as a lightning strike. Blood spurted from his broken nose. He yelled and threw his hands up to his face. She used a left uppercut to his belly which doubled him over and had sufficient force to lift his heals off the ground. Dr. Kaplan straightened him up with a right to his jaw. He stumbled backwards toward the tent's entrance but fell to his knees, gasping for air. Abbey picked him up by the back of his collar and trousers, then, with a grunt, threw him out the tent opening.

She closed the tent flap.

Abbey dropped into her desk chair still shaking with anger.

The doctor heard the captain yell, "I'm fine. I don't need help standing."

Someone said, "Sir, you've got blood on your face."

"Get away from me! Dammit. Get away."

"*I'll catch hell for this,*" Abbey thought.

***

Lieutenants Smith and Scharf sat down across from her at evening meal the same day. Both grinning broadly.

Lt. Smith said, "There's a story going around, there was a little excitement in the officer's area."

Without looking up from her mucket, she said, "Word travels fast."

"Something about a captain flying out of a tent like he was launched from a cannon."

"He slapped me."

"What?" Lt. Scharf stood with clenched fists...fury in his expression.

"Sit," Abbey told him. "It's over."

"He had no right to strike you," Lt. Scharf said while still clenching his fists. "You can press charges."

Abbey shrugged. "I should tell Dr. Fellows before the captain reports me."

"Not necessary," Lt. Smith said while shaking his head. "The captain won't tell anyone."

"Of course he will," Abbey said. She motioned for Lt. Scharf to sit.

The lieutenant slowly sat, then said, "You think he's going to complain to a superior officer, after he slapped a woman, she knocked the crap out of him and launched him out of her tent like a sack of potatoes? I think not."

Abbey giggled while the lieutenants laughed.

Two days later, another Captain arrived at the field hospital just as she was about to begin surgery.

"I'm Doctor Anthony Milton. I've been assigned to head the recovery hospital as Captain Connolly has requested transfer to another assignment."

Abbey introduced herself.

Dr. Milton said, "I believe you've been advised there is a problem with the use of chloroform and wish to visit your patients in the recovery hospital. If you give me a time, I will meet you there and we will investigate this further."

"I was refused entrance to the male wards last time I visited."

"I assure you, it will not happen again, Doctor."

"Thank you."

"You attempt to repair numerous gut-shot men. Many are surviving like the man whose appendix you removed. I'd like to discuss your procedure."

"I'll send you my notes so we can discuss them when we meet. I have three surgeries to perform so I need to excuse myself. One of them is a gut-wound."

"May I observe?"

Abbey was pleasantly surprised at his request and agreed.

Following the surgeries, Dr. Milton said, "Thank you for letting me observe. I appreciate you teaching me new techniques."

"My pleasure," she said. "I've been thinking, would you please address my lieutenants concerning the chloroform problem?"

"Certainly."

Lt. Smith and Lt. Scharf reported to them. They stood just outside the main medical tent on a cool but sunny day. The red flag snapped several times in a stiff breeze.

Dr. Milton explained, "A small number of post-surgical patients at the recovery hospital exhibited a loss of mental ability. Some experienced difficulty caring for themselves while others were incapable of the smallest tasks. We believe it may be due to overuse of chloroform."

"How many are we talking about?" Lt. Smith asked.

"A handful after each battle. Nearly all post-surgery patients," Abbey said.

"We can try to watch Pvt. Laurence more closely but he takes his job seriously," Lt. Scharf said. "Never seen him make a mistake."

Dr. Kaplan said, "Be aware we have a problem and if you see anything, let me know. We need to solve this."

She dismissed the lieutenants then addressed Dr. Winston, "Care to join me for lunch?

He nodded and they proceeded to the officer's mess area.

"How are you holding up physically?" Dr. Milton asked.

"Well enough."

"Care to expound?"

"The usual new surgeon aches in the knees and hips plus being so tall, I have to bend over when I work. It's led to lots of back pain."

"You're in charge. If you wish, have your staff raise the surgical table."

"Should have thought of that…shows you how I've concentrated on the troops well-being instead of my own."

They ate for a bit.

Dr. Milton said, "Does your team handle the horror of endless ghastly wounds adequately?"

"Yes."

"And you?"

Abbey thought for a while. "Occasional headaches but those may be from the weather."

"Sleep well?"

"Most nights."

"If you're having trouble sleeping, let someone know. We need to keep you in tiptop shape."

"I'll keep your thoughts in mind."

He stood and said, "Recovery hospital tomorrow at one o'clock?"

"I'll be there."

"Don't come alone. I hear Confederate sniper teams are roaming the countryside."

Chapter Eight: Wounded

Abbey walked to a small stream to relieve herself. She had just finished when the doctor felt as if a red-hot fire-poker was applied to the top of her thigh. A fraction of a second later, she heard a gunshot. She fell to her knees and saw a bullet had ripped diagonally across the top of her thigh. It bled profusely.

She used her hands to bring the edges together and moaned at the pain this caused. Abbey realized whoever fired at her was likely reloading. She pulled herself along on her side with one arm and one leg while she tried to keep the wound closed with the other hand. Struggling to keep moving and becoming dizzy from the pain, Abbey prayed she wouldn't pass out. She pulled herself into a stand of reeds. The doctor lay on her side in five-inches of cold water and mud. A light rain began.

"*Damn. If I don't stop the bleeding, I could die here,*" she thought then silently cursed. "No underskirt to tear into bandages this time. Damn this burns."

The doctor pulled and yanked on the shoulder seam of her shirt. Each movement causing fiery pain in her leg. She tugged and tugged but couldn't pull it apart. Abbey stopped for a moment to let some of the pain subside then pulled the seam into her mouth and forcefully chewed on it until her jaws ached. Eventually, she created a small hole which Abbey enlarged sufficiently to tear the sleeve off.

Wrapping the wound with the sleeve was sufficiently painful to cause tears to form.

She heard voices from across the stream.

"That damn Yank is out there but wounded."

"We need to search the far bank and finish him off."

Abbey took handfuls of mud and wiped her face, hands and the sleeveless arm. The sounds of men splashing across the stream reached her ears. She slowly rotated her head in their direction while removing her pistol from its holster. Each man carried a rifle with a long bayonet attached. They walked up and back along the streambank. One man entered the reeds where she was hiding. He opened the flap in his pants. Abbey, listening to his stream, felt an insect crawling across her neck. She experienced a tremendous desire to reach up and brush it off but knew she couldn't. The bug crawled up to her ear then slowly walked across her cheek then stopped just below her nose. She slowly took in a breath then exhaled. The insect walked across her upper lip, crossed her lips to her chin and, mercifully, jumped off.

The soldier closed the flap in his pants and began walking…close enough to Abbey, muddy water splashed into her nose. Her reflexes wanted her to exhale but she couldn't risk movement. A trickle of water began working its way to the back of her nose. Abbey slowly rotated her head more nose down. She felt the water running forward. The doctor stifled multiple sneezes. Abbey exhaled slowly to help clear her nostrils. The soldiers footsteps stopped. She froze. After what seemed like an interminable time, during which she dared not breath, he continued walking away from her.

"I know he's in here and I know I hit him," one of them said.

"We can't spend all night trying to find one man," a second man said. "The three of us are heading back to camp. You got five minutes more then you join us."

"Yes, Corporal."

Abbey began shivering, her body temperature dropping from the cold water she was laying in. The rainwater on her face combined with mud and ran into her eye. She jammed it shut, using all her self-control to avoid wiping it with her hand while listening to the soldier tramp up and back in the stream. Three minutes later, she heard the soldier retracing his steps then saw him entering the reeds.

"There you are," he said.

The manner he held his rifle indicated he intended to bayonet her. The fiendish triumphal grin on his face was ripped from his expression as a bullet passed through his heart. He crumpled to the reed bed with a splash. Abbey closed her eyes, said a prayer, and placed the revolver back in its holster. She wiped her eye on her left sleeve. It still stung.

"His friends may have heard the shot," she thought. *"I need to move."*

With much effort and enduring sharp pain in her thigh with every movement, she side-crawled through the reeds and muck while dragging her wounded leg. She clawed her way as quietly as possible; her hands finding little purchase in the ooze. Abbey traveled at what seemed like a snail's pace; many minutes later finally arriving at the edge of the reeds. She dragged herself onto solid ground. The doctor checked her thigh. The bandage was soaked in blood. Exhausted from the pain and loss of blood, Abbey lay still and rested for a while. Her heart beat rapidly and her chest and abdominal muscles ached from getting air into her lungs at such a rapid rate and for such a long time. She sucked in her breath and froze. In the fading light, a soldier was approaching. He kneeled. She slowly moved her hand to the pistol.

Abbey heard a whispered, "Dr. Kaplan."

She closed her eyes then whispered, "Here!" and mouthed a rapid prayer.

The man stayed low and moved to her side, his face and hands covered in mud making it difficult to see who it was. He carried a rifle and two cartridge boxes.

"I've been shot in the thigh," she whispered. "I covered the wound but it's still bleeding."

"We need to get away from here but I'll wrap your leg first." She recognized Lt. Scharf's voice.

He lifted the cover of his cartridge box and removed bandage material. The lieutenant opened his folding knife, cut the sleeve and re-wrapped her wound with the fresh bandage.

"It's getting dark now," he whispered. "Just some red sky in the west. I'll carry you on my back." He put his rifle and cartridge case straps over her shoulders.

She moaned as he hoisted her.

"Sorry," the lieutenant said.

They'd moved about twenty-yards when a shot rang out. The bullet went through the edge of a tree then slammed into Abbey's hip with enough force to knock both of them to the ground. Lt. Scharf glanced back across the stream, watching the bushes wave in the evening breeze. He noted one bush moving opposite the others then chambered a round in his lever-action. Abbey's helper fired a rapid five rounds. Abbey moaned. He checked the new wound, ripped open the cartridge case and pulled out another length of bandage which he quickly applied.

"We need to keep moving," he said.

Her expression reflected the tremendous pain she was experiencing but she managed to nod.

They heard soldiers approaching.

Lt. Scharf aimed his rifle in their direction. "Only two rounds in the magazine and no time to reload." His tightly wound body appeared to relax. "Brooklyn accents, thank God," he whispered then shouted, "Over here. I need help with a wounded soldier."

A number of men came up and helped get Abbey to the medical tent.

Once inside, Lt. Smith and Pvt. Lawrence placed her on the operating table. Lt Scharf began washing his hands.

"I need surgery to close my leg wound and get the bullet out of my hip," Abbey said. "Sober up Dr. Fellows."

"No time," Lt. Scharf said.

Abbey's attempt at saying "No. You don't know enough…" was stifled as Lt. Scharf held a chloroformed cloth across her nose and mouth.

Chapter Nine: One Mystery Solved – Another Continues

Feeling groggy, Abbey found herself back in her tent with her right hip and thigh wrapped in bandages. She saw Lt. Scharf at her desk reading and making notes.

The doctor lifted her head. "Who removed the bullet and...sutured?"

"Me."

Abbey laid back and closed her eyes.

"Either I perform the work or you'd have bled out."

"I know." She took a few deep breaths. "How long have I been asleep?"

"Roughly ten-hours."

"Best sleep I've had in a while."

"You in pain?"

"Not too bad. Pinches a bit when I move."

"Dr. Fellows gave me a white liquid if you need it."

She grinned briefly then said in a sarcastic voice, "He's not indisposed?"

"After we took care of you, Lt. Smith and Pvt. Lawrence poured enough coffee down his gullet to drown an elephant."

Abbey giggled.

"He sobered up when he was clear headed enough to realize you'd be off your feet for a while." He held up a stoppered bottle. "So, you want the pain killer?"

"Not now. Uh…I'm not wearing the same clothes."

"Your laundry lady and her daughter washed you and put you in clean clothes. You were still feeling the effects of the chloroform so may not remember."

"Thank you for all you did. And thank the team for me." She folded her arm across her eyes. "Did they enjoy seeing me exposed?"

"Lt. Smith or I would have punched the lights out of anyone who acted disrespectfully. We kept you covered as modestly as we could." He stared at her for a while. "Dr. Kaplan, after you've saved so many soldier's lives, the team respects you; even the men who don't think you should be here. It was like caring for a sister." He read for a bit then added, "By the way, when I inspected the wound in your quadriceps prior to closing it, there was no visible damage to your femur or quadriceps tendon."

"Thank you…how did you know to check…"

He held up a book. "Been working through those medical texts."

Abbey smiled briefly, then asked, "Why wasn't I moved to the recovery hospital?"

"Dr. Fellows wanted you nearby so he could check on your progress and have one of the team keep an eye on you. Also something about the recovery hospital being overrun by gangrene."

"Sorry you're assigned such boring duty."

"I volunteered."

"Why?"

"I always watch out for our assistant surgeon." He grinned. "It's in my job description."

"Just you?"

"Lt. Smith, Private Silver and Pvt. Lawrence also volunteered. They'll rotate with me for a few days. They, like me, also volunteered to search for you with an infantry unit."

"Thank them for me." She sighed. "Did you write up my injuries and your surgery?"

He held up a sheet of paper. "Right here, ready for your review. The washer lady agreed to stop by twice-a-day for a couple weeks to help with any personal stuff you might need."

Abbey thought for a while then viewed him with a questioning expression. "How is it you were the one who found me?"

"We'd split up as it was getting dark. Suddenly, I remembered you heading toward the stream when you needed to relieve yourself."

"You were right." She yawned and pulled the blanket up to her chin. "I'm exhausted. It's going to take a while to become mobile again."

***

"It's been seven days. I can stand without too much pain." Abby gently sat up in her cot.

Lt. Scharf moved to her side and helped her stand.

"Is the tent flap secure?," she asked.

"It is."

She gripped his shoulder, then turned toward him and slowly slid her arms around his neck.

He gently wrapped his arms around her.

Abbey sighed and whispered, "Thank you, for taking such good care of me," then kissed his cheek.

He stared in her eyes, kissed her forehead then kissed her lips.

A voice called from outside the tent.

"Pvt. Moss from the mess. I have Dr. Kaplan's dinner."

Lt. Scharf opened the tent flap. The corporal placed a tray on the desk and left.

Abbey sat at the desk and removed the cloth covering her dinner.

"What's this?"

Lt. Scharf said, "Gefilte fish, borscht, chicken soup, root vegetables and a challah. You know…dinner appropriate for *Shabbat*. Enough for two I see."

"What in the world? Who cooked this?"

"The mess sergeant. When he learned you'd been injured, he insisted on preparing all your meals himself. The rabbi's wife gave him a few Jewish recipes."

"But why?"

"We treat soldier after soldier without learning who they are or what they do."

"How does that relate…"

"Remember the successful gut-wound and appendix repair?"

"Yes…"

"That was our mess sergeant."

"I had no idea."

"Let's eat. Rabbi Schulman will be here early tomorrow with Cpl. Silver and some other Jewish soldiers to hold a *Shabbat* service…if you're up for it."

"Certainly." She stared at the tray then nodded toward her footlocker. "Please open my trunk. On the left side, you'll find a candle holder, candles and a bottle of wine."

Abbey blessed the candles and he the wine.

"Almost tastes like home," he said, as the lieutenant ate a second slice of gefilte fish.

"By the way," Abbey asked, "any word on the chloroform problem?"

***

"Now that you can get around using a cane," Dr. Fellows said a number of weeks later, "we're still having problems with chloroform injuries. Six additional patients experience what we believe are chloroform complications. I've kept an eye on

Pvt. Laurence and even had a surgical nurse from a neighboring regiment come over and watch him. I don't believe the problem is here."

"What about the recovery hospital?"

"I suggest you head over to examine their end of things. Pvt. Silver will accompany and drive you over there."

The rumble of cannon fire echoed in the distance.

Dr. Fellows said, "Sounds like we'll be sending patients there shortly."

Abbey and Pvt. Silver arrived at the recovery hospital. Within a few hours, a steady stream of ambulances arrived. Abbey and the Pvt. observed the wounded as they were carried into the ward.

"Dr. Kaplan," Pvt. Silver called out. He stood next to a man who had just been placed in a bed.

She turned in his direction.

"This man's clothing reeks of chloroform."

Abbey approached then bent over the man. "It does. The last chloroform he received should have evaporated by now as it's over an hour's distance from the field hospital. This is a strong smell as if someone recently poured it on him." She called to the soldier, shook him by the shoulders, then slapped the man. He was unresponsive. The doctor placed her ear near the man's nose. "His breathing is quite shallow."

"Maybe we should be checking all the men for the smell before they enter the ward?"

"I agree."

Three-hours passed without another man smelling of chloroform. The stream of wounded slowed to a trickle.

"There's a boarding house down the block from this hospital," Abbey said. "A home-cooked meal instead of Army food might be a pleasant change."

"I agree with you, Dr. Kaplan," the private said with a huge grin.

As the restaurant's owners were of German ancestry, the pair dined on *Weiner Schnitzel, Spätzle* and *Rotkraut*. Dessert consisted of *Nusstriezel* made with flaky dough, hazelnuts, apricot marmalade and honey.

"My grandparents make superb Dutch dishes," Pvt. Silver said, "but this was one of the best meals I've ever eaten."

Abbey smiled and sipped a cup of coffee. "I couldn't agree more."

They each paid their bill. Pvt. Silver pulled Abbey's chair out as she stood then both spun their heads in the direction of the entrance.

"Smell the odor?" Pvt. Silver said.

"Chloroform," she said.

They watched two ambulance drivers pass near them.

The drivers were seated at a table. Abbey and the private walked up to them.

She introduced herself, then said, "Pardon for interrupting but one or both of you smell of chloroform."

"It's from being near the wounded," one man said. The second added. "We just delivered a number of wounded right from surgery, Doctor. That's probably what you smell."

Abbey smiled, thanked them and left the establishment. "Pvt. Silver, please get the buckboard and we'll head back to the field hospital."

When they arrived, Abbey gingerly eased herself off the conveyance and thanked the private for his assistance.

"Anytime Dr. Kaplan," he said. He paused briefly then said, "I was thinking…no…it doesn't make sense."

"What?"

"The ambulance drivers administering chloroform. How would they get it and why would they use it?"

"Good questions, Private. If you find answers, let me know."

***

In the middle of camp disease treatment two days later, Pvt.'s Lawrence and Silver approached Abbey.

"Dr. Kaplan," Pvt. Silver said. "Pardon the interruption but we've been discussing the chloroform problem. We have an idea."

"I'm listening," Abbey said as she sutured a laceration on a soldier's palm.

"When I run low on the drug," Pvt. Lawrence said, "I send a note to the recovery hospital and they send me a box with containers of chloroform."

Abbey tied off the suture and a helper bandaged the injury. She yelled, "Next."

"The thing is," the Pvt. continued, "I don't always receive a full case. I always get enough to do my work but it never occurred to me I should be getting full cases every time."

The doctor inspected a large abrasion on a soldier's leg. "Keep it clean and it should be fine. If it gets red or hot, come back and see me." She turned to her team members. "Who brings the supplies out."

"Most of the time, they come in a freight wagon," Pvt. Lawrence said.

"But occasionally they are sent with ambulances returning here to pick up additional after-surgery patients," Pvt. Silver said.

"I'll send a letter to the recovery hospital," Abbey said. "Perhaps they can check the ambulances as they arrive."

Lt. Smith approached and handed Abbey a note.

"Dr. Fellows wants me to meet a doctor at the recovery hospital to discuss emotional state." She turned to Pvt. Silver. "I should be done here in an hour. Would you be available to take me over there?"

At the recovery hospital, Abbey faced an older-man with white hair on his temples and in his beard. A slim similarly-aged woman stood at his side.

"I'm Doctor Kaplan. Dr. Fellows said Dr. Siegel wanted to see me."

The man smiled and held out a hand. "I'm Doctor Bill Siegel. This is my wife Anna. She's visiting from our home in Boston."

Abbey shook hands with each of them.

"I have a patient I'd like you to see."

"Have to walk slow, I'm still healing," Abbey said, still using a cane to help her walk.

"Dr. Fellows told me of your wounds. Glad to see you're getting around."

They approached a man who was seated on a bed with his knees pulled up to his chest and his arms wrapped around his legs. He whimpered quietly and gently rocked his body.

"He's awake but unresponsive. He was discovered like this in the middle of a field near his tent. He appears to stare into the distance but not see anything."

"Is he a combat soldier?"

"Been on the nursing staff here at the recovery hospital…" Dr. Siegel paused to remove a note from his shirt pocket. He opened it then said, "for one-year and three-months."

Abbey waved a hand in front of the man's eyes. "He blinks but otherwise no reaction." She put a hand on his shoulder then gently squeezed it. "No response."

"Some seem to handle the horrors of battle but others aren't even in battle like this nurse but are affected in the same way after dealing with numerous casualties."

"How will you treat him?"

"There is no treatment we know of so we'll continue hand-feeding him for another week then, if there's no indication of improvement, arrange to have him sent to a military hospital near his home."

"Why did you want me to see him?" Abbey asked.

"A couple of reasons. From what I've observed and heard from Dr. Fellows, you're incredibly bright and a hard worker. Secondly, Dr. Fellows said you experienced nightmares after being in battle."

"True about the nightmares. They cause me occasional loss of sleep but otherwise aren't a problem."

"Watch yourself. If the sleep deprivation worsens. Let someone know."

"I will."

Dr. Siegel sighed. "We have no clue how to care for problems like this. In general those afflicted may be in excellent physical health. Dr. Kaplan, while you're working in the military, perhaps you might give thought to possible treatment."

Abbey shrugged, raised her hands at shoulder height palms up. "I'm not sure where to begin other than collecting as much information on those with altered mental state."

"Perhaps thinking about what causes your nightmares may help. There are no physical injuries but somehow...I don't even know what the mechanism might be...I believe they've suffered trauma to their mind."

Abbey stared at the doctor then the patient. She stroked her chin while considering the repeated nightmare concerning the soldier she'd shot. The doctor placed a lock of hair behind her ear then whispered. "Have to develop ideas for...trauma to their emotions."

Dr. Siegel said, "I'm guessing. Don't really know. I've found next to nothing in the medical literature. Somehow, we need to develop treatment for these poor fellows. The longer the war goes on, the more we seem to encounter."

"I'll keep an eye out for this type of patient."

"We're being advised to apply the scientific method in our medical practice. Perhaps we could begin by making observations on the patients with this phenomena and when we have enough information, begin to draw some conclusions...and send the information to Washington." He handed her a notebook. "I'm doing it now; here are some of my notes. Perhaps we could compare information at some future date."

Abbey perused his notebook. "I'll make a list of this man's symptoms and present them to you. Perhaps you'll find some I've missed." He offered her a sheet of paper. Abbey sat down at a desk and began writing.

Dr. Siegel reviewed her observations, smiled and said, "One day this war will end and we'll return to civilian practice. This is my card with my home address. If you ever develop any ideas or just want to discuss mental trauma please visit. My wife and I live on the north side of Boston. I have a surgical practice there. We have enough room, you could stay with us."

Abbey's jaw dropped but she managed to say, "Thank you, Doctor." She glanced at his wife.

Anna said, "We would be honored if you at least visited us."

Dr. Siegel added. "Even after the war's end, I fear we'll still have work with casualties like this one."

The woman turned to her husband who nodded. She cleared her throat. "Mental illness is a personal concern for us. Three-years-ago our only son, a fireman at the time, was slightly injured when a building collapsed. Unfortunately, he was the only survivor of a six-man squad. He seemed appropriately saddened initially, as I imagine anyone would. Six-weeks-later he began having conversations with the deceased men. Four-weeks of this, then not sleeping, and occasionally breaking out in tears. Ultimately, he tried to kill himself."

"I'm sorry about your son, but remember, my experience is primarily physical injuries."

"As is mine," Dr. Siegel said. "We have zero treatment for, dare I call it, mental health illness. In my opinion, we have to begin investigations in an organized manner until we can determine a procedure to treat these poor fellows. Possibly, you can start by analyzing your own thoughts which lead to sleepless nights."

Abbey nodded then turned to Anna. "Your son..."

The older woman interrupted. "Too late for him. He refused to eat until he'd starved himself to death."

"How tragic."

Anna continued. "Doctors treat those suffering trauma from bullets but must find a way to treat those with trauma which wounds their minds."

Abbey shook her head. "We have much to learn."

"As I've suggested to my husband, I believe a woman's view of these patients may provide insight lacking in a man's observations."

"I'll keep that in mind," Abbey said.

"One positive observation concerning mental attitude and its affect," Dr. Siegel said. "While observing the patients here at the recovery hospital, I've found those who believe they have a goal to complete, recover from their physical injuries quicker than those who don't."

"Suggesting a mental component to physical healing?"

"Only a general observation but something you may wish to keep in mind when you observe patients."

"Dear Lord, when will we learn enough to repair them?"

***

Abbey met with Pvt. Lawrence and Pvt. Silver.

"I hear you two solved the chloroform problem."

Grinning Pvt. Silver said, "If one of the ambulance drivers had a man who was in substantial pain, he put a chloroform soaked rag over the wounded individual's mouth; not knowing what damage he was doing by preventing enough air from getting into the soldier's lungs."

Abbey said, "You'll each be receiving a commendation and a promotion to corporal for solving this. Please know, the results of your investigation will save lives. The head of the recovery hospital put you both in for a one-week-leave. Doctor Fellows signed off on it this morning."

They exchanged grinning glances. Pvt. Silver then Pvt. Lawrence saluted Abbey.

She returned their salutes. *"What diligent men,"* she thought. *"Lord, please keep them safe."*

***

Near the beginning of Abbey's twelfth month of surgeries, the next soldier was placed on the surgical table. His entire face was covered in bandages. When they were removed, a number of her team gasped. His face was covered in blood, his eye sockets were empty his nose was missing and his right side cheek bone had collapsed.

Dr. Fellows, performing duty as lead surgeon, froze.

"An object must have passed through his eyes and across his face," Abbey said.

"I know him," Cpl. Laurence said. "He's our supply sergeant"

Lt. Smith said, "I barely recognize him."

One of the helpers began vomiting. The young doctor yelled, "Get out." The helper and Cpl. Laurence ran from the tent.

"Dr. Fellows," Abbey said to the frozen-in-place doctor.

The senior doctor continued to stare at the patient's face then took a few steps backward.

Abbey stepped in front of him and nodded to Lieutenant Smith who stepped to the head of the table and took over anesthesia duty.

Abbey put her ear over the area of the patient's nasal passages then listened to his chest. "He's still breathing but has a weak pulse. We'll stop his bleeding and close as many of his wounds as we can." She began ligations and suturing with Lt. Scharf assisting.

An hour of hard work and Lieutenant Smith said, "Doctor, he's no longer breathing."

Abbey verified his statement and checked for a pulse. "Shit. He must have had internal injuries or lost too much blood."

Abbey checked around for Dr. Fellows but didn't see him. "Next patient."

"He was the last," a helper said.

Abbey removed her apron.

"We'll clean up and get organized in case more casualties come in," Lieutenant Smith said.

"Thank you, Lieutenant," Abbey said.

Their trumpet-playing, chloroform administrator approached her as she left the medical tent. "I apologize for running out, Doctor."

"Don't feel bad. Those were ghastly wounds. Even Dr. Fellows experienced difficulty."

Cpl. Lawrence gazed at the ground while speaking, "How do you do it, Doctor Kaplan?"

"Do what?"

"With all due respect, Ma'am, my mother and sisters are strong folk but they couldn't do what you do…view ugly injuries day after day and month after month without flinching."

"I'll bet they could do it if their children's lives were at stake."

"Maybe…but they'd show some emotion, some feeling."

Abbey peered skyward and threw her hands in the air as if asking for divine assistance. "Corporal Lawrence, we don't all show emotion the same way."

He responded with a glance which Abbey thought would have been appropriate if she were an alien lifeform. "Anything else, Corporal?"

"No, Doctor."

Abbey walked to the officer's mess area.

"Tough day, Dr. Kaplan?" Captain Williams, an infantry officer, asked.

"More like a typical day…except for the last patient who sustained facial injuries which a number of my team experienced difficulty observing."

"Two men from my company received severe burns."

"I saw them. There was nothing we could do for them. In my experience, people with burns like those live for a while but their lungs seem to quit functioning within a few hours and they die of suffocation."

"Then neither made it?"

"I'm sorry."

"If you don't mind my asking…"

Abbey's pulse began pounding in her temples. She spoke through gritted teeth. "I do mind and I'm tired of people asking how I endure the horrors." She saw the other officers turning toward her.

"I didn't mean to offend…"

Her exasperated voice interrupted him. "You're in combat. You kill people. How do you manage?"

"It's not the same."

Abbey put clenched fists on her hips. "Because you're a man?"

"Well…" He spooned more food into his mucket.

"In your first battle, I'll bet you grieved over the men you killed but now it has little effect on you."

The captain stiffened and turned to face her. "I still grieve for the dead…on both sides."

"I can't afford the luxury of grieving or I fear I'd do little else."

She filled her mucket and sat at a table. Captain Williams took his and left the area. Not one of the other officers sat near her or acknowledged her presence.

***

The next patient was placed on the operating table.

"Abbey, I came to visit you and this is what happened," her brother William said. He held up bloody, handless stumps.

Horrified, Abbey stood back and put a hand up to cover her mouth. She stared at the patient's injuries and then said, "I can't work on him. He's my brother. Find Dr. Fellows."

"He's indisposed," Lt. Smith said.

Lt. Scharf said, "There's no one else. You have to operate on him."

"I can't," she shouted and ran out of the tent. The doctor was horrified to see her father and other brother with bloody injuries waiting for her surgical intervention. She heard Lt. Scharf and her brother William pleading for her to begin surgery.

Lt. Scharf grabbed her by the shoulders and shook her while yelling, "Dr. Kaplan. Dr. Kaplan."

***

"Dr. Kaplan, are you all right?" she heard Lt. Scharf yelling.

Abby sat up with a start and rapidly gazed around her dimly illuminated tent. He stood at her side.

"Dr. Kaplan," he said again. "Do you need help?"

"I'm fine," she said. Her heart beat wildly and she was short of breath.

"I apologize for entering your tent but you were shouting something about William."

"Thank you, Lt." Abbey whipped her head side-to-side trying to dislodge the memory of the nightmare. "Just a bad dream. You can go now."

The doctor checked her watch. "Seven-thirty in the morning. I'm late for camp disease duty."

Abbey rolled out of her cot and splashed cold water on her face. "My God, I could see and hear them so clearly." The doctor leaned over her wash basin, trying to remain calm while waiting for her breathing and heart rate to regain a normal pace. She shuddered. "I pray that awful dream doesn't happen again."

***

"How was he injured?" Abbey asked late in the afternoon while a child was placed on the operating table.

Cpl. Lawrence said, "We think he and a friend were playing with unexploded ordinance and something detonated. The other child died. This little guy's mother said he's four."

She shook her head, "His tibia is shredded. We'll remove his leg above the injury."

Abbey turned to Cpl. Lawrence as he administered the chloroform. "Ready?"

"Shortly," he said.

"Bless you, Doctor," the woman said after the operation was complete. "A word, please." She pulled the doctor away from the others. "Might a lost my son if you wasn't here. I don't have much to pay you."

"No need for payment," Abbey said.

The woman pulled a jar and a small piece of paper out of her skirt pocket and folded Abbey's hand around them. "Keep this to yourself doc because it ain't legal. If you find yourself in pain because you need to have a man, put some of this down there and you won't get with child."

"What is it?"

"It's a petroleum jelly mix. I've written down the recipe."

"Thank you, but…I don't…have a use for it…"

***

Abbey had just completed triage when an officer and an older woman approached her.

"Dr. Kaplan, I'm Doctor Hammond and this is Nurse Anderson who works for the Sanitary Commission. We're visiting from Washington and wish to discuss some ideas with you."

"Love to talk to you but I must begin surgery." She pointed to the wounded laid out on cots and the ambulance train of two-wheeled mule-drawn carts.

Dr. Hammond continued, "We understand. May we observe?"

"Follow me," Abbey said.

As they entered the surgical tent, Dr. Kaplan asked, "We're a bit short handed today. Dr. Hammond, do you have surgical experience?"

Appearing somewhat shocked, he said, "Quite a bit, in fact."

Abbey turned to the woman. "You?"

"I've experience as a surgical nurse."

"Excellent. From the sound of the battle, I expect many casualties today. I could use help." The newcomers nodded. "This way please."

"Lt. Smith, please setup a second surgical table for Dr. Hammond and split our team. Lt. Scharf, please assist him. Nurse Anderson, I'd appreciate you assisting me."

Numerous hours later, the last soldier's surgical intervention was completed.

"A pleasure working with your team, Chief Surgeon Kaplan," Dr. Hammond said, shaking her hand.

"I'm…" Abbey smiled, "Your assistance was a Godsend. Thank you for instructing me and my assistant in new techniques."

"My pleasure. I believe many of our questions were answered as we observed you and your team. Your surgical skill is impressive, Dr. Kaplan."

"I'm still learning."

"New techniques are being discovered all the time. Surgery is a field which requires constant learning."

Nurse Anderson concurred then said, "Dr. Kaplan, I noticed your team is cross-trained."

Abbey said, "Lt. Smith and Lt. Scharf, came up with the idea and we implemented it."

"We would like to incorporate women into the nursing corps," Nurse Anderson said. "This would free more men for combat. Some are insisting men are better at nursing. Your thoughts?"

"Let me understand; you're asking if I believe we have better medical care because the individuals performing the nursing duties have a penis? I think not."

Dr. Hammond and Nurse Anderson glanced at each other, then burst into laughter.

In the background, Abbey could see her team laughing as well.

"We came here to see how your regiment's medical work was progressing. I didn't imagine I'd have first-hand experience," Dr. Hammond said.

"The literature and circulars coming from Washington provide us knowledge and direction," Abbey said. "They are much appreciated."

"Is there something we can procure for you to advance your medical knowledge?" Dr. Hammond asked.

Abbey thought for a bit. "I could use a microscope and someone to train me in its use."

"You'll have both within the week."

They all shook hands and parted company.

"Let's get something to eat," Lt. Scharf said to Abbey.

They sat opposite each other.

Lt. Smith sat down with them. He wore a cat-ate-the-canary grin.

"What?" Abbey asked him.

"Dr. Hammond. You don't know who he is?"

Abbey eyes widened as she gasped then briefly put her hand over her mouth. "Oh my God. Was he THE Dr. Hammond?"

The lieutenant nodded.

"Who?" Lt. Scharf asked.

"General William Hammond, Surgeon General of the United States," Abbey said. "I knew his name sounded familiar but I was so worried about today's surgeries I didn't realize…"

Lt. Scharf laughed and said, "I'm glad I didn't know or I'd have been a nervous wreck."

After three-hours of camp medicine and an hour of surgery the following day, Abbey exited the medical tent.

An officer wearing Calvary insignia approached her. He walked with an odd gait…as if trying to keep his legs spread apart.

"You the Doc?" he asked.

"I'm Dr. Kaplan."

"I'm Cpt. Donovan. Calvary. Piles, Doc. Bloody piles."

"What?"

"My ass. I got piles…they're getting painful and bloody."

"Follow me into the medical tent." The man grimaced with each step.

She placed a chair near a sidewall of the tent.

"Drop your britches and bend over the chair."

As he lowered his britches, he muttered, "Kind of embarrassing."

Abbey sighed. "Not to worry. If it's one thing I've become accustomed to, it's working with assholes."

He bent over the chair and closed his eyes.

"Not good," Abbey said. She inspected the purple colored protrusion. "How long has it caused pain?"

"A few months."

"How much pain?"

"Substantial when I crap and painful as hell when I'm riding."

"It should have resolved itself within the first week."

"All the men in my family got piles. You know, dad, grandfather, uncles."

"This is the worst case I've seen. Stand up and pull up your britches."

"I'm worthless to my unit. I can't ride anymore. They're about to send me home. Isn't there anything you can do?"

"I'll see what I can learn about cures. Meanwhile, I'll give you a jar of petroleum jelly and get you a ride to the recovery hospital. Tomorrow afternoon, I'll see you there and we'll talk about what we can do."

"Yes, Ma'am."

"I can't guaranty anything."

His eyes filled with tears. "Hate to be away from my unit. We been together since the start. Appreciate anything you can do, Doc."

She called over a nurse. "Get him a cot for now then schedule transportation to the recovery hospital."

"Not trying to embarrass you Doc, but you look exhausted."

Chapter Ten: Tired

"Doctor Kaplan," Lt. Scharf said, mid-morning two-days later. Both were on their way to the medical tents. "Are you alright?"

"Tired. Nothing more."

"When's the last time you slept?"

She closed her eyes and shook her head. "I manage a couple hours each night. Loads of reports to write and samples plus drawings to send to Washington. Especially since I received the microscope."

"One of us could help."

Abbey shook her head. "My responsibility."

"Anything else preventing you from getting a decent night's rest?"

"Have an occasional nightmare."

"From what you've said previously, it's more than occasional."

"I'll be fine."

"You can request leave. It may help to go home and get away from here for a while."

"My home is in the Northwest. I'd use all my time traveling."

"Pittsburgh is less than a day's train ride."

"I went to medical college in a big city but rarely left campus. I don't think I'd like to visit a large city I don't know."

"My family regularly visited Pittsburgh to see my grandparents. I know the city. We'd have a grand time."

Abbey laughed. "We?"

Lt. Scharf blushed. "Just a thought. I'm going on leave two-weeks from this Saturday…most likely headed to Pittsburgh"

The doctor smiled at his embarrassment. "Thank you for the concern Lieutenant, but I have far too much to do."

They entered the main medical tent and checked the patients.

Lt. Scharf said, "No major surgery today. Just a few ligations. We can handle those without you if you'd like to get more rest."

"Lt. Scharf, you are not a doctor."

"I realize…"

She raised her voice. "Enough! You've made your point." The doctor wobbled slightly then steadied herself by grabbing a tent pole. "I just need some coffee." Abbey's face turned pale. Her body swayed then collapsed.

Lt. Scharf caught her. "I'll take her to her tent."

"I'll find Dr. Fellows," Lt. Smith said.

In a weak voice, Abbey kept repeating, "I'm okay."

Barging his way through the tent flap, Lt. Scharf placed her on a cot. She tried to sit up but the room began spinning. Her helper gently pushed her flat.

"You need to sleep," he said.

"One-hour. Wake me in one-hour. We have to…"

"Don't talk, Dr. Kaplan. Just rest."

"Just for an hour."

"I'll wake you," he said.

Lt. Smith entered with Dr. Fellows.

"She's resting, Doctor." Lt. Scharf said in a subdued tone.

"Just an hour," Abbey whispered.

Dr. Fellows took Lt. Scharf and Lt. Smith outside the tent. "I knew it. She's killing herself to prove she can do a man's job. This is no place for a woman."

The lieutenants glared at him with unmitigated anger.

"At least she hasn't turned to drink," Lt. Scharf said with more fury in his voice than he intended.

"Now you listen to me, Lt.…." The Major became visibly uncomfortable as he realized Scharf's face was filled with fury and his fists were tightening. The doctor cleared his throat. "Lt. Scharf, you stay here and you don't interrupt her sleep. If her breathing becomes labored or she begins sweating, you have someone find me damn fast. Lt. Smith, you'll relieve him in three-hours and you'll alternate watches."

***

Abbey opened her eyes. The light from the single oil lamp, sitting on her desk, cast long shadows around the tent. "What are you doing in here?"

Lt. Scharf looked up from the note he was writing and smiled. "Studying the medical texts you gave me, completing reports you left on your desk and keeping an eye on you...as ordered."

"How long have I been asleep?"

Lt. Scharf checked his pocket watch. "Except for the two times you woke when yelling about William, roughly ten-hours."

"I told you..."

"Dr. Fellows orders. You were not to be disturbed."

Abbey took a deep breath, sat up, rolled her shoulders then stood up. She wobbled briefly. Lt. Scharf leaped to her side and steadied her.

"Thank you, Lieutenant. I'm fine. Just a bit hungry."

"Food over here." He pointed to a cloth covered mucket. "Cup of coffee next to it but probably cold by now." He brought another chair over to her desk and motioned for her to sit. She did and consumed the meal while he continued work on the reports.

"Feel better?" he asked.

"Much."

"You need to take better care of yourself."

"Excuse me?"

"We're depending on you."

"I know...."

"You have nothing to prove."

She raised her voice. "I'm not trying to prove…you don't give me orders."

He used an angry tone to reply. "Then you understand the importance of getting enough sleep and not skipping meals."

"You don't talk to me like…"

He interrupted, raising his voice to a shout, "Abbey, if one of your team wasn't sleeping or eating properly, you'd rip him a new asshole."

Abbey opened her mouth to reply but didn't. She stared at the now miffed lieutenant, gripped his arm, closed her eyes and took a deep breath.

With a warm smile and a brief squeeze of his arm, she said, "Thank you for caring, Lieutenant."

Three days later, Dr. Fellows handed her a document. "These are your leave orders. Saturday after next, you'll have one-week to get out of here and think of something other than this damn war."

"I didn't ask for this."

"I know."

"There is so much to do."

He raised his voice. "You are not goddamned irreplaceable. An assistant surgeon from the Connecticut regiment will cover for you if needed. We'll manage without you for one-week." He regarded her with a stern expression and slowly moved his hands to his hips. "You don't have to look at me like that. I'll manage to stay off the liquor for a lousy week." The Major glared at her over the tops of his glasses. "If I have to order soldiers to physically remove you from this God-forsaken place, I will. Your leave begins

Saturday after next. You will be out of here first thing that morning."

Abbey returned his glare but said, "I'll go, Dr. Fellows, but I don't want to return and find I've been replaced."

"I'm not promising you anything but you will take this leave or that will be an excellent pretense to have you thrown out of here."

The Major was about to leave but then said, "Another thing, Dr. Kaplan. A colonel from Washington has arrived in camp and asked for a meeting with you and me. He's at the headquarters' tent."

"Be right there," she said.

She approached the top soldiers of her regiment and was introduced to Colonel Thomas.

"I'm from the Medical Museum. We've been reviewing various regiment's reports and the results they're achieving. I wanted to meet Drs. Fellows and Kaplan due to their excellent reports, contribution of medical specimens and excellent results in patient care."

He shook hands with each of them.

"Dr. Kaplan, Surgeon General Hammond sends his regards."

Dr. Fellows jaw dropped.

The colonel continued, "The general told me of your diligence and excellent surgical skills. He reported he had a brief discussion with you then you put him to work."

Dr. Fellows nervously shifted from one foot to the other.

Abbey said, "We were short-handed and the general graciously helped out on a busy occasion...even took the time to instruct me and the man assisting him in new techniques."

As she finished dinner, Dr. Fellows approached Abbey and said. "Who do you think you are? You must have some nerve asking the surgeon general to assist you."

"I didn't realize who he was when I requested his help."

"You always seem to fall right-side-up. That won't always be the case."

"I'm aware."

"I know you put my name on the reports and specimens you submit to the Medical Museum. Stop doing it. You put in the long hours. You deserve the credit. Not me." He walked away before she could say another word.

She mumbled at the receding figure. "You're right. Your name shouldn't appear." Abbey was dour faced after being dressed down by Doctor Fellows. Her mood improved as she remembered the kind words she'd heard from the Colonel. She'd walked about twenty paces, halted, then said quietly, "I need to find Lieutenant Smith."

"Assemble our team in front of the medical tents," Dr. Kaplan told him.

She addressed the men with the lieutenants at her side. They stood at attention opposite her in a straight line. Lt. Smith ordered them to parade rest. "Doctor Fellows and I received recognition for excellent results in our medical efforts. Huge mistake. This should have been an acknowledgement of our team's hard work. We earned the accolades as a team due to your diligence, learning new techniques and agreeing to be cross-trained." She paused and looked at each team member. "When I'm a civilian again, I'll put a plaque in my office concerning our unit's recognition along with the names of each one of you. Find me after the war and I'll be proud to show it to you."

Lt. Scharf said, "We wouldn't be the team we are if you weren't here to lead us, Doctor Kaplan."

"I did my part but so did the rest of you. I will always remember this as a group effort and always be proud of our achievement." She saluted and they returned her salute.

"Lieutenant Smith, you may dismiss the men."

***

"You need to go to Pittsburgh," Lt. Scharf said while Abbey stared at the train station's destination board on the morning her leave began. "We team members should stick together."

She smiled. "I'm not sure it would be right…"

His intense blue eyes bored into hers. "Have I ever treated you in a disrespectful manner?"

Chapter Eleven: First Leave

Abbey's expression went blank. She thought for a bit then smiled at her assistant. "Pittsburgh it is."

Arriving at a hotel, they booked separate rooms and met for dinner.

"I'm still tense," Lt. Scharf said. "As though I might be called to assist wounded at any moment."

Abbey giggled. "I feel the same tension."

"What would you like to do this week?"

"I think day one I'd like to take long walks. Different surroundings might relieve stress."

"Excellent idea," he said.

"Would my teammate accompany me?"

"Of course." Lt. Scharf smiled and bowed his head slightly. "I know some interesting areas and some excellent eateries." He raised a glass of wine. "To a week of stress relief."

"To stress relief," Abbey said with a laugh as they clinked glasses. With a shrug, she added, "If we can…"

He offered her his arm as they walked the following bright and sunny day.

She put her hand on his forearm and briefly squeezed it. They walked in silence for nearly three-hours.

"A pleasant Sunday morning," he said. "Is there anything you'd like to discuss this week?"

"So many things…"

"Pick one."

Abbey sighed. "I trust you to keep this to yourself…but I struggle with ugly dreams. Often, they keep me from getting a decent night's sleep."

"Is the dream why you yell about William?"

"My brother. He appears crippled or dead in some nightmares."

"Tell me about them."

She took a deep breath. "I see my family members with cruel injuries. I try to run away but I can hear them yelling for help." Abbey shuddered. "Also, a nightmare where a cannon-ball lands near me and feeling terrified as I'm thrown into the air. Then in slow motion, I watch as my limbs are ripped off."

"Ghastly."

"You?"

"Initially, I had nightmares where a soldier needed help but I didn't know enough to repair his injuries."

"No longer occur?" she asked.

"Once in a long while. My fear of incomplete knowledge is what's motivating me to study the medical books and documents you give me on war injuries." He gazed skyward for a minute then added, "Fear can be a motivator but consumes a ton of energy."

Abbey took a deep breath. "I would add two items to the list of emotions which tax my energy besides fear; tension and anxiety."

"Do they occur at some specific time?"

"Other than waiting for casualties to arrive, triage is the worst. Many of the soldiers have grievous wounds we can't treat…that eats away and drags down my emotions…depressing the hell out of me." She sighed and shook her head. "While I work on the injuries we can repair, I'm frustrated I have to leave many others to die."

"Like the ones who are gut-shot?"

She nodded. "Little hope for many of them even though I've successfully repaired a number."

"I've kept count. Two of every four you accept for surgery are surviving. Fifty-percent is one hell of a lot better than zero." He stared at the ground, his brow furrowed. "As my skills improve, I believe I understand how frustration puts sadness in one's head."

Abbey said, "Lieutenant, I'm not telling you this to make you sad."

"Trying to think of what I can do to help you feel better about yourself."

"Listening is good enough." She patted his arm. "Let's head back to the hotel and have lunch."

The following day, the team members headed out to walk near the river.

The twosome were surrounded by the sights and sounds of a neighborhood with street vendors noisily hawking their wares, horse's hooves on the pavement and the occasional screech of streetcars' steel wheels. At one point, a large, empty barrel fell off a wagon making a loud sound as it hit the cobblestones. They both jumped, looked at each other and engaged in nervous laughter.

Abbey pointed to a small park. "Let's sit on the bench over there." They sat and observed their surroundings.

"If I was an artist," Lt. Scharf said after glancing around, "that would be a fine painting." He pointed toward a washerwoman who was nursing an infant. The tiny one was held firmly against her breast by a small blanket tied around her neck and back. Seated on a low stool, the woman's back arched over her work; her legs splayed as they embraced a wide washtub set on concrete blocks. Her sleeves were pulled up over her well-defined biceps, her head wrapped in a red and white checkered scarf which was tied at the back of her neck. Clothing, clothes-pinned to a line, waved just above her. Elbow deep in gray water, she scrubbed clothing on a washboard then rinsed and wrung the water out. All the while, she laughed with and addressed two toddlers who played at her feet. Behind her, sweat covered workman hauled bricks up temporary wooden walkways to masons constructing a wall.

Abbey studied the scene for a bit then briefly stared at the lieutenant. "Thanks. I didn't even notice. What would you call your painting?"

"Motherhood?"

"Not descriptive enough."

"Mother up to her elbows in washing and children?"

Abbey laughed.

"You said you didn't notice," he said.

"Even if I look, I try not to see."

He gave her a questioning expression.

She shrugged, "Force of habit."

"Because?"

"If I don't see our patients as people, I can simply address their injuries."

"Why avoid knowing we work on people?"

"My way of preventing negative feelings. It's easier."

"Could those feelings get bottled up in your head then appear as ugly dreams?"

"Unlikely…" she gazed at their surroundings for a few moments, "but let me think."

He nodded to the South. "Four-blocks from here, is a Italian deli which serves home-cooked style and it's almost lunch time."

"Sure."

They walked in silence for the first block-and-a-half.

Abbey sighed and said, "People regularly ask me how I endure the stress of my work. I just realized I've never asked anyone else how they manage."

"Push-ups."

Abbey laughed.

"Seriously. First thing each morning then each evening before dinner. I'm up to one-hundred minimum each day."

"I don't understand how physical activity can release mental strain."

"You're the doc so if you don't know, I sure don't…but it works for me."

They split a sandwich piled high with deli meats, roasted red and green peppers, onion slivers, provolone cheese, and lettuce, all savored with sweet tea.

When they'd finished, Abbey said, "I'd like to see Congregation *Rodef Shalom.* I believe they're the oldest congregation here and have a lovely synagogue."

"It's an easy walk from here."

She took his arm again as they walked.

"Having nightmares since we've been here?"

"Only the first night." Abbey walked in silence for a while. "This is when I miss having a woman to talk to."

"Not sure what you mean."

"If I tell a man about a problem, he tries to fix it for me and feels sad when he can't."

"What's wrong with that?"

"A woman would understand just talking about it helps even without a solution."

He grinned. "Are you saying men and woman are different?"

"Different yes, but not necessarily better than one or another."

"So you should tell me about the nightmares and I'll just listen."

Abbey weighed how much to share then tucked a lock of hair behind her ear. "The nightmares wear on me in two ways. First, once I have one, it wakes me, I'm sweating, out of breath and my heart pounds. Afterward, it's difficult to get back to sleep. Second, my emotions feel like a raw nerve. Any little annoyance seems magnified."

"Is that why you seem ready to rip heads off some days?"

"Am I that bad?"

"Occasionally."

"What do you do on those days?"

"Remind the team how much strain you're under."

Abbey turned her head toward him and stared. He glanced around the neighborhood then stared at her. "Hey, it's part of my job." He again looked away for a while then said, "We're a team, doc. We take care of each other."

She gripped his upper arm then kissed his cheek. Abbey closed her eyes and rested her head on his shoulder. After a few minutes, she sighed. "I'm so tired."

"Back to the hotel?"

"I'm going to sleep the afternoon away."

At dinner, Abbey told him, "I'll be staying in my room tomorrow to read and write letters."

Lt. Scharf said, "Good idea. I'm going to visit the neighborhood where my grandparents first settled. They're long gone but I'd like to see what remains of the area."

They walked to their adjacent rooms and stopped in front of Abbey's.

She tucked a lock of hair behind one ear. "Lt. Scharf, despite my spending endless hours doing what's considered men's work, I still experience a woman's desire for a man."

"I…"

"Those big, muscular masons we saw earlier lit a fire in me."

"If you become pregnant?"

"I have a birth-prevention preparation we can use."

He didn't respond.

She wrapped her arms around him. Abbey watched as the soft press of her chest produced an expression of desire.

He slowly wrapped his arms around her. "I've wanted you since the day we met."

***

After breakfast the following morning, alone in her room, the doctor sat at the small desk.

Mom and Dad,

I hope this letter finds you well.

I know I've been terrible about writing but I'm busy all my waking hours. When battle casualties arrive, I sometimes work more than twenty-four-hours at-a-stretch, only stopping for a quick bite to eat. In-between battles, I treat camp disease and help at the recovery hospital plus do research and write mountains of reports.

I've taken pen in hand to write a missive because I've been assigned a one-week leave. I traveled to Pittsburgh as it is a one-day train ride from our current encampment. Don't worry. I'm not alone in a strange city. My surgical helper has accompanied me. He's big and awfully kind. No romantic involvement but I do feel less lonely and a bit more secure because he's here.

The fact I'm a female doctor in a man's profession causes constant frustration. As my team observed my surgical skills, they (reluctantly!) began to respect me. Unfortunately, most others don't think I should be a doctor, let alone a surgeon in a war.

Events grind me down as I suspect happen in all wars. I'm tired, both physically and mentally. If it wasn't for the sense of duty you instilled in me, I'd have quit and come home long ago. Thank you.

I'm enduring nightmares and have trouble sleeping. They don't seem to go away and may be getting worse. Not sure what I'll do.

Bought some clothes recently. Nothing cheery. Just gray and black which allows me to get my job done and, sadly, reflects my emotional state.

Abbey stood, walked to a window, and gazed at the busy neighborhood below. She returned to the desk and re-read the letter.

"*My God. This is my life?*" she thought, then sat back and closed her eyes for a while. "*Only Mom will appreciate what I'm going through.*" Abbey crossed out her father's name and addressed the letter to her mother and added instructions, the contents were for Myra's eyes only.

The doctor spent the balance of the day trying to sleep with the exception of evening meal which she ate in her room.

***

"Good morning," Abbey said with a smile at breakfast on Wednesday. In a quiet voice, she asked, "How was yesterday?"

"Wonderful," Lt. Scharf replied. "I visited my grandparents' old neighborhood in the morning and spent the afternoon reading. You?"

"The day was great. Put together a letter to my mom."

They ordered breakfast.

He sipped his coffee. "Yesterday wasn't close to wonderful..."

"You felt empty and alone."

He sat up straight and nodded. "I did...the whole damn day."

"Why?"

"Not sure." He twisted on his chair then said, "Missed my teammate. You?"

Initially expressionless, Abbey just stared at him for a minute before dropping her eyes to her lap. With a slight smile, she quietly replied, "The same."

"Because?"

"What we've endured as a team has brought us together like family."

"You've thought this through."

She nodded. "Loneliness is not a good feeling."

"What shall we do?"

"Spend the day together doing anything as long as we...well...keep the team together."

A bumpy ride on a noisy trolley delivered them to a library. The twosome sat on couches and chairs; he reading a book on physiology and she an account of Dr. Ignaz Semmelweis.

"Listen," Abbey said. "This Hungarian physician discovered doctors washing their hands before they touched women in a maternity ward reduced mortality rates from ten-percent to less than two-percent."

"How did he determine the percentage?"

"He compared the results of two clinics in the same hospital. The mortality rates in the first, where doctors performed autopsies before attending births, were higher than in the second which was attended by midwives and doctors who hadn't done autopsies."

"What did they die of?"

"The mortalities were due to post-partum infections which developed within twenty-four-hours of birth. Dr. Semmelweis discovered women delivering babies on the street rarely developed the infection."

Lt. Scharf became pensive for a while then asked, "We see numerous infections after surgery. Could it be due to dirty hands...or instruments?"

"I'll keep reading and let you know."

Thirty-minutes later, the lieutenant asked, "What did they wash their hands with?"

"Chloride of lime in solution."

"Why would it make a difference?"

"No one's figured it out but the difference is rather dramatic."

They looked at each other.

Abby said, "Our after-surgery death rate was near forty-percent at the beginning of the war. Applying the lessons of the Crimean War, we have it lowered to around twenty-eight-percent for primary amputations. If we could lower those by eight-percent..."

"Let's find chloride of lime and take it back to camp."

"I've been reminded our patients aren't experiments," Abbey cautioned.

"If we find one thing which helps them…"

"We'll see. When casualties mount, I don't see how we'll have time."

"We could try a technique one time and follow the patient."

Abbey leaned back and stared at the high ceiling. "Dr. Semmelweis achieved an eight-percent reduction in mortality. If we achieved the same…" The doctor turned to her assistant.

"We'd be heroes," he said.

She nodded.

"Perhaps we could try some things with gangrene…like additional cleanliness."

Abbey leaned back, became pensive then said, "Before I treated each of the first two of the gut-shot wounds, I washed my hands and cleaned my instruments as I thought we were done for the day. While I was working on the second, the next two arrived so I didn't clean the surgical tools before operating on the third and fourth soldiers."

"Were the first two soldiers you treated the men who survived?"

She nodded.

"Then when we're back in camp, we'll make a plan to try some things."

They were quiet for a while when he stated, "I was reading about autopsies where pus was discovered in the blood stream resulting in an always fatal condition."

"I need to spend more time with my microscope to observe similar conditions. When did you read about pus in the blood?"

"A couple months ago."

"You must have a mind like a steel trap."

He shook his head while stating, "Dr. Fellows and you keep giving me more responsibility during surgery. I make a mistake due to lack of knowledge and I kill someone. I'd rather study hard enough to remember what I've read."

They concentrated on their books for a few hours then Abbey asked, "Hungry?"

He nodded.

They found a butcher who sold brisket sandwiches then continued walking.

"How did you sleep last night?" he asked.

She shrugged. "Barely."

"Nightmare?"

"One early in the night then couldn't sleep the rest of the night thinking of all the soldiers we couldn't help or died on the operating table."

"Try push-ups."

She laughed.

As dinner ended, Abbey sipped the last of her wine, pulled him close, kissed his cheek and whispered. "I want my teammate to share my bed tonight."

Thursday morning, they found a bookstore. Each made a purchase. A kosher deli provided lunch. The afternoon was spent in his room; Abbey read on a couch, he studied at a desk. Eventually, Abbey nodded off. He covered her with a blanket and returned to his book.

After dinner, they sat on the veranda of the hotel and watched the sun go down.

"Nightmare last night?" he asked.

"Only one and it was mild so was able to get back to sleep."

He cleared his throat. "Dr. Kaplan, this week has been a great relief...being away from the constant tension of the war..."

"Makes one almost feel human."

He laughed.

A cacophony of nighttime insects came to life as the remaining daylight morphed into darkness. "Time for sleep," she said.

They both stood. Abbey briefly embraced him. "Thank you."

He slid his arms around her. "For what?"

"Listening to me, learning enough surgical technique to assist me. Protecting me during battle. Closing my wounds. Encouraging me to keep going despite Dr. Fellows criticism. Doing your best to see I'm treated with respect...I could go on but you know."

"Abbey, the things you mentioned, are the least I owe you for directing my studies to help the wounded."

"Which would have amounted to little without your hard work. You've been an outstanding assistant surgeon's assistant."

He laughed and said, "My pleasure."

Abbey leaned into him and kissed his cheek. "Assistant, keep me warm again tonight."

Friday was filled with walks along the river and occasional conversation.

After a pleasant dinner they returned to Abbey's room.

He stood in front of her. "This week…"

They stared into each other's eye's.

"I know," Abbey said. "We're two lonely people who've been thrown together and forced to endure bloody horrors. One or both of our lives might end in a fraction of a second. I don't want to get close to anyone I might lose."

He sighed. "As usual, you're right. Besides, a relationship based on mutual loneliness wouldn't last." He forced a smile. "It's been a good week. Thanks for accompanying me."

"It was…a good week."

He turned to leave.

Abbey tucked a lock of hair behind her ear. "Wait."

Lt. Scharf looked back at her.

She stepped toward him and put her arms around his neck. "One more night together, please."

Lt. Scharf embraced her. He kissed her lips. Abbey wrapped herself around him as tight as she could.

On the train back to camp, he said, "The closer we get, the more anxious I'm becoming."

She sighed. "I sense the same."

Chapter Twelve: Evaluations

At the recovery hospital, Drs. Kaplan and Fellows examined patients in a large ward and determined a few would need further surgical intervention.

"Hey you," a young lieutenant called to Abbey. "I need some help over here."

She ignored him.

He shouted, "Hey You, I'm Doctor Peter Dillon and an officer. I'll make your life hell if I don't get a response when I talk to you. I need to talk to Dr. Kaplan."

A number of nurses in the ward turned to watch Abbey.

Unsmiling, she walked up to him, put her hands on her hips and glared down at the slightly more than five-foot-tall man. She spoke slowly and succinctly. "I'm Dr. Kaplan. Not,

Hey You. Please rest assured, you won't be giving me or anyone else hell, little man, or your first medical intervention will be to remove the boot I'll bury in your ass."

A number of nurses turned away, covering their mouths to stifle laughter.

His cheeks reddened. In a trembling voice he said, "I've been assigned to your team for training before I'm sent to a regiment."

"We'll be performing two surgeries shortly. I'll be leading today, so you stand next to me and observe."

He swallowed hard. "Yes, Doctor."

After the surgeries were complete, Abbey told the newcomer, "Head to the kitchen and get a ten-inch-square of pork belly with skin attached. We'll begin your training by cutting and sewing the pork."

A nurse, standing next to a man on crutches, called to Dr. Kaplan. The doctor crossed the ward. The nurse lifted the patient's shirt. Abbey removed a large, square bandage and examined a burned area the size of a dinner plate.

Dr. Dillon whispered to Dr. Fellows, "Excuse me Major, but will I have to take orders from a woman at my new regiment?"

Dr. Fellows squinted at the newcomer. "I'm forced to put up with her on a daily basis, so you'll manage to follow her orders while being trained."

"Work for a woman? I'm more of a man than that."

His eyes glaring, Dr. Fellows said, "I've noticed the team emptying bed pans is short staffed. I can arrange your assignment to use your medical education to perform that duty…if you prefer…"

The newcomer appeared horrified, gulped, then spat out, "No," quickly adding, "Major."

Putting his hands on his hips, Dr. Fellows said, "Then I suggest you learn to follow Dr. Kaplan's orders."

The soldier swallowed hard and said rapidly, "I can follow her orders, Sir."

Abbey talked to the nurse and burn victim, "Keep it clean and it should continue to heal."

Dr. Dillon approached Abbey. "A ten-inch-square of pork belly with skin attached. On the way, Doctor Kaplan."

Abbey spent the next two-hours working with the new arrival. He was sent back to the mess area for more pork to practice on.

She shook her head while examining Dr. Dillon's attempts to duplicate her technique.

Abbey found Dr. Fellows staring out a window in an office they'd been assigned. He offered her a drink.

"No thank you."

He lifted his glass and downed a large swallow of dark liquid. The elder doctor coughed once then wiped his lips with the back of his hand.

Abbey rolled her shoulders a few times, attempting to relieve stress then sat in a chair and folded her hands in her lap. "He doesn't have sufficient dexterity for surgery."

"How bad?"

"Dangerous bad. One glance at his work and you'd think he wore hams at the ends of his arms instead of fingers. He can barely cut a straight line and has little ability to suture. Most of his incisions were irregular and too shallow or too deep." Abbey closed her eyes and shook her head. "Although his book knowledge may be adequate, the man shouldn't be allowed anywhere near a patient needing surgical intervention."

"I'll send a letter to the medical board but it's not our decision." He downed another belt then briefly stared at her. "On the other hand, you like paperwork. You send them a letter."

Using more sarcasm in her voice than she intended, Abbey said, "Hitting the bottle kind of hard, Doctor?"

His face reddened and he growled, "You think it's easy for me to remove limb after limb from these young men?" He stared at the floor and shook his head then gave her a dismissive wave. "I don't know how the hell you can remain so reserved."

"It's our job."

He stood and began pacing. "For more than thirty-years, I enjoyed a quiet practice in a small town. If someone needed surgery I'd stop their bleeding and send them to a hospital." He gestured toward the recovery wards. "Think of all those cripples. Who knew this damn war would endure for years instead of months? Now I'm mired in this…shit. I've witnessed enough horror for a hundred goddamned lifetimes. The cries and the terror in the eyes of those casualties will be in the forefront of my memory until the day I take my last breath." He collapsed into a chair and stared daggers at Abbey. "Go back to the ward, Dr. Kaplan." He refilled his tumbler. "If anyone asks for me, tell them you don't know where I am."

"You trust my medical decisions?"

"As long as you're not performing experiments. If you feel the need…get my permission first."

***

"Talia! Mrs. Warshawsky," Abbey called out when she saw them just after camp disease treatment.

"Dr. Kaplan, how are you?"

"I just received a document specifying how to surgically repair a hare lip."

Talia's eye's grew wide. With a hand covering her deformity, she yelled, "When?"

"I've never done this so there's no guarantee."

The young teen grabbed Abbey wrists and begged, "When?"

"I'll assemble my team. Be at the medical tent in an hour."

After the procedure, Abbey gave care instructions to Mrs. Warshawsky then added, "The stitches will fall out on their own. Don't pull on them and keep the repaired area as clean as possible. Let me see her again in three days. Sooner if it becomes warm, red or the swelling increases."

Talia patted Abbey's arm and tried to form a word but it was too painful.

"I know," Abbey said. "You're welcome."

***

"Excuse me. Are you Doctor Kaplan?" a slim young woman of medium height asked a few weeks later during breakfast near the field hospital tents.

"I am." Abbey downed the last of her coffee.

"Pardon the interruption. I'm Margaret Herzog. I've sufficient medical training which qualifies me to become a surgical assistant but the only work I'm given is bathing patients and emptying bed pans."

"A surgical assistant requires a medical degree and completing an examination."

"I'm aware. If I can work with you and learn about camp disease and surgery, I'm certain I could pass the exam."

"Have you completed your medical studies?"

"Completed both years but ran out of money, so didn't receive a degree."

The doctor regarded the thin woman whose expression pleaded for help. "What do you propose I do?"

"Assign me to your team. I want to put my book learning to use and become a surgeon like you."

Abbey looked away and said, "I have little control over assignments."

"I've heard surgeons can request personnel."

"Someone high up the chain-of-command assigned me to this regiment's chief surgeon. Try asking your superiors."

Margaret's posture stiffened. "They're men who don't think I should be here. As it happens, they don't think you should be here either. They talk down to me and don't listen. Sorry to have bothered you." The woman's expression was bitter as she turned to leave. She took a few steps. Margaret stopped, hesitated then spun around and glared at Abbey. Red faced, fists clenched, and body shaking, she shouted, "If a woman won't help me, who the hell will?"

Chapter Thirteen: Expanding Educations

The sound of distant cannons followed by exploding shells rumbled across the sky. Abbey stared at the newcomer then wondered what her mother would do if faced with a similar situation. She smiled then tucked a lock of hair behind her ear. The doctor leaned back and sighed. "Get something to eat and we'll talk."

Still red-faced, the woman spat out, "I'm not hungry."

Another volley of distant cannon fire followed by small-arms-fire echoed across their camp. Abbey nodded in the sound's direction. "We can expect to begin numerous surgeries within the hour. We may not have time for evening meal until long after dark. You'll need your strength."

An expression of relief flooded Margaret's face. "Yes, Doctor."

The woman filled a mucket and sat opposite her.

"You're willing to work as a helper until you learn surgical techniques?" Abbey asked.

Margaret nodded.

"Tell me about yourself,"

"I'm from Toronto."

"No you're not," Abbey said. "When you were angry, your southern accent became pronounced."

"I try to suppress it for obvious reasons." Margaret's voice dropped to a near whisper. "I was raised in Vicksburg, Mississippi. My father owns a cotton wholesaling business. When war became imminent, he thought it would be safer for me to attend college up north. In truth, I attended medical college in Toronto." She ate a few bites then in full voice, continued. "If you don't mind my asking, how did you decide on a medical career and what college did you attend?"

"I was ten and watched a doctor sew up a wound. Ever since, my only plans were for medicine and particularly surgery. I attended the Female Medical College of Philadelphia.

"I've heard of it."

"A great school. It was founded in 1850. I believe it was the first college to train women for the degree of medicine. Philadelphia, also called the City of Medicine, is home to the nation's first hospital and medical school. The Quakers, who lived in Philly and the surrounding counties, promoted egalitarian causes including women's rights. They were instrumental in creating the college."

"When I was of similar age, my older brother, who was strong as an ox, became weakened over a handful of days. A number of doctors came to the house to examine him but he died."

"Poliomyelitis?"

Margaret nodded. "I'd love to research disease causes and cures."

"So your parents sent you to study medicine?"

The southerner twisted uncomfortably. "They weren't aware of my plans to attend medical college."

Abbey's eyebrows went up.

"According to my mother," Margaret sat up straight, switched to a high-pitched-voice, put her nose in the air, and placed her hands on her hips. "It is quite unacceptable for a genteel lady to enter a career which may require placing her hands on the private areas of a man or woman."

Laughter burst forth from Abbey. "What do they think you're doing?"

"Studying to become a teacher."

Margaret ate a bit then asked, "How did you become a surgeon in the medical corps?"

"One of my professors at college was related to the man who financed and organized this regiment. She knew of my desire to develop skill as a surgeon. After passing the examination, I was assigned to Dr. Fellows, this regiment's chief surgeon. Unfortunately, rather than choosing a skilled surgeon to be chief, the regiment chose a political appointee. I suspect he performed little surgery during his civilian practice. The strain of endless casualties caused him to turn to drink. I've acquired a surgeon's skill as a result."

Margaret gave her a questioning expression.

"The more he drinks, the more his hands shake. Initially, I spent my time on camp disease; sutured small lacerations, then removed bullets and shrapnel from shallow wounds. I began closing for him then some months ago, he was shaking so bad I took over in the middle of an amputation. Since then I've performed innumerable surgeries without him."

"Without an assistant?"

"Fortunately for the wounded, the regimental band's lead percussionist has amazing dexterity, a mind which soaks up information like a blotter and has a stomach which doesn't try to empty itself at the first site of blood."

A short, rotund sergeant approached wearing an ill-fitting uniform. His jacket buttons strained to contain his protruding potbelly. "Miss Herzog, I need your assistance immediately."

"From now on she'll be working with me," Abbey said with a pleasant smile.

The officious appearing little man clasped his hands behind his back, smirked and rocked onto his toes. "I make her assignments."

"Then you're assigning her to me."

"Not hardly," he said with a grin and a leer at the doctor's large chest. "I'm a sergeant so I decide." He glared at Dr. Kaplan.

No longer smiling, Abbey unfolded to her full six-foot height. She returned his glare and put her hands on her hips. In a slow and succinct voice she said, "I'm Doctor Kaplan, assistant surgeon with this regiment, therefore rank equivalent of lieutenant. I've decided I will need her skills."

"But…"

"If the chief surgeon, who holds the rank of major, finds out someone is impeding my ability to give our brave men the best care I'm capable of, he will be most displeased...Sergeant."

He held up his hands in an apparent gesture of surrender. "She's assigned to you, Doctor...er...Lieutenant. I'll need a written request from the chief surgeon."

"You'll have it before day's end."

He saluted and said, "I'll arrange the transfer."

Abbey returned his salute. "Thank you, Sergeant."

The crestfallen little man spun on his heel and hurried away.

"Dr. Kaplan," Margaret said, "you should work on your salute. It was kind of sloppy."

Both women laughed.

"You have a good relationship with the chief surgeon?"

Abbey sat down and grinned. "He hates my guts."

Margaret chuckled.

"He's desperately in need of a skilled surgeon so puts up with a woman. I cover for him when he's indisposed so he quit trying to push me out."

Abbey rolled her shoulders.

"How is your body holding up after numerous long days of surgery?"

"It hurts. I'm tall and the tables are such that I lean over during most of the surgery. The first few weeks, I was in so much joint and muscle pain, I thought I'd have to quit. But my body adjusted...somewhat. The soreness doesn't end. Nor does the stream of wounded once a battle begins. Worked over forty-eight-hours straight a few times."

"Aren't you worried about becoming so tired you'll make mistakes?"

"Yes but there's so few of us. Our regiment of twelve-thousand men has one chief surgeon, an assistant surgeon and roughly ten helpers. It will be a blessing if you can learn procedures quickly…but…"

Abbey waited until she had the woman's full attention.

"Please understand, I'm giving you an opportunity without a guarantee. Your success will depend on your having been born with skilled hands. Not everyone who has the requisite book learning has the manual dexterity to perform surgery."

Margaret nodded. "I understand."

Abbey closed her eyes for a moment then smiled. "My younger brother, who had no interest in medicine or surgery when he was young, used to sew cooked noodles together without tearing them…prior to the age of ten."

Miss Herzog's eyes widened.

"As an early teen, he was called to the side of a newborn. With the guidance of a community doctor, he used his skilled hands to perform tiny ligations, remove minute shards of glass in the infant's leg wound and closed it with tiny sutures." The doctor sighed. "There are certainly days when I wish he was at my side."

Margaret ate in silence for a while then leaned forward. "Dr. Kaplan, how do you deal with the strain of seeing so many soldiers with torn bodies? I've only been here a few weeks and the more I see, the more depressed I get."

"The sight of bloody injuries hasn't bothered me since childhood."

"But the severely wounded…the amputees." Margaret's brow dropped and her eyes narrowed. "Some are little more than children."

"The War Department allows child enlistees from nine to seventeen."

"Losing limbs, their lives are irreversibly altered. I feel their pain."

"I may have at first but now that I'm the one doing the surgeries, I can't afford the luxury of feeling their pain."

"How do you ignore it?"

"I concentrate on the work in front of me and studying the documents coming from Washington which explain new techniques."

"But then afterward…"

"Except for occasional nightmares and the accompanying loss of sleep…" Abbey looked down then took a slow, deep breath. "Miss Herzog," she looked in the newcomers eyes, "have you ever watched a carpenter build a house?"

"Of course."

"They show no emotion when they work. We must do the same."

Margaret twisted on the bench and leaned forward. "Carpentry is a mechanical task."

"As is surgery."

Abbey's new acquaintance gazed at her dinner. Without looking up, and trying to avoid seeming confrontational, the woman said in a quiet voice, "We're not working on houses. We work on people."

"Perhaps you'd be better off bathing patients and emptying bed pans?"

Margaret rapidly shook her head and sat up straight. "No, Ma'am. I wish to assist you. And learn, learn, learn."

"I live alone in an officer's tent. You can share it with me and I can direct you to literature I have to further your education."

"I'd love to."

Abbey smiled. "Miss Herzog, you may become the first friend I've managed out here." She became pensive then added, "You may wish to wear britches."

"Never in my life would I consider...but why?"

"If you have to crawl rapidly across the ground when bullets are flying over your head, you want all the speed you can manage; a skirt slows one down."

"Can I assume you're speaking from experience?"

"Yes."

"I know it will feel odd...but I'll follow your suggestion."

"Also, I'll introduce you to a washerwoman. I suggest you follow my lead and begin each day with a clean apron."

"Whatever you suggest, Doctor Kaplan."

"Call me Abbey."

"And please address me as Margaret."

Abbey nodded.

"Abbey, given any thought to what you'll do after the war?"

"A doctor who's dealing with war weariness, I don't know what else to call it, asked me to visit him in Boston. The subject intrigues me. Afterward, I'll return to my family in the Northwest to pursue a lifetime of surgery."

"You mentioned war weariness. Please tell me about it."

"Another day," Abbey replied as she watched an ambulance-train rumble into view. The doctor nodded at the two-wheeled wagons. She stood. "Finish eating. Your surgical education will begin shortly."

***

Eight-weeks later, Margaret again assisted Abbey while she treated camp disease. A colonel presented himself with a two-inch-long infected lesion just below his knee.

"Dr. Herzog, would you please lance and clean this?"

"Yes, Dr. Kaplan."

Abbey watched briefly then said, "Good work." She turned to the waiting soldiers. "Next."

Whenever appropriate, she assigned patients to Margaret. When the last patient was treated, Abbey checked her watch. "That's little more than half the time it usually takes when I'm working alone."

"The last eight-weeks have consisted of more doctoring than I'd imagined could be squeezed into such a short time. I appreciate you referring to me as Doctor Herzog."

"Most soldiers appreciate being treated by a doctor. Even female. Besides, with the hard work you're putting in on the study materials plus the work you performed with camp disease and surgery, I think you're on your way to becoming an excellent doctor."

They began walking back to their tent when they heard a soldier calling for Doctor Kaplan. He carried a boy wrapped in a blanket.

"He was playing near a fire and fell in," the soldier said. The boy sobbed and quivered while a woman walked next to them.

"Bring him to the medical tent," Abbey said. The soldier put the wide-eyed boy on one of the surgical tables.

"What's your name?" Margaret asked while she and Abbey began removing his charred clothing.

"Henry Carmine," the boy said. "I'm nine."

"Henry," Margaret continued "I'm Doctor Herzog and this is Doctor Kaplan." She turned to the older woman. "Who are you Ma'am?"

"His mother."

Margaret said, "Come around this side and stand where he can see you, please."

"The burns are not too bad," Abbey said after examining them.

Margaret smiled at the young patient and said, "Hear that Henry? I know it hurts a lot now but Dr. Kaplan says your burns are not too bad. We're going to clean and bandage them."

With an occasional whimper, the boy was treated. His mother expressed profound thanks to the doctors.

The two lady medics walked to their tent.

"Margaret, your conversation with the boy and his mother…"

"Too much?"

"No. Not at all. I noted their expressions. The more you talked, the more they relaxed. What a marvelous quality. I limit my conversation to what I need to know for a diagnosis."

"Should I limit my conversation?"

"No. Even during camp disease treatment, you did the same with the soldiers and had them smiling. I admire your ability as I know I'm lacking in that area."

***

Mrs. Warshawsky and her daughter approached Abbey and Margaret just before they arrived at their tent.

"I'm here to thank you," Talia said.

"Let me see your lip," Abbey said. The doctor ran her finger along the repaired tissue. "Properly healed. Only a barely visible scar."

"What did you do?" Margret asked.

"This was a hare lip."

"You closed it? I've never heard of…"

Talia interrupted with a shout. "She fixed me." Her eyes filled with tears. She threw her arms around Abbey and began sobbing.

"Hey," Abbey said while embracing the teen. "You're supposed to be happy; not crying."

Talia took a step back and nodded while wiping her eyes with the backs of her hands.

Her mother put an arm around her daughter's shoulders and said, "She's happy. You've no idea how happy."

***

Abbey and Margaret relaxed in their tent, each sipping a steaming mucket of coffee.

"Twelve-weeks working together," Margaret said.

"I firmly believe you will be passing the medical board exam with ease."

"Do I hear a but coming…"

"You remind me of our family's doctor back in Seattle. In my mind, Dr. Beckham is the epitome of a community doctor."

"But not a surgeon."

"Correct. Your hands will allow you to perform limited surgery but…"

"Lt. Scharf has better hands than I do."

Abbey laughed. "Don't feel bad. Besides my brother William, few people on this planet have Lt. Scharf's level of manual dexterity…but it doesn't mean you won't be a marvelous doctor."

"What do I do now?"

"Keep learning and you'll take the medical board exam."

"Will Doctor Fellows recommend me?"

"I'll see to it."

"He doesn't like me and was furious when he realized he'd signed my transfer paperwork while in a drunken stupor."

"If I ask him, he'll do it. He may not like it but he'll do it."

"Why?"

"Shortly before you joined our team, we received acknowledgement for the excellent reports and samples we send the Medical Museum plus the results of our medical efforts. A colonel came from Washington to congratulate us. Since then, Dr. Fellows has done his best to ignore me but given me free reign on most medical and surgical decisions."

"Any assignments this afternoon?"

"Word has spread concerning Talia's hare lip surgery. I...sorry...we...have seven soldiers, most from other regiments and a number of civilians from the surrounding area, including one adult man, two grown women and a two-month-old baby; all with hare lip. We'll begin their surgeries at one o'clock."

Just before she began the last repair, Dr. Fellows entered the surgical tent.

He approached Abbey. "I heard you're repairing hare lip today. Could be useful when I return to civilian practice. May I assist, Dr. Kaplan?"

Shocked, Abbey replied, "Of course, Dr. Fellows."

***

"Abbey," Margaret said, "I received word on the boy who fell in the fire some days ago. He's doing fine other than some scar tissue on his right cheek. His mother is a...I believe the polite term is...camp follower."

"I suspected such. A number of them trail after us and service the men."

They each spooned breakfast from their muckets.

"The boy's mother and quite a number of others have diseases we could treat. Lesions on their genitals and the like. We would need supplies."

Abbey thought for a while then said, "A woman is here from the Sanitary Commission. We'll ask for the supplies and let her know we believe it is in the best interest of the soldiers to keep the...camp followers...healthy as possible."

An hour later, Abbey and Margaret examined a soldier who died while on picket duty.

"Carefully examine his eyes," Abbey said. "See the tiny red dots?"

"Barely," Maggie said. She squinted. "Yes, tiny red dots definitely present."

"They're called petechiae. When someone is asphyxiated these appear."

"An enemy soldier caused this?"

"Possibly. Although, soldiers use a garrote or knife to silence a picket. Consider his neck. You can see bruising where thumbs pressed on the front of the man's windpipe and where fingers dug in toward the rear."

"Yes. So this was a murder?"

Abbey nodded. "I suspect so. We'll find the unit's commander. We need to inform him."

***

"Not many in line for camp disease this morning," Abbey said a few days later.

"Shall we head out to the camp followers?" Margaret said.

Abbey checked the heavens. "Clear sky. Perfect day to see patients. A nurse would help."

"May I suggest a female nurse? When we treat our patients…down there so to speak, I think they'd appreciate that."

Abbey nodded. "There's one in the Connecticut regiment to the east. I'll head over."

A brief buckboard ride in the cool spring air and Abbey approached a young woman with wide hips, narrow shoulders and a warm smile.

The doctor detailed her request. The woman brushed her unkempt hair out of her face and said, "Your reputation precedes you, Dr. Kaplan. Been wanting to meet you. I'll check with my Captain and explain your mission."

"If you believe it will help, tell him a woman from the Sanitary Commission has provided supplies and encouraged us."

The nurse returned shortly with a broad grin.

"A soon as he heard the words Sanitary Commission, he approved." She tied her hair into a bun as they walked.

"Did you know the commission was primarily run and organized by woman?," Abbey said.

"Had no idea."

"They found out how poor our soldier's diet was and were motivated to organize food drives in thousands of towns and cities. The food, especially the fresh meat and vegetables seem to keep the men healthier and they recover more quickly when sick or wounded."

"They say the Sanitary Commission brings train loads of produce. Ate a Michigan peach for the first time, last summer. Sweet as honey."

Abbey urged their horse into a trot then asked, "How are you treated?"

"Well enough." They rode in silence for a bit then the woman added, "My fellow nurses, men of course, resent me but the casualties don't mind. Even a woman of my odd looks is appreciated by them."

"Odd looks? You show the world a warm smile."

"Thank you, Doctor Kaplan. I know my looks don't recommend me but I find infinite satisfaction in my work. I'm not clever enough to be a doctor or surgeon like you so I do my best with the skills I have and try to emphasize my strengths."

"Such as?"

"Patience. Sometimes soldiers wish to tell me a story about their life or loved ones. When I'm off work, I can sit and listen as long as they wish. Also I'm gentle."

Abbey raised her eyebrows in Laura's direction.

"I know. They're rough, tough soldiers but when they're wounded, I'm certain a gentle touch is appreciated when treating their wounds. No reason they should suffer unnecessary pain."

"Dr. Herzog," Abbey called out as they arrived at the Massachusetts regiment's medical tents. She brought their horse to a stop. "Please meet Nurse Laura Grafton."

Margaret nodded and offered her hand. "Welcome."

"Dr. Herzog just passed her medical board exam."

"A fine accomplishment, Dr. Herzog," the nurse said.

"Thank you." Margaret turned to Abbey. "Lt. Scharf and Cpl. Silver packed our supplies in a freight wagon and will accompany us."

"Lt. Scharf," Abbey said, "we'll need some privacy…"

"Cpl. Silver and I have loaded a small tent. It's tall enough to stand up along the center line and there is room along each side for a cot. We'll have it up shortly after we arrive."

A brief ride and a camp filled with a rag-tag assembly of woman and children, came into view.

Abbey glanced around as the wagon came to a halt then she and Lt. Scharf decided where to pitch the tent. Four women noticed the men about to erect the tent, determined its purpose then assisted them.

A few women gathered around Margaret and Laura while others walked around spreading the word, doctors were available. A small parade formed and lined up at the tent.

A long day under a sunny, warm sky ensued. They treated everything from diseased genitalia and lacerations to children's rashes and fevers.

A mother entered with a one-year-old. The boy had a hare lip.

"I can repair this," Abbey said as she examined him. "Come by the 222nd regiment's medical tent tomorrow around," she mentally reviewed her schedule, "...eleven."

The mother smiled and said, "I never. Thought he'd been branded for life."

Margaret smiled and said, "We've repaired a number of adults, a teen, and a two-day-old with the same condition."

"Medical tent at eleven. We'll be there. Doctor, I got this bad sore on my side."

She turned to Abbey who examined it and said, "Dr. Herzog, please clean and bandage this."

One of the women inquired, "Do you work with Lt. Smith?"

"He's our hospital attendant," Abbey said.

"Tell him we miss him," she said then whispered, "Pays in gold coin that one. We all likes that."

Abbey and Margaret exchanged shocked expressions.

"Surprising he has gold coins but I'll let him know," Abbey said.

The woman nodded at Lt. Scharf then whispered to Abbey. "He's a real looker, your lieutenant. Me thinks he's got a special eye for you."

"We work together. That's all."

"You take care of him or some other girl will."

"I beg your pardon?"

"When a man's willie tells him it's time, he'll find somebody to put it in."

"Thank you for telling me but we need to get back to camp," Abbey said, trying to end the conversation.

"Even the best of them goes wandering occasionally. I know."

"Yes. Thank you. Appreciate you telling me," Abbey hurried away.

They were nearly packed when they heard a scream.

A woman ran up to them. "Need a doc right quick. We've got a birth happening and it ain't goin' well."

The team hurried to the stricken woman's side. Abbey examined her, swore under her breath then said, "Lt. Scharf, I'll need my surgical kit and chloroform. I have to perform a caesarian. Laura, please clean her belly."

Margret comforted the mother but noticed Abbey seemed uncharacteristically on edge throughout the procedure.

Abbey placed a healthy but screaming infant on her mother's belly, then had Laura tie and cut the cord.

They re-packed the wagon and headed back to their regiment.

"Abbey," Margaret said, "The breadth of your surgical background is amazing. When did you first perform a caesarian?"

"Roughly an hour ago."

"That was your first?" suddenly wide-eyed Laura asked.

"I saw one many years ago performed by our community doctor in the Northwest." Abbey smiled while remembering a pleasant memory. "And helped my mother deliver my sister Ciara when I was quite young…between those and my school work, I remembered enough detail to get through it."

The nurse said, "I'd heard you had top notch surgical skill but you must have a superb and detailed memory as well."

Abbey shook her head, her expression deeply saddened. "Which is not always a good thing. I graphically recall horrors which torment me."

Margaret turned to Abbey. "Which horrors?"

"Later. Cpl. Silver, please accompany Nurse Grafton back to her regiment."

"The minute we unload, Doctor," he said with a pleasant smile and nod to Laura.

Abbey and Margret walked to their tent.

Margaret checked their surroundings and, not seeing anyone nearby said, "Do you ever feel the desire to have a man?"

"Last week, I glanced at a group of men cutting down trees near a river. One of them had superb muscle definition."

"Abbey, you're blushing."

"If I could manage it in complete secrecy, I'd certainly have encouraged him to put out the fire he started."

"But, medically speaking, why the fire?" Maggie asked.

"All women feel desire, I suppose."

"Yes but why?"

Abbey engaged in a long sigh. "I've been trying to understand our sexual desire since my teen years. I'm not a philosopher but I'd say nature demands it."

"So women don't have control but follow nature's demands?"

"We have control in some ways."

"What about men? Does nature control men as well?"

"I suppose but in a different way."

"How so?" Maggie asked.

"Women tend to follow nature because…I suppose we're closer to it." Abbey thought for a while then continued. "Nature reminds a woman of her closeness on a monthly basis. But…women tend to go with nature but men try to…bend nature."

"I think you're over-analyzing. Men and woman want to have relations in order to have children. It's as simple as that."

"Yes. Simple…but no…if women are closer to nature then I must consider their closeness as a component of a woman's well-being. As well as considering men wish to bend…"

Maggie raised her voice. "Abbey, like I said, you're over-analyzing."

Abbey turned to her friend and smiled. "Sorry. Yes. I'm sure you're right." She didn't speak for a while then thought, *"What other behaviors demonstrate women are closer to nature?"*

***

Abbey carried a large box into the administrative center of the recovery hospital where a number of regiment's medical records and specimens were organized and sent to the Army Medical Museum. She dropped off a stack of reports and placed the box holding specimen jars on a table. The doctor felt a pair of eyes burning holes in her back.

"Dr. Kaplan. More reports and specimens?"

She turned toward the voice and discovered a set of eyes glaring at her. "Dr. Dillon. I didn't know you worked here."

He was seated at a desk off to the side of the room. "They won't let me work with patients and I know it's your fault. I was shown the letter you wrote. They assigned me three assistants and now I'm busy organizing reports and shipping specimens instead of caring for the wounded."

"Not everyone has hands for surgery."

"I'm good enough."

"No you're not."

He banged his fist on the desk. "A woman doesn't have any business deciding a man's future."

"The letter was co-signed by Dr. Fellows."

"But you made the decision as to my skill."

"I did. I'm the one who witnessed your unsatisfactory attempts with pig skin."

He seethed and spoke through clenched teeth. "And, damn you, the name you called me stuck."

"Name?"

He balled his hands into fists. "Little Man. I hate the name. I know it's used behind my back all the time."

Abbey saw his helpers snickering…and leering at her chest. She briefly glared at them until they turned away.

"I'm sorry things didn't work out according to your desire but we all take what life gives us and have to manage."

"This ain't over."

"Yes it is and there's nothing you can do about it."

***

A week later, Margaret looked around as she and Abbey walked to dinner.

"No one can hear us if we speak in low tones but…the longer I'm here…"

"Again? Conversation about having a man?"

"As I said, the longer…"

"The more you want one."

"Abbey, how do you handle it?"

"I was on leave some weeks before you arrived. I let someone take care of me."

"Someone from here?"

Abbey warmed at the memory. "A kind, gentle man with a sense of discretion. We've done it a few times since our leave."

"Do I know him?"

"You've met."

"And you weren't worried about becoming pregnant?"

"I have knowledge of birth prevention which…if you like…I'll share with you."

Margret's eyes widened and her jaw dropped.

Abbey whispered, "I know. It's not legal."

"Bullshit," Margaret said. "So only a man can decide when I become pregnant? I'm not allowed to decide how to use my own body?"

Abbey grinned. "Margaret Herzog, you've thought this through and reached the same conclusion as I have."

"But, dammit, the laws are written by men."

"And written to their advantage, of course. Men are the only ones who can vote…" Abbey's smile turned mischievous. "More bullshit. One day we'll need to do something about that."

They both chuckled.

"Abbey, you'll show me the birth prevention method?"

Abbey nodded. "Of course. Someone specific you're thinking of?"

"One of our helpers has been especially kind to me. His smile makes me…you know."

Chapter Fourteen: Maggie Disappears

As first light appeared over the encampment during late June of 1863, Abbey rolled out of bed and was surprised Margaret wasn't in the tent. She washed, dressed, then reached into her trunk and unfolded a clean apron. Two newspaper clippings fell to the ground. Abbey picked them up. They each detailed the terrible conditions endured by the populace as the siege of Vicksburg, Mississippi, progressed.

Abbey gasped. "Margaret's family."

The date on the news clippings indicated they had been published recently.

After a few hours without hearing from Margaret, she thought, "*She couldn't have gone to Vicksburg. Margaret is a great doctor but delicate physically. I cannot envision her traveling cross-country and, my God, crossing battle lines.*"

While completing camp medical duty, Abbey's shoulders slumped thinking of the danger her friend might be in.

During the day, a number of people asked where Dr. Herzog was. Abbey simply replied she didn't know.

***

Two days later and just before sunset, a Captain appeared at her tent entrance.

"Dr. Kaplan, I'm Captain Wallace of the Military Investigative Service. May I speak to you?"

Abbey sat at the table in her tent. She invited him in.

He removed his hat as he entered. "Sorry to bother you Doctor, but we believe someone from this regiment is keeping track of the numbers of our wounded and killed. This, and other information, is being forwarded to the Confederacy. We intercepted a satchel with coded information but couldn't determine who was carrying it or its source."

"Why are you telling me this?"

"A few people reported Dr. Herzog occasionally spoke with a southern accent. Know anything about that?"

"She said she lived in the south at some time in her life but as to her being a spy…"

"Dr. Kaplan, I understand she's been absent for two days. We'd appreciate you telling us if you had any idea where she might be?"

"I woke two days ago and she wasn't here."

"Would you mind if we searched through her things."

"Is that necessary?"

"It is."

"Go ahead."

The Captain called two men into the tent and the trio rifled through Margaret's belongings.

"Ma'am…" the captain said.

"Go ahead," Abbey said as she stood, "examine my things as well." She watched them rummage through the reports on her desk then searched her trunk; all the while, the news clippings seemingly burning a hole in the pocket of her britches.

She tried to compensate for her anxious state by talking. "Dr. Herzog is a hard worker and a compassionate doctor. Two weeks ago, she passed the medical board exam. We attended a stage play last week to celebrate. Her kind demeanor managed to get us into the actor's dressing room so we could meet the performers. She's a sweet woman and an excellent doctor. I can't imagine her as a spy."

"It's been reported someone matching her description was seen boarding a train bound for the Mississippi River. Why would she do that?"

"No clue…if, in fact, it was Margaret taking the train."

"Thank you for your time and cooperation, Dr. Kaplan," the captain said. Then, with an icy expression, added, "Please keep in mind, spies and their associates are shot." He stormed out of her tent.

Abbey slumped into a chair. Her hands were shaking and her heart pounded. She waited ten minutes then burned the news clippings in her tent's stove.

"Please Lord," she prayed while she watched the newsprint turn to ash, "bless and take care of my good friend."

Chapter Fifteen: A Major Battle

"We're getting information a major battle is about to take place," Colonel Wilson said to Abbey as their regiment completed a two-week march.

"How major?" Abbey asked.

"We have roughly seventy-thousand combat-ready soldiers here and on the way."

"Confederate compliment?"

"Hard to say with any accuracy but at least fifty-thousand."

"Our regiment?"

"Will be in the thick of it."

"Any estimate of when?"

"Most likely two or three days from now. That'd be July 1st. All leaves have been cancelled."

"I'll let my staff know to begin prepping supplies. Thanks for keeping me informed, Colonel Wilson."

He shook his head. "It will be difficult to get your team setup. The medical supply trains are being held back until the Army can bring their artillery and troops up. You'll be setting up in the open in yonder orchard."

Abbey found Lieutenants Smith and Scharf.

"Without the medical supply trains, how will we handle wounded?" Lt. Smith asked.

She shrugged. "Let's gather what supplies we can."

"Someone sober up Dr. Fellows, please," Abbey said. "We'll need him when this battle starts."

"Cpl. Silver and I will do that," Lt. Smith said.

"Lt. Smith, I'll give you a note to take to the Connecticut regiment, requesting Laura Grafton. We'll use her as a surgical assistant."

He nodded and said, "I'll send a messenger immediately."

"I fear this will be a Fourth of July we won't soon forget," Abbey said.

"I was hoping to visit a town close to here," Lt. Scharf said. "Some cousins live there."

"Name of the town?" Dr. Kaplan asked.

"Gettysburg."

***

"At least with all this surgery, my mind doesn't have time for nightmares," Dr. Kaplan said to Lt. Scharf, then used her teeth to tear meat off a roasted turkey leg. They'd taken a break from the seemingly endless parade of wounded and sat on the ground with their backs against a tree.

"You managing any sleep?" Lt. Scharf asked.

"In this heat and humidity? I've managed, at most, a couple hours the last few days. You?"

"The same. Eat anything?"

"Just this, beef and barley soup yesterday, pancakes with jelly and bacon, two days ago."

"How's your body holding up?"

"Knees, back and hips are killing me." She flexed her hands then spooned lima beans with cubed ham and carrots, out of her mucket. "Was getting cramps in my hands for a while last night. How's it going assisting Dr. Fellows?"

"He's working hard. Covered in sweat and shaking the first day. Dr. Fellows is directing me…actually training me, to do much more surgery than you allow me. The more his hands tremble, the more he instructs me instead of trying to do it himself. Since some time yesterday, I've done entire amputations under his direction."

"Excellent training."

"I notice he regularly asks your advice."

"Since roughly a month ago, he treats me as if I'm the chief surgeon."

"He should."

"Thanks for learning enough to be his assistant."

He shrugged then flexed his shoulders forward and back. "You put me on this path." He ate for a while then asked, "How is your assistant?"

"After the first few hours, Laura anticipates what I need and has it in her hand, ready to pass it to me. She has enough dexterity to help with ligations and some suturing." Abbey turned toward the nurse, who sat a number of yards away. She shouted, "Laura Grafton is a medical angel."

Laura smiled then turned toward Abbey and mouthed a thank you.

The doctor closed her eyes for a while, put her head back against the tree then said, "Your and Lt. Smith's suggestion about cross-training has been a life saver; allowing rotation to give our team a chance to eat and rest." Abbey yawned then asked, "How long has it been?"

"Over seventy-hours, I believe."

"The cannon and rifle-fire have died down."

More mule-drawn-ambulances rumbled into view. Their wheels creaked and thumped along the rutted path from the battlefield.

They both stood and Abbey stretched.

"Off we go," she said. "Not sure how much more of this I can take."

After another ten-hours of surgery, Dr. Fellows took Abbey aside.

"The fact that you're a woman still disturbs me but I'm no fool. Better than anyone else, I know your surgical and medical capabilities; which surpassed mine months ago. You regularly repair gut-wounds I wouldn't even attempt...and you've been successful over half the time you perform them."

Abbey's eyebrows went up in surprise.

"Yes. I've been keeping track of survival rates. If only a quarter of them survived it would border on the miraculous but half is a God-send. The men in this regiment don't know how lucky they are. You have my word as an officer, your position is secure as long as you desire it."

***

Dr. Kaplan approached the corporal with the tear streaked face who leaned on his crutches. His right lower leg and foot were wrapped in bandages. She'd decided to walk a field which would become known as the location of Pickett's Charge. The engagement ended a number of days previous. "Are you in pain?"

"Just a little Ma'am. Thanks for asking." He slowly shook his head. "We was behind breastworks up Cemetery Ridge yonder," He nodded to the ridge. "The Confederates came across this field to attack us." He sighed. "Lost many a good friend on that damn ridge."

"You survived the battle."

"Wasn't a fair fight."

"Little is fair about war."

He eyed the tree line one-hundred-yards behind them. "The Southern soldiers who came out of them trees; they had to know."

"Know what?"

He surveyed the trampled wheat field then the one-hundred-yards up to Cemetery Ridge. "Their officers must have known as well."

"Corporal, know what?"

"A suicide charge, Ma'am."

"How so?"

"They were all experienced soldiers…as were we. They arrived here after an exhausting march. Casting their eyes on this field, having to attack a fortified, uphill position after crossing an open area like this which is totally lacking in cover; they must have known few would survive." He lowered his eyes and slowly shook his head. He wiped a tear away with his shoulder. "Many of us used rifled muskets and rifled lever-action long-guns. They used smooth-bore muskets."

"I'm sorry but I have little familiarity with munitions other than the damage they do plus the Spencer I've used in combat."

"Rifling a barrel means it's accurate out to two-hundred-yards. Them Southern boys' smooth-bores were only accurate to fifty-yards. In other words, they had to wait 'till they were fifty-yards from us to begin shooting while we could begin picking them off at two-hundred-yards." He gazed around the field for a bit and sighed. "Disrespectful of me to refer to them as boys. They were men. If they crossed this field and attempted to attack up the hill, they damn sure were men." He turned and pointed to a nearby stream. "That there water ran red." The soldier took off his hat, bowed his head and mumbled a prayer. Abbey bowed her head, clasped her hands and recited her own prayer.

The corporal continued, "Anyway, a number of us used lever-action rifles like your Spencer, which could fire seven-rounds-a-minute as opposed to the one- to two-rounds-a-minute of the muskets. Didn't have to stand to re-load them either."

They walked further into the field.

"One man with a lever-action could put out as much fire as six or seven men with muskets. Or twenty men with lever-actions equaled one-hundred-forty with muskets."

"Terrifying."

"The left side of our line would have collapsed but for snipers with repeating rifles. Held off a much larger force from Little Round Top until reinforcements arrived."

"Lucky."

"Odd thing I remember. The cannon-balls fired in our direction exploded behind us."

"How are they timed?"

"With fuses. We talked to a captured Confederate artillery soldier. He said they'd just received a new shipment of fuses right before the battle. Probably didn't have time to test them." He paused to view the torn and shredded trees around the battlefield then added, "Let's get off this area. I feel like I'm trampling on the souls of the men who died here."

Abbey nodded. "Couldn't agree more." They walked a distance away then turned to look at the battlefield again. She said, "It took numerous days to bury them. The line of those needing surgery seemed endless and quite a number died before we could treat them."

"Gettysburg was terrible, maybe the worst in terms of total men lost, but so were other engagements. In the Battle of Shiloh, more Americans died in two days than in the Revolutionary War and the War of 1812 combined. At Cold Harbor, Virginia, over seven-thousand men died in less than thirty-minutes."

"You seem knowledgeable concerning war."

"History teacher before this." He glanced at Abbey's face. "You all right Ma'am?"

"I seem to tear up lately."

"I heard you're having trouble sleeping."

Furious, Abbey spoke through gritted teeth. "Does the entire fucking camp know?" She turned away from the soldier, kicked at the dirt and folded her arms across her chest.

He put a hand on her shoulder. "I reckon the entire camp cares, Ma'am."

Abbey took a few deep breaths as she regained her composure. Then, after dropping her arms to her side, said, "Thank you, Corporal. Sorry I spoke like that."

"Don't you be upset, Doctor. Lots of death here but you've saved many a life. You deserve to be proud of your work here."

"Believe me, I'm too emotionally and physically worn to be much of anything let alone proud."

***

"Lieutenant Scharf," Abbey said while sitting at the desk in her tent, the lieutenant was seated at her side peering through her microscope. "It's been three-months since our move from Gettysburg, I'd like to change your routine. Dr. Fellows…"

"Has been quizzing me on my book knowledge for hours at a time."

She laughed. "We agree you have sufficient experience and book knowledge to help me perform camp medical duty each day. You'll still be under my direct supervision but we have little doubt you can perform many procedures on your own. In addition, I've lined up more texts for you to study."

"So much for my drumming."

"We'll make you a doctor yet."

"Amazing," he said while slowly shaking his head. The lieutenant's smile slowly disappeared. "I appreciate your and Dr. Fellows' guidance. It gives me the opportunity to do more for the wounded." He gazed in her eyes for a long time then said, "Are you sleeping?"

"Adequately. Still have some really bad nights where sleep seems to be impossible or I don't want to sleep because of the nightmares."

"But some days your lack of sleep is written all over your face."

"Some days are bad."

"Abbey, you will please, tell me if you reach a point where you're feeling overwhelmed from lack of sleep?"

She nodded and said, "I promise." They stared at each other for a while then she smiled and said, "You're the only person I don't explode at when you use my first name."

"Sorry…come to think about it, we're both lieutenants so it's allowed."

Abbey giggled. "May I call you Jordan?"

"Yes Ma'am."

"It's getting late. Camp medical duty at sunup, Lt. Jordan."

He stood and saluted, "Yes, Lt. Abbey."

She laughed, stood at attention and returned his salute.

He turned to leave.

Abbey grabbed his arm, turned down the oil lamp with her other hand then embraced him. She whispered, "I might sleep better if Lt. Jordan spent the night."

***

Two-days later, Cpl. Silver stood at the opened flap of Abbey's tent.

"Please come in," she said.

He entered, removed his hat and saluted. "I was wondering if you ever heard from Dr. Herzog."

She returned his salute. "Margaret?"

"Yes. We were friends."

"I suspected there was someone." Abbey smiled at the wiry soldier. "I'm glad it was you."

"Do you have any idea where she might be?"

"The Military Investigative Service interviewed me and I told them I had no idea."

His shoulders drooped. The corporal's expression saddened. "Sorry to have bothered you."

"Cpl. Silver, I know you enjoy scenery."

He evidenced a puzzled expression. "Ma'am?"

"You might want to visit Vicksburg, Mississippi when the war ends. I believe you'll find the scenery there is just what you're looking for."

He grinned broadly. "Bless you, Dr. Kaplan."

***

At the recovery hospital, she watched an officer as he finished reading a letter to a soldier with bandages covering his eyes. The soldier thanked him and the major moved to another patient. Abbey approached him and offered her hand.

"How do you do?" Abbey asked the major. "I'm Dr. Abbey Kaplan."

He stood. "Major Benjamin Sokolov. A pleasure to meet the doctor who's done so much for our troops."

"Thank you. What do you do for our regiment?"

"Not in your regiment. I'm on the general staff. My specialty is maps and battle planning."

"Have you been in combat?"

"Not specifically. On two occasions we were attacked close to where I work. I grabbed a rifle and joined an infantry squad until we could break contact and escape."

"Break contact? Why?"

"The information in my head would be most useful to the Confederate forces. Being captured would be unthinkable." He gazed at the scar on her cheek. "Battle wound?"

She nodded. "One of a number."

"Shall we step outside?"

They walked to the porch of the old building where they were cooled by a pleasant breeze.

Abbey regarded him for a bit then said, "You make plans and our boys carry them out."

"Yes. A mentally painful task, I assure you."

"How so?"

"It's easy to move lines on a map and discuss how many casualties we may expect in the abstract. But I regularly visit the recovery hospital to talk to the men. Doing so, reminds me how deadly a mistake can be for the human beings carrying out my plan."

"But you don't have to visit."

"True. But visiting and talking to the men...listening to their hopes and dreams..." he looked down for a moment, "as well as destroyed hopes and dreams...forces my mind to plan carefully."

"I thought the war might be over after Gettysburg."

His voice became tinged with anger. "After that battle, I screamed until my face turned purple and jumped up and down as high as a dining table trying to get people's attention."

Abbey envisioned the rather large major jumping table high. She giggled and said, "Because?"

"The Confederates were on the run. We could have pursued them and likely destroyed most of Lee's remaining forces. Our military leaders, and I use the word leaders with reservation, decided otherwise. Rumor is, the White House was shaken to its foundation by Lincoln's anger after he was informed we didn't pursue Lee's Army of Virginia."

"I barely ate or slept while performing surgery for multiple days during and after the battle."

"The Army of the Potomac has better equipment, more men and better supply channels than the South. The longer this goes on, the more cruel it is. It pains me to say this but...if General Lee led the North, I believe the war would be over. We don't have the leadership we need."

"Where I work, a field hospital, we don't hear things like this."

"Perhaps it's better I don't discuss dissention among our leaders."

"I can keep my mouth shut." She regarded him briefly. "Your thoughts give me perspective on the war."

He stared at the cobblestone street which fronted the old building which held the recovery hospital. A buckboard clattered by. He sighed, then said, "Consider for a moment, the Northern home-front. While men are dying by the thousands, elite colleges are still having..." he pronounced with contempt..."rowing competitions."

Abbey's eyes went wide. "I had no idea! How absurd!"

He checked his pocket watch. "I have to report back to headquarters now. I've enjoyed our talk. Perhaps we can find time to continue this discussion."

"Love to," Abbey said, "when we can both find time."

Chapter Seventeen: The Enemy Gets Close

Just after lunch, Dr. Kaplan spoke to Lt. Scharf, "I received a note from Dr. Fellows. A recovery hospital a long day's ride from here is in desperate need of surgical assistance. I've been asked to perform a number of surgeries. I'd like you to assist."

"Yes, Doctor."

Lt. Smith overheard and said, "You'll want to get there before dark. Each of you should carry a rifle and ammunition. Southern patrols are rumored to be scouting the roads between here and the recovery hospital. I'll send Pvt. Theo and Cpl. Wilber from the infantry unit with you. Theo is good with horses and an extra rifleman might be useful."

Abbey carried her Spencer carbine, two cartridge boxes strapped over her shoulder; one with cartridges for the Spencer and one filled with bandage material, plus a pack with her surgical instruments. As usual, she strapped her Colt pistol to her hip.

"Think you'll need your pistol and belt? Lots of weight there if we have to hike some," Lt. Scharf said.

She glanced at her sidearm. "It saved me before."

"True enough," the lieutenant replied.

With Pvt. Theo at the reins and the horse's hooves trotting a steady rhythm, Abbey said, "I don't believe I've ever heard the surname, Theo, before."

"My full name is Taki Theodoracopulos."

"Therefore we call you Theo," Cpl. Wilbur said with a grin.

Abbey's melodic laughter filled the air while the others grinned. "Where is your home Pvt. Theo?" she asked.

"A dairy farm in central Massachusetts."

"Your home, Cpl. Wilbur?"

"Pittsburgh, Ma'am."

"Your family?"

Cpl. Wilbur replied, "Three generations of coal miners but me."

"Why not you?"

"My daddy said he'd break both my legs before he'd let me work in the mines. Said I've got enough brains to get a thinking job."

"What will you do?"

"Good with numbers. I'll become an accountant."

"Tell 'em about the letters," Theo teased.

Cpl. Wilbur appeared embarrassed. "My wife sends me at least two letters a week…full of stories from home and lovey stuff." He thought for a while, sighed then said, "Can't wait to get home to her and the kids."

Lt. Scharf said, "Our horse seems to be moving at a steady trot."

"This could be the last trip for Beau," Cpl. Theo said.

"Why?" Lt. Scharf asked.

"He's old and seemed reluctant to get in position for hitching to the wagon. Normally he can't wait to get hitched and begin pulling. Some horses live to be ridden but this guy, until this morning, lived to pull."

The road they traveled, climbed slightly for a couple miles then followed between a series of multiple mile long ridges, each of which attained a height of a couple-hundred-feet above them.

"We'll proceed between ridges for a number of hours," the private said. "Another hour and we should stop to let Beau rest."

They stopped in a small glen between the ridges.

"This is beautiful country," Abbey said while gazing at the lush hillsides. She alternated raising each arm above her head, while twisting and stretching. "So green. I'm from the Northwest and we have green like this all year long."

Pvt. Theo shook his head while Beau slurped water from the bucket he held. "Can't imagine a place where the trees are green all year long."

For the next few miles the only sounds emanated from the jingle of the horses harness and the rhythmic sound of the horse's hooves plus an occasional bird call.

217

They crossed a low ridge and entered another narrow valley with steep sides covered in a lush growth of bushes and trees. A small stream paralleled the road. Another two-hours passed.

Their horse slowed. Despite Private Theo's urging, the horse continued to slow then stopped. "We should give him a chance to rest."

Abbey got off the buckboard and stretched as did Lt. Scharf. Abbey watched as dark clouds approached.

"Looks like rain coming," she said.

The horse slowly kneeled, then rolled on his side.

The doctor asked, "What's going on?"

"He's old and he's dying," Pvt. Theo said.

"If he's going to die, why not put him out of his misery with a bullet?"

Cpl. Wilber said, "Because we don't want to attract unwanted attention."

Abbey slowly gazed at the seemingly empty hillsides. "Whose attention?"

The corporal said, "Don't look now, but for the last hour, at least four Confederate soldiers have been just below the lip of the ridge yonder, paralleling our progress and gradually coming down the ridge. We need to get into the greenery on the opposite hillside."

"Were you ever in combat?" Lt. Scharf asked Pvt. Theo.

"No Sir, but I'm a hunter."

"Everyone grab your rifles and ammunition," the lieutenant said.

Cpl. Wilber said, "Once we're in them woods on our left, we'll split up. I turn left and you right. I'll attract their attention then catch up with you. Once together, we Alabama High Shuffle back to our lines."

Abbey asked, "Alabama High what?"

"We'll be moving fast and quiet; fast like with our knees nearly hitting our chest and quiet like we're careful where we step to minimize noise."

Abbey's pulse rate increased as she looped the ammo boxes' straps over her shoulder. "Please Lord. No combat today," she implored.

"Abbey," Lt. Scharf said, "your surgical pack."

"Too heavy to hike anywhere. I'll hide it when we leave the trail and come back for it another day."

They walked directly into the woods on the hillside and into tall brush.

"I'm turning left to drop back and setup an ambush," Pvt. Wilber said. "You three head right and we'll meet up later."

Once in the trees, they began moving parallel to the road and angled their progress slightly up the ridge. They moved for an hour then rested under the cover of a grove of four- and five-foot-tall bushes. Shooting broke out behind them.

"Should we go back to help?" Abbey asked.

"The lieutenant shook his head. If he's okay he'll join us but if not, going back will endanger us. We need to keep moving."

After another hour of hiking through the woods, Pvt. Theo said, "I'm going to climb a tree and see if they're still following." He slowly climbed an oak.

Abbey examined the steel-grey sky and shivered, "The wind is picking up and the temperature is dropping."

Pvt. Theo dropped out of the tree. "They're still coming but not gaining on us."

"How many?" Abbey asked.

"Six—possibly eight."

"Let's move," Lt. Scharf said.

They hiked for an hour then dropped into cover as they heard running footsteps approaching.

"Over here," Lt. Scharf called to Cpl. Wilbur.

The corporal said, "There's at least six soldiers following us. Maybe more."

They'd walked a number of hours when Abbey felt a single cold rain drop slide down her neck. The wind picked up. She shivered. They heard more rain hitting the leaf-lined canopy above them. Large drops began falling off the trees. Each hit them with an audible sound. A bright flash and thunder exploded causing her to jump. The intensity of the rain increased. She felt the rain slowly soaking through her shirt and britches. The sun going down didn't help as the temperature dropped considerably.

"We should make camp for the night," Lt. Scharf said over the sound of the rain and thunder.

"Won't they continue following us?" Abbey asked.

"Unlikely in this weather," he said.

They gathered pine branches and sat on them.

"We need to establish watch," Lt. Scharf said.

"Hour on, three-hours off?" Pvt. Theo said.

"Sounds right," Cpl. Wilbur said.

Lt. Scharf and Abbey nodded.

"The off watch should spoon to conserve body heat."

The three men turned to Abbey who was shivering, her arms wrapped around her upper torso. "Fine with me," she said. "I'm freezing."

"I'll take first watch," Theo volunteered.

They were so chilled the following morning they shivered uncontrollably and their skin was blue.

"Let's get moving," Abbey said through chattering teeth. "Maybe we'll warm up."

"At least it's not raining," Pvt. Theo said.

"We need to conserve our ammo as we're out numbered," Lt. Scharf said. "If you have to shoot, make sure they're close enough to hit what you're aiming at."

After four-hours in hot, muggy air under a sunny sky, they stopped to rest in an area where they could conceal themselves in a large stand of shrubs.

"I think the squad is gaining on us," Abbey said. She raised up to get a better look.

Pvt. Theo yanked her down. "Keep your head down. Lots of soldiers get their brains blown out trying to see what's going on." He shook his head. "Keep quiet and we'll see them coming when they're close enough."

Lt. Scharf peered through binoculars, pointed then handed them to Cpl. Wilbur.

The Confederate soldiers, in a straight line, followed their tracks in the damp earth. The lead soldier kneeled and studied the foursome's boot-prints. He showed four fingers to his trailing compatriots, slowly stood and continued following their footsteps.

Cpl. Wilbur whispered, "When they get to the bush with red and gold leaves, open fire. Spread out."

They positioned themselves on a line perpendicular to the trail and five-yards-apart. They aimed back the way they came.

They opened up on the Confederate patrol. The first two were hit but the rest dove into the brush and crawled rapidly away.

"Let's move," Cpl. Wilbur said.

They hiked in and out of the canopy of tall trees. While the trees provided occasional shade from the blazing sun, the humidity caused profuse sweating.

Abbey's body was wet and uncomfortable as if she'd been dunked in a river of warm water. Her clothing stuck to her body.

Cpl. Wilbur kept watch to the rear.

Five gray coated soldiers suddenly jumped up in front of them, rifles shouldered and pointing at them.

"Shit," Cpl. Wilbur muttered. "They got around us."

"Drop your guns," one of the gray-coated soldiers said.

"Damn, this is the one," another said while Abbey and the others slowly began lowering their rifles to the ground. "She looks just like this picture."

"You Dr. Kaplan?"

"Yes."

"She's the one we want."

"What?"

"You the surgeon who's fixin' gut-wounds?"

"Not all."

"You're gonna come with us. Put your rifle down. Slowly."

Just before Abbey's rifle was at ground level, she fired at one soldier, hitting him in the abdomen, she dove to the ground then rolled over as bullets narrowly missed her. The doctor racked the lever on her rifle then shot a second soldier in the belly.

The soldier's eyes went wide as he put both hands over the bloody wound. "Damn. Never thought…" he stared at Abbey in disbelief, "you killed me."

The third and fourth soldiers, having fired their muskets, attacked Wilbur and Theo who engaged them in hand-to-hand fighting.

The fifth soldier tried to bayonet Lt. Scharf. He twisted to the side but the blade pierced the side of his shirt slicing across the side of his abdomen. He used the butt end of his Spencer to slam the soldier in the face, fracturing the soldier's eye socket. Yelling in pain, the soldier again tried to use his bayonet but the lieutenant managed to chamber a round and fired into the man's chest.

Cpl. Wilbur retrieved a small knife from his pocket and used it to cut the throat of the man he had engaged and then did the same to the man wrestling with Cpl. Theo.

"We need to get moving," Cpl. Wilbur said. "I'll lead."

Pvt. Theo said, "I'll take the tail and watch behind. Any one hurt?"

Lt. Scharf yelled, "Me. But not bad." He enlarged the opening in the side of his shirt and saw a four inch long cut about three inches above his pelvis. "Need to wrap this."

Abbey quickly bandaged the area. "How the hell did they get this drawing of me?"

"This was a setup. They knew we were coming."

They began hiking again but with a bit more purpose in their steps. Lt. Scharf said to Theo, "From now on, while we hike, point your rifle in the direction you're looking so you can take a quick shot from your hip."

Theo nodded

Abbey, her hands shaking, took another glance at the drawing then folded and pocketed it. She put her canteen up to her lips and downed the balance of its contents.

Hiking up a long ridge, Abbey remembered Andre the trapper, teaching her to shoot rifles and pistols from the hip and other odd positions. "*Thank heavens we played what seemed like games back then,*" she thought.

The foursome hiked for an hour then found it necessary to cross a wide dust covered road. Theo shinnied up a tree to see if they were being followed.

"At least one still trailing us," he reported.

Cpl. Wilbur said, "We'll run across the road one-at-a-time and get in the bushes on the other side. I'll go last and provide covering fire if needed."

Abbey ran across the road and into the cover followed by Lt. Scharf. He motioned to Pvt. Theo to head across.

The private made it to the middle of the road then yelled as he collapsed midway. His legs appeared to have quit working. He used his forearms to pull himself along, grunting with each pull and choked on the dust his arms stirred up. More rounds kicked up dirt as they hit around him. Lt. Scharf and Cpl. Wilbur fired at their pursuers.

Abbey broke cover and ran to Pvt. Theo.

"Go back," he pleaded. More bullets were throwing dust into the air as they struck the ground around them. Lt. Scharf's rapid return fire filled the air. Abbey felt something like razor burn on her upper arm. She ignored the pain, grasped the private's hands and pulled him into concealment. A three-inch cut had opened her skin. She pushed a bandage against it. Abbey took another bandage and wrapped the wound.

Lt. Scharf joined them and stared at the bandage "Abbey?"

"A scratch."

"Pvt. Theo…"

"Sorry Sir. Something hit my lower back. Can't move my legs."

They examined him and found a small injury on his spine.

"We'll have to take turns carrying him," Lt. Scharf said. Abbey nodded and packed Pvt. Theo's wound.

Cpl. Wilbur came crashing into their position. "We took out most of them. The others are heading away from us for now. It's going to be dark soon. We need to find a place with decent cover. I'll scout around." He stood, took one step and a rifle round slammed into his chest. He looked at the others with shock written on his face then collapsed. Abbey checked for a pulse but found none.

Abbey and Lt. Scharf took turns carrying Pvt. Theo on their backs.

They traded their human cargo for an exhausting two-hours then stopped at the base of a large, steep hill.

"We get two-hundred-yards up the hill," Pvt. Theo said, "and we're across Union lines."

Abbey peered up the considerable incline.

"Nervous sentries will shoot at anything that moves," Theo told them. "We got to be careful and quiet."

Lt. Scharf said to Abbey, "If you can get him up the hill, I'll stay behind and ambush anybody trailing. For God's sake keep low. They're gunning to capture you."

She nodded then dragged Pvt. Theo slightly up the incline.

Dropping on her side, she moved an arm's length up the hill, reached for Pvt. Theo's hands and pulled him towards her. She repeated the process until her arms and back ached. Abbey felt pain in the tendons on the inside of her elbows. She pulled his arm over her shoulder then used her other arm and legs to push up the hill. He moaned with each movement. An hour of dragging the wounded man and Abbey panted heavily, her body drenched in sweat. She glanced back down the hill and realized they hadn't moved far.

"I've got to rest a minute," she said.

Theo's face showed substantial pain while he nodded.

They heard gunshots further down the hill. "Never mind," she said and began dragging him again.

Abbey's legs were aching; particularly her right calf. She stopped for a moment and glanced back down the hill. No sign of Lt. Scharf. In the dim light, she saw steam coming off her sweat soaked clothing then returned to hauling Theo's crippled body up the considerable incline. She quietly grunted with each exertion. They were ten-yards from the top when a bullet struck next to her. Abbey flattened herself and Pvt. Theo.

"Union Soldiers," she yelled. She wasn't heard as gunfire from the top of the hill erupted.

Burying her face in the dirt, she thought, "*Will I die on this damned hilltop shot by our own soldiers and thrown into a grave that my family will never find?*"

"We're Union soldiers," she yelled again.

A voice yelled. "What unit?"

"222nd Massachusetts. I'm Doctor Kaplan and I've got Pvt. Theo with me. He's wounded."

A head partially exposed itself and carefully peered down the hill.

The head exposed itself further and an agitated voice shouted, "Doc? What the fuck you doing out there?"

She recognized Cpl. Silver's voice then shouted. "I need help down here, damn it."

The doctor checked Pvt. Theo. He was still face down in the dirt.

"Oh no. Please Lord, no."

The doctor lifted Theo's head and saw a bullet hole in the left side of his forehead. Abbey rolled on her back and gazed at the sky. "Why?" She shook her head. "After all the shit we survived to get back to our lines. Why now?"

Three Union soldiers came down the hill.

"Let me help you, doc," Cpl. Silver said. "There's Confederates down there. He put an arm around her and assisted her in climbing up the hill.

"Lt. Scharf is still down there. Don't shoot him please."

"Thought you said you had a wounded man with you," one of the other soldiers said. "This one's dead."

"He was alive until one of you shot him."

Cpl. Silver said, "You shouldn't a been out there."

"But we were and…" Abbey took a deep breath, "Shit. Never mind."

"I see Lt. Scharf," Cpl. Silver said.

"For God's sake, don't shoot him," Abbey said.

The lieutenant approached her but stopped to stare at Theo's body.

In a voice filled with disgust, she said, "Shot by our own troops."

She turned and took a few pain-filled steps. "Damn." She waved Lt. Scharf over. "I've pulled my calf muscle. I can hardly walk." Lt. Scharf put an arm around her and she put her arm around his neck.

Cpl. Silver moved to her other side.

They walked to the officer's area.

"We were surprised and overrun," Cpl. Silver said. "Lots of hand-to-hand fighting. Cpl. Lawrence hasn't been seen since."

Abbey asked, "Tell me. How did the enemy surprise our troops?"

Silver said, "They took out our pickets an hour before dawn, seemed to know right where they were, and moved two companies close before first light. They poured cannon fire on top of us initially. As their infantry attacked, the cannon fire was directed beyond our initial position thereby killing many who tried to escape by scattering into the fields around our camp."

"Glad we missed that," Lt. Scharf said.

The two men assisted Abbey to her tent. She stood leaning on her desk. "Thank you, Cpl. Silver. You can go now." He did and she turned to Lt. Scharf. "Please secure the tent flap then help me out of these clothes. My entire body aches and it's difficult to stand on my right leg…pulled my calf muscle. I'll need your help to get cleaned up and dressed."

"I can get the laundry lady."

"Please. Don't want to wait. I'm filthy and tired. Hell, I ache in places I didn't know I had. I need help and I'd prefer it be you." Abbey managed a weak smile and put a hand on his shoulder. "We'll pretend we're on leave again."

"I'm filthy as well," he said then held up blackened hands.

"You clean up first." Abbey nodded to a wash basin then gently lowered herself into a chair.

He pulled off his shirt and britches, poured water into the basin, then soaped up, rinsed and wiped off. He refilled it and washed his shirt and britches.

"Take a pair of my britches," she said. "Don't wear your wet ones."

Buttoning a shirt, he said, "Ready to help."

The lieutenant re-filled the basin then assisted while getting her britches and blouse off. She leaned on his arm and shoulder.

Washed and in clean clothing, Abbey was helped to her desk. She was about to sit but turned and wrapped her arms around him.

"Abbey…"

"Don't say anything. Just hold me."

After a few minutes he kissed her cheek.

She turned to her desk chair then slowly sat in it. He sat in a second chair.

"My Lord, I'm exhausted and my muscles ache all over," she said.

Lt. Scharf shook his head. "So sad about Pvt. Theo. We made it back to our lines…"

"And our own soldiers cut him down."

Abbey moved to her cot, then pulled out the drawing. "My wanted poster. Who the hell drew this?"

"Only Pvt. Tomlinson has that kind of skill as far as I know. I heard he died this morning. The military police said they found petechiae and bruising around his neck. They think he was killed."

"Even so. How did the Confederates get the drawing?"

"A spy?" he said then seemed pensive and quiet for a while, just staring at Abbey. "I should go back to my own tent…"

"Stay here. You can use the other cot," she said. "I'd prefer company."

He nodded. "Cpl. Wilbur died a hero."

"We need to write-up his actions."

"I've had my fill of war," he said.

She slowly shook her head. "When, dear God, will it end?"

Chapter Eighteen: Bromine

Late one evening, Abbey was called to the medical tent. A man in obvious discomfort was sitting on a cot.

"My feet are messed up. I can't walk, Doc."

Abbey unlaced his boots. The soldier grimaced and occasionally moaned as she removed them.

"This is a mess." His feet were covered in blisters, infections and cuts.

"How many weeks were they like this?"

"Lost count."

"I can clean this but you'll have to be off your feet for a week or so to give these injuries time to heal."

"If you could just give me something for the pain. I left my buddy at a guard post up yonder ridge but he's alone."

"How did you get down here?"

"Mostly crawled." He winced as she cleaned the sores. "Have to get back in case we hit the shit. Lots of Confederate movement west of here."

"Sorry but no. You need to give these wounds time to heal. Recovery hospital for you after I'm done."

The soldier didn't reply.

Abbey cleaned out wounds, lanced blisters and wrapped his feet. "Get some sleep. You'll be moved by ambulance in the morning."

***

Early the following day, an ambulance driver approached Abbey in the center medical tent. "Someone needs a trip to the recovery hospital?"

"One patient. Has torn up feet." She nodded toward one of the adjacent medical tents. "Check the medical tent over there."

Abbey unwrapped the bandage covering her left forearm. She thought, *"Damn, warm and looking worse…I wonder…I may have brushed this laceration against the gangrenous wound on the soldier I helped move at the recovery hospital. Is this the beginning of gangrene?"* The doctor shuddered. *"Could lose my arm, or worse, to that disease."*

The ambulance driver returned. "No one in the medical tent, Doctor."

"Should be in there."

"It's empty except for a dead body…which had good feet."

"He couldn't have gone anywhere. His feet were torn up so bad he couldn't walk."

"Where was his unit?"

"He said something about an observation post where he'd left a buddy by himself."

They proceeded to the medical tent. Abbey pointed. "The soldier was in this cot last night."

"Looks like he dragged himself out of here," the soldier said pointing to the trail in the dusty earth.

"To get back to his buddy," she said while shaking her head. "My God, their sense of duty is astounding. How does a soldier develop the attitude which would cause him to endure such pain to help his fellow soldiers?"

"Don't have an answer. But Doc, that there lesion on your forearm don't look too good."

***

Abbey dug through the stacks of paper on her desk.

"It's experimental but…" She thought as she perused numerous documents.

"Here…bromine treatment…applied four-times-a-day for two weeks then daily for four weeks. Initially tried on a man with severely diseased tissue on his lower upper arm, elbow, and forearm. Prior to treatment, only amputation considered as a cure." She read further and muttered, "Injury fully healed, but severe warning on the tremendous pain when bromine applied. They ended up using chloroform during initial treatment." Abbey reread the document. "My wound isn't as large. Perhaps it won't cause as much pain." She examined the formula. "Bromine. Where the hell can I find bromine?"

Abbey proceeded to the communication tent where a telegraph was located.

"I need to get a message to the Medical Museum. I need a few jars of the chemical bromine."

The operator suggested, "How about I also send the message to the supply house which provides chloroform?"

"Excellent idea, Corporal."

Later the same day, a man came down the officer's row of tents calling for Dr. Kaplan.

She left her tent. "I'm Dr. Kaplan."

The telegraph operator approached and saluted. "Telegram for you Ma'am."

"Thank you, Corporal"

Abbey read the message and smiled. "Yes. A messenger carrying bromine will be arriving by train from Philadelphia in one day."

Chapter Nineteen: The Chemist

At the train station and near the freight office, Abbey sat on a bench reading a few documents while awaiting the arrival of the day's train from Philly. She stood as it approached. A young woman, small-boned and short in height but possessed of an upright stature, descended from the train and marched to the freight office. Under her arm, she carried a small wooden box.

"I have a package I wish to deliver to Dr. Abbey Kaplan of the 222nd Massachusetts."

Abbey rushed to her side.

"I'm Doctor Kaplan."

"Melissa Morgenthau of Falstaff Chemical." She extended her hand to Abbey then handed over the box. "This contains two jars of bromine. I have a document for you to sign."

"There you are," Abbey said as she signed then placed the box under her arm. "I didn't expect a woman to accompany my request all the way out here."

"Normally I wouldn't deliver supplies but when I saw your name and thought you might be one of the scarce female doctors in this war, I decided I needed to meet you. As my father owns the company, I have freedom to do things like this."

"Have time for lunch?"

"Definitely, Dr. Kaplan. Please call me Melissa."

"Homestyle cooking at the hotel up the street and please call me Abbey."

As they proceeded into town, their footwear made a hollow sound on the wooden planks of the walk which fronted all the buildings in town.

"I'm curious and a bit surprised at your attire, Abbey."

The doctor laughed. "I attended surgeries this morning and didn't have time to change before rushing out here to meet the train. During a battle, where our position was overrun, I discovered britches and combat boots are more utilitarian when one is in a survival situation. In addition, I carry a pistol on my hip for the same reason."

"Are you part of the military?"

"Yes but as a contract surgeon. I'm given the equivalent rank of lieutenant but don't wear the insignia."

They were seated at a table in the hotel's restaurant.

"How did you decide to work in chemistry?" Abbey asked after reviewing the handwritten signboard with the day's menu.

"My father is a chemist and, as I said, owns Falstaff Chemical. I've been around chemistry all my young life. Although I have a Masters in Chemistry, in truth, I consider my profession as a pharmacist."

"A what?"

"Someone trained in the field of pharmacology. The drugs you receive from our company are certified by me as to the purity, accuracy of compounding, strength and contents of the formulation. We pharmacists are trying to move our field from the *ad hoc* nostrums of the past and bring scientific basis to the medicines we produce."

"A laudable goal," Abbey said. "The men in your field accept you?"

"Certainly not," Melissa said but then added with a grin and a twinkle in her eye, "but, at least in my case, it helps being the owner's daughter."

Abbey laughed.

They each ordered the special of the day, consisting of baked rosemary chicken, garlic roasted red potatoes, and asparagus.

"Even my father," Melissa continued, "resisted my desire to become a pharmacist but my mother is a strong woman and insisted he support my educational and professional goals."

Abbey smiled remembering a fond memory. "My father talked to me about attending college from a young age. In our home it wasn't a matter of...if...I would attend college but…which…college I would attend." Dr. Kaplan thought for a while then asked, "Do doctors accept your findings?"

Melissa sighed and shook her head. "Not many. The old-timers in particular are set in their ways."

"How do you test the efficacy of new or, for that matter, old products?"

"To a huge degree, we depend on reports from doctors and hospitals. Many of which refuse to give us details on the success or failure of drugs and nostrums…certain ones we've found to be terribly toxic despite being widely utilized."

"Which do you suggest I no longer use?"

"Calomel. A deadly concoction. I'd strongly recommend against using it."

"The chemical which caused the controversy resulting in William Bennet being fired as surgeon general?"

Melissa replied, "Yes. He wanted it banned but the old-timers insisted on its continued use. The general put his career on the line for the sake of the troops and was forced to resign."

"He did so much to modernize medicine. A pity he was forced out," Abbey said.

"I'm learning that politics are most distasteful."

Their lunch was served.

"Smells wonderful," the doctor said.

"The toxic effects due to the mercury content in calomel are deadly. My research demonstrates it shouldn't be used for any reason."

"But…"

Melissa interrupted. "I know. Doctors have been using it for decades and refuse to give it up."

"Why won't they follow your advice?"

"Pharmacy is viewed as a subset of medicine rather than our own field. As such, our research holds little sway with those who see themselves as the only healers."

Abbey shook her head. "I swear my chief surgeon believes medicine is an art rather than a science. He ignores the research I perform as well as the results of other's work."

Melissa asked, "And you? Accepted by your peers?"

"Grudgingly these days. Barely at all at first." Abbey stared at her plate for a bit. "Initially, I was mocked and our chief surgeon did everything in his power to replace me. After struggling for many months, I ultimately received sufficient support, I can accomplish my task…consisting of putting my medical education to work, expanding my knowledge of medicine, surgery and altered mental status. Even our chief surgeon is allowing me to perform as I see fit." Abbey thought for a while then asked, "Do you have a man in your life?"

"I was engaged." Melissa showed a smile as if reliving a pleasant memory. The expression slowly turned dark. "We were unwrapping dishes we'd received as a wedding present from my grandmother. I mentioned women should be able to vote."

"His reaction?"

Melissa stared at the floor as she explained, "He laughed for a good five-minutes then stated, 'Women weren't smart enough to vote'. I reminded him I graduated at the top of my nearly all male class. He ignored that and further stated, when we married, I'd have to give up my career."

"I'll bet that hurt."

"Not as bad as his nose."

Abbey was confused. "Nose? What does that have to do…"

"Somehow, one of grandmother's gift china salad plates flew across the room and struck the bridge of his nose, breaking it."

Abbey tried not to but burst out laughing. "Melissa…"

"Give up all the work I'd put into my career? Bullshit."

Abbey laughed again. "I understand. I agree. We need the vote and those of us who wish to pursue careers need the freedom to do so." The two finished their meal then sipped their coffee for a bit, each lost in her own thoughts.

"Melissa, do you think women having the vote would change men's attitudes toward our professional goals?"

"Unlikely in our lifetime. Actually, I feel like we'd be fighting for our daughter's future. I've met pitifully few men who think women having the vote is a good idea. At a minimum, as a voting-block, the politicians would have to respect women's views."

"That would be an improvement…"

The pharmacist sat up straight and said with conviction, "I'm also concerned about child labor and working conditions in mines and these new manufacturing businesses. All are quite cruel."

"Melissa. You fascinate me. I hope we'll stay in touch."

"Thank you. I agree…staying in touch…we'll work at that."

Abbey smiled as she remembered Maggie. "I trained a mentally strong and driven doctor named Margret Herzog. We'd have made a formidable trio."

They went back to sipping their coffee until Melissa said, "I'm curious about the bromine you requested. How do you intend to use it."

"It will be used experimentally to cure diseased tissue."

"Abbey, we've just met but I'd appreciate looking over your shoulder for a few days. I promise not to get in the way."

"Combat wounds are terrible to observe as are the surgeries, most of which consist of amputations."

"We produce chloroform for the military but I've never observed it's use. I have vast experience in chemistry and I've been researching new pharmaceuticals; some of which I've brought with me."

"Melissa, I'm going to be trying the bromine treatment on myself, beginning when I return to my quarters. I have a dime-sized-lesion which doesn't seem to be healing. I'd appreciate it if you'd help apply it."

"Glad to."

"Besides the bromine, tell me about the pharmaceuticals you have and how should they be utilized?" Abbey asked.

"Among others, collodion. It comes as a liquid but forms an adhesive seal when it dries. When a Dr. Howard closed sucking-chest-wounds with sutures then placed alternating layers of lint and linen bandages, followed by a few drops of collodion, the soldiers could breathe normally and survival rates increased by a factor of four."

Abbey's jaw dropped. "A factor of four, did you say?"

Melissa nodded.

"Astounding. I rarely see a non-fatal sucking-chest-wound. And they occur in every battle. Your arrival is certainly propitious." The doctor tucked a lock of hair behind her ear. "Where are you planning on staying?"

"The nearest hotel."

"If you don't mind primitive conditions, I have an extra cot in my tent…we do, however, exist near the front lines and occasionally take fire."

The pharmacist's face brightened. "Then, after this meal, we must proceed to the nearest dry goods establishment so I may procure britches and appropriate footwear."

***

Abbey's eyes watered and she moaned at the intense pain caused by the bromine. "My Lord, it feels like my arm is on fire."

Her new friend said, "I believe chloroform must be administered when the bromine is applied to large wounds."

"I understand why. This burns like hell. I have much to do today so let's get this wrapped and we'll treat it again in six-hours."

The following morning, just when camp medical duty came to an end, a messenger arrived on horseback.

"Message for Dr. Kaplan or Dr. Fellows," he shouted.

"I'm Dr. Kaplan," she called out.

He dismounted, saluted and handed her a document which she quickly read.

"A Connecticut regiment was ambushed early this morning. Their field hospital is overwhelmed as most of their medical helpers were killed. They're requesting surgical assistance." She turned to the messenger. "Tell them I'll be on my way with a surgical team within the hour."

"Yes, Ma'am." He saluted, climbed on his horse and galloped away.

"Lt. Smith, I'll need yourself, Corporals Evans, Silver plus four general helpers, along with chloride of lime and our usual surgical supplies. In addition, teamsters with the necessary conveyance to transport us to the Connecticut regiment's field hospital. We'll meet back here in thirty minutes."

Abbey addressed Melissa. "You're welcome to join us but I must warn you, they are likely still taking fire."

"How can I help?"

The doctor smiled. "Bring your new pharmaceuticals. For now, we'll help load the wagons. Lt. Scharf will provide the supplies and we'll estimate how much we'll need...Um...Melissa, this may involve combat. Are you certain..."

Her new friend interrupted. "We may encounter a sucking-chest-wound. Imagine what I could learn from observing your treatment...not to mention observing other procedures."

***

Abbey introduced herself to the Connecticut regiment's chief surgeon. "Thank you for coming, Dr. Kaplan. We need to split your team as my helpers were wiped out by shell-fire last night," Major Carracciola said while shaking Abbey's hand. He stood just outside the field hospital's main tent. Rows of wounded needing surgical intervention were arrayed on stretchers and cots.

They walked among the injured and performed triage.

"It smells like defecation over here," Melissa said.

Abbey explained, "Some lose control of their bowels when grievously wounded or the odor could occur when their intestines are split."

The major asked, "Dr. Kaplan, I understand you've successfully treated abdominal wounds."

"Only some. If the wound is near the surface and hasn't torn too much of the intestine plus I am convinced I will be able to find and ligate all the bleeders, I'll attempt repair. We use instruments rinsed in chloride of lime solution and utilize clean, dissolving suture material to repair the wounds or they quickly become diseased."

She bent over, lifted a soldier's shirt and gently pulled up his bandages. "This type of wound is worth attempting repair."

Dr. Carracciola peered at the injury. "Survival chance?"

"Roughly fifty-fifty...as opposed to one-hundred-percent fatal."

Dr. Carracciola nodded.

"We'll do our best for you," Abbey said to the gut-shot soldier who whispered thanks and did his best to smile through his pain.

Abbey returned his smile then continued, "More damage than this and the patient will likely bleed out during surgery or soon after."

"Let's begin with him and with your permission, I'll assist," he said.

They entered the surgical tent.

"Dr. Neal," the chief surgeon called out to his assistant surgeon, "please start the next patient without me."

With a nod from Dr. Kaplan, Cpl. Silver administered chloroform to the gut-shot patient.

Melissa stood next to Abbey while the doctor performed and described the procedure.

"Thank you, Dr. Kaplan. Most informative." The chief surgeon of the Connecticut regiment moved to his own table.

An hour later, a high pitched whistling sound could be heard. "Incoming," Lt. Smith screamed.

Melissa, wearing a puzzled expression, turned to Abbey. The doctor grabbed the pharmacist by the shoulders and roughly pushed her to the ground then flattened herself to the soil as well. A tremendous, "Whump," occurred, followed by the ground seemingly jumping up and slapping their prostrate bodies. Melissa noted, the men had learned to lay on their bellies but kept their family jewels out of harm's way by keeping their hips slightly above the soil.

Another projectile whistled its arrival. It exploded near the first, showering the medical team and patients with dirt and debris.

After the second explosion, a spinning piece of pie plate sized, jagged-edged, cast iron came whirring through the tent. One soldier ducked at the sound of the explosion but didn't flatten himself to the ground. Melissa watched as the flying debris neatly sliced his head from his body as if cleaved by a cutlass. Blood spurted up from the neck of the headless body. The head rolled to a stop near her; eyes still open as if they could see her. The head belonged to Dr. Neal, the surgical assistant. She jammed her eyes shut and curled into a ball with her hands over her loudly-ringing-ears. More whistling and explosions occurred which, mercifully, exploded beyond the medical tents.

After a few minutes without further cannon fire, they began to stand and assess the damage. One side of the tent was shredded as well as part of the roof.

Abbey sat up then stood. She helped Melissa to her feet. The pharmacist sputtered, "His head...it was sliced right off."

"I'm going to need your help, Melissa."

"Help...?" She watched, wide-eyed, as two men respectfully placed the body and head on a stretcher and left the tent.

Melissa wobbled slightly. "His severed head...it looked right at me..."

Abbey steadied her then shook her by the shoulders.

The pharmacist slowly shook her head. "I'm sorry, Dr. Kaplan but I'm not made for this."

"This is war and we do what is needed to save these soldiers. Therefore you'll find the necessary strength and do, goddamn, what I tell you."

Melissa used both hands to briskly wipe her hair out of her face. "Yes...you manage the horror..." she swallowed hard "...so will I..." she stood tall and said, "We...save these men...I will, Dr. Abbey."

"Listen to me. Clear your head. My assistant will be working with Dr. Carracciola. I need you to assist me."

"Assist...," the new acquaintance muttered in a quivering voice while her entire body trembled. She strained to remain standing tall. Melissa bowed her head and whispered, "I'm needed here, Jesus. Please give me strength that I might help these brave soldiers."

The doctors and their teams began treating those wounded in the tent. Medical helpers continued to remove the dead and stage the injured.

Melissa followed Abbey as she evaluated the soldiers and helped bandage many.

Abbey helped her into a surgical apron then directed her to rinse her hands in the bowl of cleaning solution.

Dr. Kaplan yelled, "Next."

A soldier was placed on the table.

"Cut open his clothing so we can see the damage," Abbey directed her new assistant.

The soldier's foot was missing and his ankle was crushed. Abbey felt along his lower leg bones. "Crushed up to mid-calf. We'll amputate just above." Abbey demonstrated applying the tourniquet strap. "I'll amputate just below this but leave a flap of skin from the lower section to close the wound. I need you to grip below the location of the amputation and gently pull down on the tissue, away from the cut I'm going to make."

Melissa put her shaking hands on the injured leg. "Oh no. It's still warm…and it's covered in sticky blood."

"Steady Melissa. This man needs our help."

Melissa nodded but continued to tremble as Abbey began a circumferential cut into the leg muscle. Melissa didn't watch but felt the tissue she held moving slightly downward as Abbey sliced. A quick glance revealed only the bones attaching the upper and lower calf; the tissue she pulled on had moved away from the incision in a cone shape.

Abbey put the bone saw to work.

"I feel the vibration of the saw's teeth," Melissa whispered. "What an awful sensation."

A moment later and the severed limb was free.

"Place it in the wheelbarrow," Abbey said.

Melissa didn't move but stared at the bloody remains she held.

"In the wheelbarrow behind us please, Melissa," Abbey repeated in a louder voice.

As if in a daze and still staring at the severed limb, the chemist turned and slowly walked to the wheelbarrow. She placed it on top of other previously severed arms, legs, hands, feet and fingers.

"She's going to vomit," Cpl. Silver said.

Sure enough, Melissa turned pale then wretched numerous times.

Abbey used a tenaculum to pull arteries to the surface so she could tie them off then used a file to round and smooth the end of the bone. Last, she began suturing the flap to close the wound. She nodded to Cpl. Silver then indicated Melissa. The corporal approached the chemist.

He put a hand on her shoulder. "Happens to most their first surgeries, Ma'am. Don't feel bad."

"Hoped I was stronger than this."

"You're doing fine but Dr. Kaplan still needs your assistance."

Melissa took a few deep breaths then repositioned herself across the surgical table from Abbey. She straightened. "Ready, Dr. Kaplan."

Around midnight a number of children were brought in.

"We'll suture this laceration," Abbey said, indicating a shoulder wound. "I need you to pull the tissue together while I sew."

"Yes Doctor," Melissa said. She brought the edge of the child's wound together, gritted her teeth and mumbled to herself, "I'm doing this. I won't get sick. This child needs me. I refuse to get sick."

When she'd placed the last suture, Dr. Kaplan said, "Next," then whispered to Melissa, "You're doing great."

A soldier was placed on the table. His skin tone was blue. "Found a sucking-chest-wound as requested," Cpl. Silver said. "We've kept him on his side per your instruction. He's the last of the wounded for now."

Dr. Carracciola's eyebrow's went up. "You can treat a perforated chest?"

"First time but with a new pharmaceutical, courtesy of Miss Morgenthau, who also brought me a description of the technique we need to implement," Abbey said.

"May I observe?"

Abbey nodded. She kept her hand over the soldier's chest opening, allowing better airflow to his lungs.

Dr. Carracciola, Lt. Scharf and other members of the surgical team, all gathered around Abbey as she performed the new procedure with Melissa assisting.

"The soldier's skin color," Dr. Carracciola said a few minutes later, "is steadily improving." He turned to Abbey and Melissa. "Brilliant work by the female medical team." He shook each of their hands but seemed to have a special smile for Melissa. "Miss Morgenthau, when can you supply me with collodion."

"I have extra," Melissa said, "but, if you'll direct me to the communications tent, I will send a telegram to my company. You'll have it within a day."

"As we're done here and with your permission, I'll take you myself." He offered his arm.

The following morning, Abby and Melissa walked around the men waiting for transportation to the Connecticut regiment's recovery hospital.

She encountered a man with a distorted face. His right side cheekbone and a segment of his upper jaw had been ripped off but healed. The poor man was alive but left with a ghastly facial expression.

He noticed their stares. "I can scare kids with this kisser."

Melissa whispered to Abbey, "I've read of surgery to replace bone with material used by dentists."

"As have I," the doctor said. She turned to the soldier. "We know of a procedure which will attempt to replace some of the missing bone. Would you be willing to let us try?"

"Hell yes, Ma'am."

"We're going to take some measurements, then craft the missing bone and perform a surgical procedure to place it below your skin."

"Measure away," he said.

Abbey did while Melissa made notes of the measurements, then sketched a dimensioned drawing.

With the assistance of a dentist, the twosome crafted the shaped material and fasteners then a discussion followed with how he used implants.

The following day, Abbey led the surgical team with Dr. Carracciola assisting and guidance from the dentist. Melissa and Lt. Scharf made notes as the surgery progressed.

"A tremendous bit of surgery," Melissa said after the last bandage was applied. "But will it work?"

***

The following morning, back to her own unit, Abbey noted a tall, broad shouldered man of dark complexion and grey flecked hair waited at the medical tent next to a wagon pulled by two large mules. He wore overalls and held a wide brimmed sun hat which he nervously fingered. His hands were rough and callused. A young boy stood at his side. Four bushel-baskets, each covered with a cloth, were adjacent to the wagon.

The man talked to a corporal then approached Abbey. "I'm Trent Booker, Ma'am. Got a truck farm a few miles up the road. That corporal said I should talk to a Dr. Kaplan. Word reached me, there's a surgeon by that name from the 222nd Massachusetts who repairs hare lip."

"I'm Doctor Kaplan and I perform that procedure."

He seemed shocked. "You?"

"If it's a problem I'm female..."

The tall man quickly interrupted. "No Ma'am! Just surprised." With a twinkle in his eye, he added, "Hell... long as you can help my son, I wouldn't really care if you was mule from the waist down."

Abbey chuckled and glanced at Melissa whose laughter filled the air.

Mr. Booker asked, "You don't mind working on folks like us?"

Dr. Kaplan pointed to the soldiers waiting to be transported to the recovery area. "As you can see with your own eyes, we perform surgery on everyone needing it."

"Bless you, Doctor." Mr. Booker put his hand on his son's shoulder. "Matt is ten. Any chance you can help him?"

"Let me see your lip, Matt." Abbey ran her finger on his lip and examined the gums behind the lip. "I can repair this."

"Will it hurt?" the boy asked.

"You'll be asleep during the work I do. Afterward, the area will be sore for a few days. But if you and your dad follow the instructions I give you, your lip will heal just fine. Can you put up with pain for a few days?"

The young man straightened and nodded. "Yes, Ma'am. I'll manage."

"I have two-bushels of sweet potatoes and two-bushels of carrots for payment," the man said.

"Not necessary. The Army pays me. I'll need an hour to perform the repair."

"Excuse me, Dr. Kaplan, but I pay my own way. Always have. I'm sure the soldiers 'round here would enjoy these carrots and tubers."

"That's most kind of you, Sir. I'm certain the men will appreciate your produce," Dr. Kaplan said. She reached out and shook the farmer's calloused hand. "Cpl. Silver, notify the mess sergeant then please assist Mr. Booker and get these provisions to the mess area." She turned to the man's son. "Matt, come with me," then called to the father, "Mr. Booker, would you have basil leaves? I could use some for their medicinal qualities...upset stomachs and the like."

"I'll gather a pound or so when I return to my farm...one more thing Dr. Kaplan. My niece just graduated from medical school. She's going to setup a community practice in our town. Would you mind teaching her your hare lip technique?"

Abbey thought for a moment. "I can teach her a number of techniques useful to a community doctor. If possible, have her here in two days at seven in the morning and tell her to bring enough clothing for a few day's stay. I'll schedule appropriate surgeries."

Another day later, Abbey walked Melissa to the train station.

"It was proper of the mess sergeant to pay for Mr. Booker's produce."

"All but one-bushel of carrots...which was declared payment for his son's surgery." Abbey giggled. "So if anyone asks the value of our surgical skills, you tell them we're worth precisely one-bushel of carrots."

Melissa laughed then said, "How's the bromine working?"

"The inflamed area is obviously healing."

"What about the soldier with the implants?"

"Much better. Not perfect but won't scare anyone."

"Thank the Lord."

They walked in silence for a few minutes.

Melissa seemed sullen. She sighed. "I feel like I'm leaving a sister behind...even though we've only known each other for a handful of days...a sister who's going to be in grave danger."

"Such is the price of war. I knew what I was in for when I volunteered for this assignment."

"I don't know how you manage."

"Our discussions on pharmaceuticals were most beneficial and your help with the surgeries was a Godsend. You should be proud of yourself. I'm sure it wasn't easy."

"Truthfully, it was hell. Pure and simple, it was hell. Even now, I have many varied emotions swirling around which are empowered by ghastly visual and tactile memories. I'm certain the wounds those poor soldiers endured will haunt me for years to come."

"But you did it. You're tougher than you previously thought...sister."

Melissa turned and briefly embraced Abbey. "At one point, I felt like I couldn't go on. In my estimation, the only reason I found the inner fortitude, was the strength the Lord suddenly provided me." She sighed and nodded. "It was a blessing meeting you, Abbey Kaplan. When I have research on new pharmaceuticals, I'll write or send them with instructions on their use."

The loud hissing sound of the approaching train blowing down it's boiler, shattered the air.

Melissa smiled at Abbey and said, "Thank you for allowing me to work at your side. I'll pray, sister, you remain safe and we'll meet again."

"When we meet again, we're going to work at gaining respect for the field of pharmaceuticals," Abbey said. With a twinkle in her eye, she leaned toward Melissa and said in a quiet voice, "And getting women the vote."

Chapter Twenty: Second Leave

Abbey was spending the day examining soldiers at a nearby recovery hospital. She stopped at the bed of a patient whose head was wrapped in bandages. Only his face was exposed. He smiled at her but only one side of his lips formed the smile.

"He was my assistant surgeon." An older man approached wearing captain's insignia. "Walked out in the middle of an amputation, returned to his tent and shot himself in the head."

"Surprising he wasn't killed."

"Poor aim. Dented the side of his skull though." The older man held out his hand. "I'm Paul Brantley, chief surgeon of the 209th Ohio Infantry Regiment."

"Abbey Kaplan, assistant surgeon with the 222nd Massachusetts."

"Heard about you."

"Good things I hope."

"Indeed. Thank you for taking care of, or should I be honest and say covering for, my friend from medical school, Dr. Fellows."

"He allowed me to learn many surgical techniques and gain the ability to be a lead surgeon."

"He indicated he has boundless admiration for your skill."

Abbey laughed and shook her head. "I doubt it."

Dr. Brantley's face became serious. "Dr. Kaplan, please know, Dr. Fellows stated to my face; if the time ever comes when he needed surgical intervention, he would want you holding the scalpel."

Abbey's jaw dropped. She slapped her forehead in disbelief then said, "Are we talking about the same Dr. Fellows? Of course, it would be nice if he told me those words in person."

The captain laughed. "Dr. Kaplan, I have a delicate surgery to perform shortly. I will attempt to repair broken bones over a soldiers left eye with an experimental procedure. Will you please assist?"

"Certainly."

"Afterward, I'd like to discuss repair of hare lip and your experience with abdominal surgery."

***

Dr. Fellows, the following day, found Abbey and Lt. Scharf at the mess area. "Dr. Kaplan, orders have come through for your leave. You start this Saturday."

"Last year, Lt. Scharf accompanied me."

"Yes. I have his leave orders as well," Dr. Fellows said, "I hate to have you both gone at the same time as I understand what an excellent team you've become." He turned to Lt. Scharf. "Your skills have progressed to the point, after some review and a practice test, you will take the medical board exam shortly after you return."

Lt. Scharf grinned and said, "I understand, Sir."

The chief surgeon turned to Abbey. "Certainly you must agree, he's on his way to passing the medical board examination?"

"Yes, Sir. He'll do well."

They saluted. Abbey and Jordan walked away together.

He glanced at her. "Think we'll get as much tension relief as last year?"

"I'll make up more petroleum jelly."

He laughed. "Abbey...I'm serious. After all we've gone through since our last leave...Will we be able to achieve a better mental balance?"

***

The twosome walked along the train platform in Pittsburgh.

"What would you like to do first?" Abbey asked.

"I've been dreaming of a long, hot bath and finally feeling clean."

Abbey laughed.

He continued, "I was hoping to repair some of my stress-induced mental scars." He gazed in Abbey's eyes. "Perhaps we'll make time to listen to each other. It might do us good."

A slow groan was heard as overstressed metal gave up its load. A deep rumble was followed by hundreds of terrified screams. Their heads snapped in the direction of the sounds.

"What the hell was that noise?" he said.

"Sounds like it's coming from the train station."

They began running.

"Alabama High Shuffle time," Abbey shouted, lifting her skirt to keep up with him.

"I don't dance," he yelled.

Abbey giggled.

"Never saw anyone run that fast in a skirt."

"You'd be amazed how fast you can move when trying to outrun cannon fire."

They rounded a corner and both became wide-eyed. "What happened?" she asked.

A dense cloud of dust blew out the entrance as panicked travelers poured out of the station like disturbed fire ants leaving their mound. Screams and shouts for help assaulted their ears.

They approached the entrance as the dust cleared. Jordan peered inside. "Some of the roof beams collapsed."

The screams of injured pierced the air. They arrived at the base of a twisted pile of roofing material and beams.

"I hear a child's voice inside this pile," Jordan said.

A man ran up. "I'm a nurse."

Abbey asked, "How far is the hospital."

"Two blocks."

"I'm a surgeon. I need a surgical kit with thread and a suturing needle plus chloroform."

The man just stared.

Jordan screamed, "Don't stare at her asshole. Get the damn shit."

The man yelled, "Yes, Doctor," as he spun on his heel and began running.

Abbey took off her underskirt and the underskirt of a dead women. She handed one to Jordan.

"Tear these into strips."

Two woman followed Abbey's example; stripping off their underskirts and tearing them as she did.

Jordan began moving material. Additional moans and cries for help were heard. He climbed the debris pile. Abbey followed. The twosome plus another man and a woman began gently removing bodies and handing them to others. They moved lower in the twisted mass with each removal.

Dr. Kaplan cocked her head to the side. "I can hear a child whimpering."

"There," Jordan said. He pointed to a young girl. She was pale, and they could see she suffered wounds to her scalp and legs. Her crushed left forearm was pinned by a large beam.

"We have to amputate her arm at her elbow or she'll bleed to death before they move all this debris to get her out."

They heard an out of breath man climbing the twisted material. He yelled, "Got your surgical kit Doc!"

Jordan passed it down to her.

Abbey quickly applied a tourniquet to the child's arm then closed the unconscious girl's scalp wound and one tear on her thigh while instructing Jordan in bandaging both.

She cut through shoulder muscle and was about to start sawing when the girl began to stir. Abbey grabbed the chloroform and poured some on a length of cloth. She held it to the girl's face until she quit moving.

"Hold this about an inch above her nose."

"Yes, Doctor," Jordan replied.

A fireman yelled from above them. "Need anything Doc?"

"I'll need help lifting this girl out in a few minutes."

"I got two guys heading down to help."

Two burley fireman tunneled their way in.

Abbey finished the last suture and covered the wound. She and Jordan slid their arms under the little one and passed her to the first of the firemen who lifted her to the second. A cheer went up as the child was passed out of the wreckage.

The firemen steadied Jordan and Abbey as they climbed up and out of the twisted debris.

The station was littered with bodies. Abbey began closing wounds with Jordan closing some and the nurse assisting. An older man approached Abbey. "I'm Doctor Blackmun. What are you doing there?"

Abbey asked, "Where did you go to medical school?"

He appeared shocked at the question, but answered, "Boston."

She continued to work and said, "Then you should know it's called ligation."

"Are you a…"

She yelled, "I'm a surgeon with the 222nd Massachusetts. If you're a doctor get busy."

He didn't move, just stared at her.

Abbey examined a woman. She turned to the immobile doctor. "This woman's leg needs to be amputated. Prep her and I'll be right back."

He spat out a hurried, "Yes, Doctor," and began cutting away the woman's bloomers.

More medical personnel arrived along with wagons to transport the injured.

Three-hours later, Dr. Blackmun thanked Abbey and Jordan.

"A pleasure," she replied, "although I'm supposed to be on leave."

They laughed and shook hands.

Jordan offered his arm. Abbey grabbed it and squeezed it against her.

"An honor to have assisted you, Dr. Kaplan."

"You performed well. Well enough to pass the medical board."

He laughed. "We'll see."

***

Abbey spent the balance of the night and into the following afternoon, sleeping on a luxurious down-filled mattress.

She awoke around four and found an envelope had been slipped under her door. The doctor opened it.

"A formal invitation to dinner from Jordan." Abbey smiled. "How thoughtful."

Chapter Twenty-One: Dialogue Between Friends

At dinner, Jordan pulled out a chair for her. She wore a dress with a low-cut top which displayed much of her ample chest. With pleasure, the doctor noted his glances at it when she wasn't looking directly at him.

He was clean-shaven and wore a neatly tailored suit.

Abbey said, "Your civilian appearance is professional."

"When I return to civilian life, I'm going to be a doctor and a surgeon so thought I should look the part on this leave. You look lovely, Dr. Kaplan."

"Thank you."

They perused the menu.

"Where were you born and where will you live after the war?" he asked.

"My parents were from Ireland. I was born in Philadelphia, then moved to Boston, Massachusetts, Independence, Missouri, then Portland, Oregon and Seattle, Washington."

"Well traveled. My parents came from the German-speaking area of the Austro-Hungarian Empire. They arrived in Philadelphia then moved to Pittsburgh to be with family. My father found work and we stayed until I left for the war. Sadly, my parents died in a boating accident about two months after First Bull Run."

"Three sisters as I remember?"

"Correct."

"What will you do after the war?"

"Secure a position in a hospital as a surgeon. You?"

"I'm returning to the Northwest."

"How has the last year affected you?"

She eyed him while deciding how much to tell him. "Painfully, in a mental sense although my medical skills have blossomed. As you know, I arrived to the war immediately after medical college. Almost the entirety of my surgical training has been on war injuries."

A wine bottle was placed on their table. Jordan sampled it then filled their glasses.

He raised a glass. "To our mental health and a rapid end to the war."

"Amen." Abbey said with a smile. They clinked glasses.

Jordan thought for a while and said, "Was the price in emotional pain worth your participation in the war?"

She leaned back, sipped more wine, and sighed. "Since shortly after I arrived at our unit, I've felt like a wrestling match is going on in my head. Pressure to stay and continue saving lives while enduring the daily horrors and abuse versus feeling like the horrors are drowning me. At times I'm winning and at others, feel I'm within an inch of having my shoulders pinned."

He seemed confused. "Explain abuse."

"A female doctor is resented by many if not most. I've had to beat people over the head with my ability and dedication until they give me, grudgingly I admit, a modicum of respect." She shook her head and took a long drink of wine. "Thank the Lord, he provided me with an assistant who helped keep my depression from drowning me." She raised her glass to Jordan and they clinked glasses again. "If being mentally beaten down by others was the only difficulty, my emotions may not have suffered as much but the hordes of wounded, crippled and particularly those I'm unable to help, weigh heavily." Abbey swirled the wine in her glass and downed the balance.

He picked up the wine bottle, refilled her glass and topped off his.

Abbey contemplated the soup placed in front of her. "Smells delightful. Jordan, I'm going to depress you if I keep talking."

"After the war we'll go back to our own lives and likely never see each other again. Feel free to talk about anything you wish."

"You may not enjoy that."

"Abbey, you mentioned your, what shall we call it, emotions; improved during our last leave."

"Yes, my overall sense of well-being improved, but I don't know why."

"Delicious chicken soup," he said.

"My mother is a brilliant cook. She uses celery root among other flavorings."

"Sounds wonderful. Adds an aromatic note I would say."

Abbey became pensive then said, "I had something of a breakthrough on the train ride to Pittsburgh this year."

He stopped eating, sat back and sipped his wine. "Tell me."

"Occasionally, I…we…make a mistake which costs a soldier dearly…sometimes fatally. Initially I was devastated; couldn't sleep and tried to forget what happened."

"Forget?"

She nodded. "I didn't forget, but gradually, the incidents didn't become a source of horror."

"The breakthrough?"

"Something, perhaps, you might emulate. By accepting I'm human and will make mistakes, I improved my mental balance in regards to my errors."

"Perhaps you could apply the same thinking to the other things which keep us awake at night."

"I've been trying but with little success."

The twosome ate quietly for a bit then Abbey asked, "How do you manage when the mental pain grows."

"Poorly, I'm afraid. Bad results leave scars on my humanity which I fear will never heal."

"Jordan, your sense of compassion is commendable."

He smiled, "Thoughtful of you to say."

"In truth, the primary reason I joined the war effort was to advance my medical knowledge and ability as a surgeon."

"As a woman, do you miss putting off having a family and, if so, is it a source of pain?"

"I'm busy all day, seven-days-a-week. Not much time to contemplate a family." Abbey sighed and saw warmth in his eyes. "*Jordan remains a most pleasant, man,*" she thought. The doctor put a lock of hair behind her ear. "But...my body longs to have a man. It becomes painful to ignore."

"With nothing but men around, I'm desperate for a woman."

Abbey put her hand on his. "How are you managing?"

"Not well." A twinkle appeared in his eye. "Last week, I found myself admiring a mule with wide hips."

Abbey laughed hysterically.

When she quieted, he said, "Even contemplated buying sex."

She shook her head. "Don't. You'll likely get a dreadful disease. I treat many of the camp followers and their customers. They both develop ghastly sores on their genitals."

"How repulsive."

"And occasionally deadly."

"I understand it's easier for females to ignore their sexual urges."

Abbey slammed her hand on the table. "What crap! Men have such a distorted view of womanhood."

He blushed. "I apologize."

"Unnecessary." She stared at him briefly. "Perhaps it's our mother's fault for not explaining to their sons the urges we feel."

He shook his head, "Believe me. The last thing men need is knowledge which increases their libido."

Abbey burst into laughter. They were served grilled chicken and root vegetables.

"So how do you manage the urges? Um…if we're getting too personal…"

"Not at all. It helps to talk. A year ago, we…took care of each other."

"This year, perhaps you'll allow me once again…"

Abbey experienced an ache in her lady parts. She stared at her lap while her cheeks warmed .

"I'm sorry. It was rude of me…"

"Not at all, Jordan." Abbey sat up straight and composed herself anew. She grabbed a lock of hair and stuffed it behind her ear. "As you said earlier, we'll go back to our own lives after the war and likely never see each other again." She looked in his eyes. "When we've completed dinner, perhaps you'll accompany me to my room?"

***

Abbey unpinned her hat and carefully placed it in its box. Jordan slipped out of his clothing. She sucked in her breath and brought her hand up to cover her mouth. The doctor stared for a moment then said, "My Lord, such a well-muscled body."

"Thank you. Since our last leave I perform nearly two-hundred push-ups and sit-ups on a daily basis."

"The result is magnificent."

She reached out to touch his rippled abdomen then hesitated. "May I?"

"Please."

He flexed for her. She ran a hand across his chiseled pectorals, washboard abs, then around to his back, across his butt and down one leg. Abbey's insides throbbed. "You could pose for anatomy studies."

"Thank you. Your figure?"

Abbey turned her back to him then lifted her hair off her collar. He unbuttoned the back of her dress. She stepped out of her clothing.

"Beautiful," he said.

She cupped her breasts. "Fallen a bit I'm afraid."

Still lovely," he said, then kissed each one.

They wrapped their arms around each other and engaged in a long kiss.

"Abbey, I must admit, even after our trysts last leave, I know little about a women's body. I would know better what to do if you told me where and how you like to be touched."

Abbey's heart pounded. "I'd love to."

As if she weighed nothing, he lifted her and carried the doctor to bed.

***

"People's feelings are so strange," Jordan said during one of many walks which meandered through Pittsburgh's downtown.

"How does that apply to those of us experiencing a war?"

"Emotions have no shape or form but…" He seemed to be struggling to find the right words. Jordan gazed about then pointed to a robin standing on the edge of its nest. Its three young, mouths opened wide and peeping away, begged to be fed.

Abbey viewed the nest and smiled.

"A sight which warms us," he said. "A feeling which wraps around us like a lover's arms." He took a deep breath and shook his head. "But the horror of war invades our soul, overshadowing positive thought and experience. Our vain attempts to sustain our emotional balance leave us feeling incomplete…like we've landed alone in the middle of an ocean where the horrors of war drag us down into greater and deeper depths of depression and despair."

"Drag us down…deeper depths of depression and despair…let me contemplate that for a bit," Abbey said.

They walked in silence for a couple city blocks.

"Then, Sir, what do we do to maintain our sanity?"

He sighed. "Not sure."

"Perhaps, remembering we are contributing to a great cause?"

"That may help in the long term but in the short term, I believe I need small victories to sustain me."

Abbey stated, "For me, saving patient's lives, learning more about medicine, training others and contributing to the museum are all victories."

He shook his head. "I guess I should see saving patients' lives as victories but I seem to dwell on those we can't. Little victories rarely come my way."

"What about our victory at Gettysburg? Didn't it help?"

"The Union victory certainly buoyed my spirits…until the reports on the number of casualties tempered my celebration." With saddened expression, he added, "Including Confederate losses, we believe over 50,000." He sighed, gazed across a river then turned to Abbey. "Once alone in my tent, I cried like a baby…was despondent for days afterwards."

"The stream of those needing surgical intervention seemed endless. Plus countless follow-up surgeries at the recovery hospitals."

He stated, "I remember. When we witness man at his cruelest, as during a war, why isn't our sexual desire suppressed?"

Abbey thought for a moment, then replied. "Perhaps to remind us of our humanity."

"Or do our base instincts surface no matter what the emotional environment?"

"Instinct?" she asked.

"I doubt there is logic involved when I desire a woman. Wanting to have relations is built into our mind. It's not like we can turn it on and off at will. It's more like a steam engine with someone other than ourselves at the control. Well…that's how it seems to me."

"Excellent thoughts," Abbey said. "War and its associated horror does temporarily depress desire…but only when I'm exhausted, under great stress or in the middle of surgical intervention."

He forced a smile. "Enough about war. How about dinner?"

***

The following morning they walked arm-in-arm along the river.

Abbey said, "I began considering differences in the way men and women think, a bit over a year ago. When I communicated my ideas to a colleague, she accused me of over-analyzing."

"What differences specifically?"

"I propose women are closer to nature than men and this difference influences our behavior. I believe women admire nature while men are born with a desire to bend nature."

They walked in silence for a few minutes.

Jordan asked, "What proof would you posit, women are closer to nature?"

"Nature causes women to have a monthly reminder they are intended for child-bearing."

She glanced at Jordan who was deep in thought.

After another few minutes silence, he said, "Another example, please."

Abbey studied their surroundings. She pointed to a grove of trees across the river. "I see a stand of Oak trees and admire their beauty. A man sees the same but the image in his head consists of material to build something."

"I'm not sure I understand what you're saying."

"Let me think of another example..." Abbey became pensive as they walked. She watched geese paddling along the edges of a nearby stream. Her expression brightened. "Not long ago, I watched a number of geese. They were resting at the edge of a reed bed at the side of a wide river. On a sylvan day, wind-driven-waves caused them to slowly bob up and down. With a mighty flap of its wings, a goose lifted partially out of the water then used its legs to run across the pond while using its wings to help it gain speed. Eventually it lifted its legs and was carried up and away by wings alone."

"A beautiful sight."

"But a man stood next to me who saw the same thing. Instead of commenting on the beauty, he wondered aloud what it would take to build a machine which copied the bird to achieve the same and fly away."

"A flying machine? Amazing."

Abbey seemed lost in thought. In a barely audible voice, she said, "I experienced natural beauty but he wanted to bend nature to his own will."

"Fascinating concepts. How will you use them?"

"Not sure. As my interest in people's mental difficulties increases, and by keeping those suppositions in mind, I may be able to better assist those with melancholy or other emotional disturbances."

Jordan asked, "Have you considered most inventions are produced by men?"

"Is it because they wish to bend nature or most women's lives are consumed raising a family?"

"Piercing questions, Doctor."

"Lunch?" Abbey asked.

"Yes, but let's continue discussing this topic."

***

They stood on the platform and waited for the train back to camp.

Abbey said, "As I said to my leave companion last year, two lonely people, governed by their urges, does not a relationship make."

"Again, I understand," Jordan said, then smiled and gazed into her eyes. "Abbey, you satisfied much more than my physical need this year."

"Such as?"

"All our discussion of personal struggle, emotional state and the war…we've engaged each other on an intellectual level which was deliciously satisfying."

Abbey registered contentment. "I…I experienced the same feeling as well."

"If you're ever looking for a friend after the war…"

"If I'm ever in need of a friend, I'll find you." She kissed his cheek.

Their train whistled as it approached the station.

"Oh well," Abbey said with a sigh. "Back to the war."

Chapter Twenty-Two: Dr. Scharf

It was a cool day in December of 1864.

"Are you in much pain?" Jordan Scharf asked a soldier with a piece of shrapnel sticking out of the middle of his ribcage. He lay on a cot outside the medical tents having just been delivered by ambulance.

"Gets painful as hell if I take a deep breath."

He opened the man's shirt. A small, flat piece of metal, roughly half the size of grown man's palm stuck through his skin. "Not much bleeding so not too deep. We'll remove this, dress your wound and have you on your way." He gripped the metal. It slid out easily...followed by blood spurting out of the soldier's chest.

The man's eyes went wide as his face displayed abject terror. Jordan covered the opening. Copious amounts of blood oozed out between his fingers. He screamed for Dr. Kaplan. When he looked at the soldier's face, his mouth was open and eyes were staring straight up. He'd quit breathing.

"What happened?" Abbey asked.

"This little piece of metal was in his chest. I pulled it out and blood spurted everywhere...and he died."

"Likely his heart was pierced...or you pierced it when removing the metal."

"But he wasn't in much pain so I imagined the metal wasn't deep."

"If it wasn't deep we might have had a chance to remove it without more damage but once it pierced his heart...we couldn't do anything."

"So I killed him."

Abbey nodded. "It happens."

"Lord forgive me."

"Surgeons are human. We all make mistakes."

"Have you killed anyone?"

"You know I did. You were there."

"When?"

"You might remember, I treated a conscious soldier for an entry-wound while he was bleeding out from a huge exit-wound. If I had checked for and treated the exit-wound before I started on the entry-wound, I might have saved him."

"Dr. Kaplan, I could use a break."

"I have a wound that requires your immediate assistance in the medical tent."

"But..."

"A child needs your attention."

"Give me a minute."

She yelled, "Now, Lt. Scharf."

He slowly stood then followed her into the main medical tent.

"He has a cut on his upper eyelid just below his eyebrow, it's nearly the width of the his eye," A trembling women cradling an infant said..

"We have to suture this with tiny stitches," Abbey said.

"The little one screamed as Abbey administered chloroform but quieted quickly.

Lieutenant Smith and Cpl. Silver ran into the tent with a few members of the team.

"I need you to suture this with tiny stitches," Abbey told Lt. Scharf

He stared at the wound. "Normal suture material will be too thick."

"What can we do?"

"Hold a piece against the table and I'll split it." They cleaned their hands and he retrieved a scalpel.

Abbey stretched an eight-inch-piece of gut-suturing-material.

Lt. Scharf checked the sharpness of a scalpel then slowly ran it down the material, neatly splitting it in two. He held it up. "Still too thick." He looked at Abbey.

"I agree."

She secured the split material a second time while Lt. Scharf divided it. He pulled on it to check it's strength.

"Perfect," Abbey said.

"Dr. Kaplan, please make sure his head stays still."

"Yes, Dr. Scharf."

He raised his eyebrows then completed the first tiny suture and began a second. "I could use a much smaller suture-needle for this."

Lt. Scharf tied off the last suture. Abbey placed a bandage over the child's eye.

Abbey cradled the tiny one and said to his mother. "Come back in two-days so we can check him."

The woman threw her arms around the lieutenant. "Thank you, Doctor Scharf."

"I'm not..."

She kissed his cheek. "Thank you, Doctor. God bless you."

"You're welcome," he said, appearing a bit overwhelmed. Abbey handed the child to his mother.

"Coffee?" Dr. Kaplan asked the lieutenants. They nodded. She sat across from them at a picnic table sipping a steaming mucket of dark brew.

"I'll have a small-suture-needle made for you and put it with your surgical instruments," Lt. Smith said to Lt. Scharf.

"I don't have surgical instruments."

"After today," Abbey said, "You should. You're capable of numerous procedures which will free me up to do other work. I'll sign a request form."

"I'm not a surgeon."

"I couldn't have split the gut like you did and doubt I could have duplicated your tiny, precise movements. That's why I requested you perform the surgery. Your hands are capable of the finest movements" she grinned, "like my brother William."

"I'm not..."

"The little one would have lost his eye without your intervention."

"Thanks but..."

"When we've finished here, I'll need today's lead surgeon to fill out the medical report on the child's surgery. When complete, I'll co-sign."

"Abbey..."

"We have directives to follow. They are orders, not requests." She downed the last of her coffee and grinned. "I'll expect you in my tent in one-hour..." She put a hand on his shoulder and squeezed..."Dr. Scharf."

Lt. Smith slapped him on the back. "Saved a kid's eye. Not bad, buddy. Proud of you...Dr. Scharf." They shook hands and Lt. Smith walked away.

Jordan smiled at Abbey and took her hand in both of his. "I'd like to talk about a future for us. When the war ends, we can marry. You could stay home and raise our children..."

"Stay home..." She yanked her hand away. "When the war ends we'll talk. Not before."

***

Dr. Kaplan kneeled over an injured man. He lay on a stretcher having just arrived at the medical tent. He was in substantial pain, sweating and blue-grey in skin tone. The man couldn't seem to breath properly.

"The right side of his jaw is crushed. Possible further damage causing breathing problems."

"Oh hell," Dr. Fellows said. "This is my nephew."

"I'm sorry," Abbey said. She quickly opened her instrument case. She poured a liquid on her scalpel then brought the blade up to the man's throat.

Dr. Fellows screamed, "No," and grabbed Dr. Kaplan's arm which held the scalpel.

Abbey yelled, "Get away." She jerked her arm free.

Lt. Scharf briefly stood between the two doctors. Any thought the older doctor had about reaching for her again were quashed by a brief glance at Lt. Scharf's expression which promised quick and drastic repercussion for such a move.

"But she can't…" Dr. Fellows pleaded.

Abbey made a cut at the center base of the nephew's trachea then gently held the incision open with her fingers.

The patient began taking deep breaths.

Abbey glared at Dr. Fellows while saying, "Now he can breathe. Lt. Scharf, please carefully hold this open while we transfer him to the surgical tent."

Dr. Fellows sputtered, "But…you…cut his…"

"Yes and I've done it numerous times. A fact you would have known had you attended the surgeries I've performed or read my summaries before they were sent to the Medical Museum."

They walked to the medical tent with the injured nephew. Dr. Fellows followed behind the group; the chief surgeon's head hung like a scolded puppy.

The nephew was placed on the surgical table.

"Anesthesia to the trachea-hole please," Dr. Kaplan said. "And gently maintain his airway until the little breathing tube we made is cleaned and placed there."

The anesthesiologist complied and said, "Yes, Doctor."

Abbey nodded to Lt. Smith who rinsed the tube in cleaning solution then carefully placed it in the nephew's neck opening.

"I'll assist," the chief surgeon said.

In a firm voice and with an expression which would have frozen an erupting volcano, Abbey stated, "No. You won't. Lt. Scharf has assisted me at least a dozen times on this type of repair. He's familiar with the procedure so he'll assist. If you wish, you may observe."

"But…"

"Or you can perform the operation yourself. You're the chief surgeon. The choice is yours."

"I…" the old doctor wearily shook his head. "I'm the chief surgeon in title only. The actual chief surgeon is and has been for some time, Dr. Abbey Kaplan. I prefer to observe, Doctor."

Abbey turned to her team. "Is the dental material cleaned and ready?"

"Yes, Doctor." Cpl. Silver said.

"Dental material?" Dr. Fellows said quietly. In full voice, he said, "Dr. Kaplan…please…this is my nephew…"

"The team will do its best for him," Abbey assured him.

Chapter Twenty-Three: The End in Sight

"As our regiment's involvement in the war is winding down, we may be disbanded, although some soldiers will be folded into other units," Dr. Fellows said to Abbey while she and Lt. Scharf ate breakfast on a bright, early April day in 1865. "Rumors abound, Lee will surrender shortly."

"Please Lord, that should happen," Abbey said.

The older doctor smiled and said, "In a letter I just received, my nephew's wife sent her thanks for caring for him. She said he's healing nicely."

A small volley of rifle-fire echoed across the camp. They looked in its direction.

Dr. Fellows shook his head. "That sound is the execution of Lt. Smith and his courier."

"What? No!" Abbey was incredulous, wide-eyed and her jaw dropped.

"He was caught in the act of handing information on casualties, battle strength and placement to his courier."

"He didn't sound southern," Lt. Scharf said.

"The man was a well-paid spy. The day our pickets were overcome was the result of knowing precisely where they were. When a Confederate headquarters company was overrun, his name was on a document in possession of a Southern colonel."

Abbey shook her head. "I'm astounded. He was the head of our team...good to everyone."

"As we are taught, the love of money is the root of all evil." Dr. Fellows appeared deeply saddened. "A banker was instrumental in turning him in. He reported to the Military Investigative Service, Smith's sister made monthly deposits in gold coin. The funds were far in excess of what they could have earned from their farm. He was the conduit for your likeness reaching the Confederates."

"The drawing...so then he likely killed Pvt. Tomlinson."

"A war, and money, does strange things to people." Dr. Fellows shook his head and walked away.

***

The following day after camp disease treatment, Dr. Kaplan heard men shouting and an occasional gun shot.

Cpl. Dan Silver came running up to her. "It's over!"

"What?"

"Lee surrendered." He picked her up, spun her around then gently placed her back on the ground and stepped back. "Oops, sorry Doctor."

Abbey threw her arms around him in a warm embrace. "It's over. Thank God Almighty, it's over."

Their brief reverie was cut short by the rumble of an explosion.

They gazed at the rising smoke cloud roughly two-hundred-yards distant. "What the hell was that?"

They heard men yelling for help. The twosome ran in the direction of the sounds. In the distance, Abbey observed a large crater. A number of men could be heard moaning while others yelled for help.

Dr. Fellows approached and blocked her path. "I'm sorry Dr. Kaplan."

"Sorry? Why? What happened?"

"The crater was caused by an exploding powder wagon. It broke a wheel and a number of men were trying to push it off the road. For whatever reason it exploded. Those close to the wagon were torn to shreds." His face was etched in sorrow. "Abbey, it pains me to inform you but Lt. Scharf was killed. You don't want to see what's left of him." He paused then continued in a somber tone. "I know you two were close...I'm so sorry." He put a hand on her shoulder. "A number of the wounded need surgery. If you'll head to the medical tent, I'll take care of things at this end."

She took a step back, feeling light headed. "The medical tent...right away."

"Cpl. Silver, please accompany Dr. Kaplan to the medical tents."

As Abbey walked, she slowly shook her head while muttering. "No…Not Jordan…Can't be…After all the shit we've survived…"

Abbey stopped and felt light headed again. She sensed her knees weakening. Cpl. Silver noticed and threw an arm around her waist to steady her. She put an arm around his shoulder then slowly shook her head. The doctor thought, "*My friend and confidant…my assistant…my lover…the one who cared more about me than anyone else…and did his best, always, to watch out for me.*" She took a deep breath, steadied herself and, with an uneven gait, continued walking.

Wearing an expression of sorrow, Abbey realized the loss of her friend tore every bit of joy from her soul which the war's end created.

The doctor stopped briefly in front of the medical tents and gazed at the red flag. After years of use, it was little more than a torn and frayed rag; it's tattered remains hung limply in the still air. Like many of the soldiers, it was a pale and faded reminder of what it once was.

Dr. Kaplan entered the medical tent. She glanced at Cpl. Silver as he and another soldier gently lifted a wounded man onto the surgical table. "*Dan looks old and tired beyond his years,*" she thought. Abbey viewed the other men around her. "*They all do. No more innocent faces. Likely, I appear the same.*"

Abbey began her last surgeries as a member of the 222nd Massachusetts.

***

April 1865

Dear Mom,

Thank the Lord, it's over. I should be full of joy but find I'm only experiencing a sense of relief. I yelled and screamed when I learned the war ended but then, I suspect like many others, I began thinking of those who didn't survive, which deeply saddened me. Even the day we learned General Lee surrendered, I lost a good friend…a man who, from the first day I arrived, assisted and supported me in more ways than I could list in one letter. His death was caused by, of all things, an accident. I doubt he suffered, but his death drove home the heart-wrenching grief and emptiness which so many families came to know during this dreadful war.

I performed my last military surgery today. As I gazed into the faces of my medical team one last time, they appeared old and worn beyond their years. When they first arrived, they were innocent and enthusiastic boys who were anxious to win a war. The horrors they faced as we repaired grievously wounded men, robbed them of their innocence, and caused them to dig deep inside to find the emotional strength to endure innumerable hideous sights. Soldiers witnessed horrors which caused revulsion and ripped pieces from their sanity causing sleepless nights, terrible nightmares and, for too many, mental breakdown which prevented them from functioning…even pushed some to suicide. We surgically repaired men, occasionally women, and a number of children. But had no medicine or treatment for those whose altered emotional balance caused them unbearable pain and suffering.

Each of us tried to adjust to the horror of war in our own way. I fear many of the men will be going home to families who won't recognize them. Many of the men can't articulate what they endured. And if they can't…how will their families understand how they've changed…and what happened to them? An old-timer told me many will suffer long after their last day in combat.

I received a commendation today for the medical and surgical work I performed. It was signed by the top officers in the 222nd Massachusetts regiment. A meaningful and well appreciated gesture. In the future, I suspect it will have more meaning but for now, my mind is still occupied with thoughts of those I couldn't help.

I've become the surgeon I dreamed of…but have a burning desire to learn about a person's mental health. Little information exists so my current goal is to find like-minded doctors and, together, pioneer a new area of medicine where we learn to heal injuries of the mind.

The happy, upbeat child you raised has become a woman who rarely smiles. She has scars on her body…and deep wounds in her mind that will take time to heal; if they ever do.

In a few days, I'll be traveling to Boston for a few weeks. A doctor and his wife invited me. He will help me exorcise some demons. Heading home afterward. When I do, I may still be limping from a hip injury. Don't worry. I expect it will heal completely.

Mom, I've reread this letter. Again, please don't share it with anyone other than to tell them I'm safe and expect to be home in a month or so. Having endured the pain of so many deaths during the Irish Potato Famine, I know you'll understand what I've been going through, but doubt others will.

Along with this letter, I've included a document which details how to repair hare lip. Please pass it on to William. Tell him his big sister successfully used the procedure on male and female adults, a teen girl, a ten-year-old boy, a two-year-old and a two-day-old. You would have loved the expression on the teen girl's face when she came to thank me for the repair. She literally cried for joy.

At times during this ordeal, I've confronted situations which left me utterly clueless. When this happened, I said to myself, What would Myra do? and most often found a solution.

Thank you for instilling in me a love of all our fellow men and the importance of perseverance. Those values have served me well.

Love,
Abbey

***

Three-days-later, Dr. Kaplan left her tent for the last time. She walked to the train station.

Abbey stood on the platform with many others headed home. Anytime someone looked her way and knew who she was, they smiled and nodded.

The train gradually pulled into the station. Footsteps approached.

"Dr. Kaplan, leaving without saying goodbye?"

"Dr. Fellows. Sorry…I…I was busy getting some final reports completed."

He held out a hand. "An honor to have served with you, Doctor."

She shook his hand.

The major. asked, "Where will you go?"

"Boston for now. Dr. Siegel asked I contact him."

"My hometown isn't too far from there. Perhaps we'll meet again."

"I'm planning a brief stay. I have some demons to excise then home to the Northwest."

"I…have something to say that's long overdue…but the truth is, I should have told you long ago. After working with you and seeing the results of your surgical efforts on my nephew and countless others…it's obvious anyone needing serious surgical intervention…they'd best pray to the Lord Almighty, Dr. Abbey Kaplan is holding the scalpel."

"Dr. Fellows…"

"If I'm rewarded with a place in heaven, precious lady, it will be a reward for the modicum of training I provided you. Take care of yourself, Dr. Kaplan."

He spun and walked away before she could reply. Abbey was shocked to note his eyes were filled with tears. She mumbled to the receding figure, "You take care as well, Doctor Fellows."

Her attention was refocused on her immanent travel as the railcars screeched to a halt. After a few passengers disembarked, she entered the coach and found a seat. The railcar jerked as it started moving then rocked side to side as it slowly picked up speed. Two-rows in front of her, she saw a trio of soldiers' slide into adjacent seats.

They were quiet for a while then one said, "It'll be good to be home and get a good night's sleep."

Another said, "I wonder how long I'll be listening for incoming or jump at loud noises?"

The third laughed and said, "I been gone five-years. Ah wonder how long it will take my kids to adjust to having a daddy in the house?"

Abbey took a deep breath and let it out slowly, then thought, *"It's over...wonder if I'll ever relax...ever have a decent night's sleep?"* She watched the passing fields. *"Is my mental state altered due to my war-time experience? I'm not the same person my family knew. I'm certainly not the young girl they remember sending off to medical college."* Another long sigh and she thought, *"I wonder what became of Margaret? My dear friend, Maggie. Such a good woman and friend."* She stretched then enjoyed watching a number of newborn calves struggle to remain standing on wobbling legs while a few older calves ran and jumped in the bright sunshine. *"New life. Life not knowing the horror of war. That's what we need...but many of the soldiers are going home with severe mental pain."*

She unpinned her hat and placed it on the seat beside her.

"Who will be there to help and understand their suffering? I'm proud of what I've accomplished but...after all the horror plus mental and physical pain I've endured, I wonder what will become of me?" She closed her eyes and prayed aloud.

"Lord, please give me strength and direction for the tasks that lie before me."

"For the last few years, my life had such meaning and purpose. Will I find that again? Will I find a friend and confidant like blessed Jordan Scharf?"

She stared at the passing sylvan countryside while pleasant memories of the lieutenant flooded her mind.

A deep voice interrupted her reverie. "Excuse me. Aren't you Dr. Kaplan?" a fashionably dressed man said.

Her expression brightened. "Major Sokolov, the battle-planner who visited the recovery hospitals."

"You remember me. Thank you. May I...?" Abbey motioned to the seat across from her.

He sat then asked, "Boston bound?"

She nodded.

With a pleasant smile, he inquired, "We never found time to continue the conversation we began at the recovery hospital. Perhaps now?"

"I would enjoy that, Major."

~~~ *The End* ~~~

Author's Notes and Resources

Readers interested in further learning about female doctors and nurses in the Civil War may wish to research the following women:

Dr. Elizabeth Blackwell, the first woman to earn a medical degree in the United States. When the Civil War began, this prodigious organizer, assembled four-thousand women to form the Women's Central Association of Relief.

Dr. Mary Edwards Walker; First volunteering as a nurse for the Union in 1861, then an assistant surgeon, Dr. Walker earned a commission for her work as a surgeon in 1863. In 1864, she was captured by Confederate soldiers, suspected of spying, and forced into Richmond's Castle Prison. She became the only woman to receive the Medal of Honor.

Captain Sally Louisa Tompkins of Richmond, Virginia; Created a private hospital for Confederate wounded. This hospital treated 1,333 soldiers. Of this number, only seventy-three died. Of all military hospitals during the war, Capt. Tompkins' had the lowest death rate.

To learn more about medicine during the Civil War, I recommend, "Learning from the Wounded," by Shauna Devien. Also, "Civil War Medicine" by C. Keith Wilbur.

To learn more about the Civil War in general, I highly recommend, Shelby Foote's brilliant, three-volume series, "The Civil War." His insight and analysis of the motivations of each side, conditions of the troops, descriptions of the battles and the home front are, in this author's opinion, peerless.

To appreciate the terrain and troop emplacement where the battles were fought, I recommend, "Great Maps of the Civil War," by William J. Miller.

On our way to somewhere else, we stumbled onto a Civil War prison, Camp Ford, near Tyler, Texas. While it is currently under re-creation by the Smith County Historical Society, it none the less provided me with a feeling for prison life in East Texas. Camp Ford is located just south of Interstate 20 at the intersection of Loop NE 323 and highway 271. The Historical Society's building in Tyler holds artifacts from the site.

To plan your own trip to many Civil War battle sites, I recommend "The Complete Civil War Road Trip Guide," by Michael Weeks.

While researching this novel, I traveled to a number of Civil War battle sites. Among the notable is the Vicksburg National Military Park located in Vicksburg, MS. We arrived in late June to find identical hot and humid weather conditions as those during June of 1863 when the battle and siege of Vicksburg took place. There is a perimeter road through the park and numbered sign posts that correspond to audio from a CD which can be purchased at the gift shop upon entering the park. Battle lines are demarcated and cannons placed as they were during the battle.

While at the Military Park, as a former combat soldier, I experienced anxiety and trepidation when I stood where Union troops gathered before their futile attack at Thayer's Approach. As I hiked the battlefield, the sun beating down and sweat drenching my clothing, my imagination filled my mind with the screams of the wounded and dying, the sound of their guns firing, the buzzing sound of rounds from the Confederate lines at the top of the hill and cannon shells exploding in our midst. Even the smell of gunpowder seemed to assault my nose. Hopefully, dear reader, you will find my writing reflects what Civil War soldiers and medical personnel endured.

From the heights of Vicksburg, one can view where waterborne cannon lobbed shells from the Mississippi into the town during the siege.

Lastly, during your visit to Vicksburg, book lovers must visit Lorelei Books at 1103 Washington St. I stopped in after our tour of the Military Park and asked about books concerning civilian life during the siege. The proprietor directed me to many useful books, one of which, "My Cave Life in Vicksburg," by Mary Anne Loughborough, will be the basis for at least two chapters in my next novel. Also found at Lorelei Books was "Reluctant Witnesses – Children's Voices from the Civil War," by Emmy E. Werner. The grit and wisdom of the youngsters' perception of war inspired a new character for my next novel – a young girl whose life is tempered by the crushing weight of her war time experience.

If you enjoyed this novel, please consider giving it a positive review. Thanks!

Printed in Great Britain
by Amazon